A LEGACY OF NIGHTMARES

Copyright © 2021 by J.M. Wallace

This is a work of fiction. Names, characters, places, and incidents either are the product of the author's imagination or are used fictitiously. Any resemblance to actual persons, living or dead, events, or locales is entirely coincidental.

All rights reserved. No part of this book may be reproduced or used in any manner without written permission of the copyright owner except for the use of quotations in a book review. For more information, address: jmwallace.author@gmail.com.
ISBN978 -1-7378806-1-5

Editing by Suzanne Buono
Cover Design by GetCovers
Map by Melissa Nash

ISBN 978-1-7378806-1-5

For Alyssa

A LEGACY OF NIGHTMARES

J.M. WALLACE

ALSO BY
J.M. WALLACE

Books
A Legacy of Darkness

Novelettes
A Smuggler's Tale Series:
The Princess of Sagon

To the girls who grew up riding their ponies as if they were unicorns, and who have always known that magic is real.

THE BEYOND

NORTH ASTERION

Druid Tribe

North Pass

Blight

Ravenwood

Ceasy Lagoon

Norbrach

Living Sea

Summer Palace

Blight

Patsu Trade Route

Spreading

EASTERN ISLES

SAGON

Patsu Trade Harbour

SOUTH ASTERION

ASTERION MAGIC SYSTEM

Magi – Those born with the ability to wield magic.

Sorcerer
The highest order of Magi, trained extensively in the arts of alchemy, enchantments, and incantations. Their magic is driven by invention rather than nature.

Mage
Ranked under Sorcerer, these Magi are still undergoing training to rise to Sorcerer. Some are not powerful enough to advance to the next level.

Druid
The first Magi, an ancient people who once wielded powerful magic gifted by The Mother herself. Their magic is derived from the land, tying them directly to nature and the divine.

Witch
A lower caste of Magi, deriving their magic from herbs and concoctions. These Magi are rumored to be distant descendants of the Druids, resulting in magic more reliant on nature and the divine.

Ancient creatures and Forest Dwellers
Less powerful Magi with ties to the land. They do not rely heavily on their magic, but rather their *connection* with nature.

Nefari
Dark Magi who derive their power through sacrificial magic. They are dangerously powerful, but at a great cost. These Magi are outlaws in both human and Magi society.

PROLOGUE

A reading from: *The Final Judgment*

In a time after creation, following the great war in The Beyond, three Magi brothers were tested. They were granted objects of powerful magic—each a test of their true nature and their ability to forgive. The first brother, Leto, was gifted a stave to amplify his power. The second brother, Roth, was granted a gilded sword, powerful enough to cut down any threat he faced. And the third, Pris, was given an obsidian stone to protect him from harm.

These brothers had witnessed the fall of their country, and to rebuild their forces and exact revenge, had ventured south to a new land. The Mother found them and blessed them with these objects, granting them her favor and the opportunity for a fresh start. But no magic can be wielded without sacrifice. Their sacrifice would come in the form of a test: that test was forgiveness. To demonstrate that they were worthy of such power, they would have to give up their thirst for vengeance, or otherwise reveal their unworthiness by seeking out those who had wronged them.

The first brother used his chance to forgive and in return he found love. Leto hid away his stave and was rewarded with a companion. The second brother put away past grievances, threw the sword into the abyss, and was rewarded with peace. Driven by such hate, however, the third brother was unable to let go. He chose vengeance, and a river of blood was spilled in his wake. As a result, his object was cursed and lost to the world, destined to spread greed and destruction to any who came upon it.

CHAPTER ONE

Shaye, In the darkness

The darkness was all consuming. It shrouded Shaye like a warm blanket on a cold winter's night. She felt safe here… Safe from herself and the horror that awaited her on the other side. It had been days since she had succumbed to it, allowing herself to fall into its depths, where pain and guilt could no longer reach her.

Bastian had been right when he had promised the power she would feel if she would just give in to him. There were no nightmares here… No memories to torment her, only strength and the urge to use it. Still, something tugged on her heart and soul, calling her to return. Something shifted within her mind, and once again she could not remember why she had been so consumed with helping the son of her enemy, the man who had betrayed her people; why she had let that man's son touch her, kiss her, and manipulate his way into her heart.

You are safe here. Bastian's promises echoed in the darkness. He would set everything right, she knew that now. King Sorin did not deserve her forgiveness, nor did the people who had allowed his father, King Allerick, to take her magic away. Magi had suffered for too long under a rule that had made them give up a piece of themselves. Now, that part of their soul was crying out to be released.

How could she have let herself become so lost? Shaye was determined to make them pay for what they had done. Something in her mind was telling her that the Nefari were not her enemy, not anymore. No, she would rise with them, a force more powerful than anything Asterion had ever seen.

By Bastian's side, she would take back her magic, and they would claim what was rightfully theirs. He had only ever wanted to protect her, from the moment they met in the palace as children, when he took a beating for her from that bully. Nobody would ever hurt the two of them again, not if she did as he asked. The voice inside her head assured her of that.

Shaye, Bastian's voice beckoned her in the darkness, *it is time for you to wake. We have work to do.*

She did as he bid, pushing through the darkness that enveloped her. She awoke. Bastian smiled down at her with his solid black eyes, black like the obsidian pendant he wore around his neck. The whites of them were gone now, but she was no longer afraid. She felt no anger towards him, and she could not remember why she had ever been angry with him to begin with. He was like a dark prince, *her* dark prince.

He extended a hand to her, their jet-black fingers linking together. She felt her power answer to his. Lightning coursed through her and the black magic she had wielded in the abandoned camp flared to life. It was time.

CHAPTER TWO

Sorin

Sorin's body ached, almost as much as his soul did, by the time they reached the first clan. The blast from Shaye had done a number on them all, and the feeling of defeat was even worse. He had promised to protect her; but in that promise, he had never imagined he would need to protect her from herself. All he knew now was that he would go to the ends of the world if it meant getting her back. He hoped with all his heart that he could do it.

Their journey into the Raven Wood had been a blur. He had been too consumed with his nerves over asking the Forest Dwellers for help. It is something his father, King Allerick, never would have done, after all. The only thing that brought him any confidence was the small, pale-green girl who had become their friend over the last few weeks. Mavka had promised to help them find allies here in the magical forest that she called home.

Although the Raven Wood had been part of Asterion since the beginning of creation, it wasn't until a few weeks ago that Sorin had ventured into it for the first time. The forest stood on the outskirts of Brenmar where the Winter Palace had been built over two decades ago by the late King Idor. As a child, Sorin's father had kept him far from Brenmar. That is, until the night of the Winter Solstice ball when his father had brought Sorin along to witness the coup against Idor.

Sorin supposed he could have visited this part of Asterion once his father had become king, but there were too many painful memories of the bloody night in the ballroom. It wasn't until the blight had started spreading through the land that Sorin had returned to the North. Once there, he had tracked down the Stave of Leto in hopes that fixing it would suppress the dark magic that was killing the land.

A lot of good that did, Sorin thought, cringing at the memory of everything that had gone wrong. He had known Bastian could not be trusted, and still they had let him sleep under the same roof as them, share their meals, and manipulate his way into Shaye's mind. Sorin shifted in the saddle and Shaye's moody, dapple-gray gelding, Finn, bucked slightly underneath him.

Mavka whistled, drawing their attention to movement in the distance. "Almost there!"

Mavka was riding with Bron on his warhorse, Altivo. She was sitting in front of Bron, and Sorin could see his friend pull the small girl closer to him before taking off at a gallop. Sorin took a deep breath before encouraging Finn to keep up.

He was nervous about how this encounter would go, but it brought him comfort knowing that Mavka was fiercely loyal to him, Shaye, Bron, and Ingemar. He also knew that Mavka held influence with the clans who had spent the last twelve years hiding out in wait. They had control of their magic and had simply been awaiting the right time to stand up and fight back against the Nefari; the dark magic users who had invaded and fed on their land and who had been thwarting Sorin's attempts at ridding Asterion of the blight. If Sorin could gather enough of the clans together with Mavka's help, then they would have a significant force with at least a fighting chance against Bastian and the Nefari.

The first clan they approached was made up of Dwellers who looked like Mavka. The women were petite in size, standing no taller than Sorin's chest. They were dressed in the same fashion that Mavka had worn when they had first met her: scant clothing made up of flowers, vines, and moss. In comparison, the Dweller men stood tall and ferocious with intricate blue tattoos covering their bodies. By the way they greeted Mavka, he knew that this was her clan. She had not spoken of her family much since joining Sorin and the others, and from the way she had acted, he had thought she'd been living alone all these years.

The moths, who acted as Mavka's constant companions, danced around wildly, seemingly happy to be home as well. A horn echoed through the dying trees, sounding out to announce their arrival. There were Dwellers scattered throughout the area; some sat on the limbs of the trees, while others were sitting around small fires. Every one of them eyed Sorin and his friends curiously.

They approached a group of proud-looking men, and Mavka grabbed the hand of the tallest one. His skin was a green pigment like hers, but his hair was short, the color of bark. He too had blue tattoos coating his arms and legs; they depicted scenes of battle and magical creatures that he had faced over the ages.

Sorin bowed his head to the tall Forest Dweller whom he suspected was their leader. The man tilted his head to the side in response, as if curious as to what Sorin was doing. He was much taller than Mavka, with the same strong, winding horns as the Dweller they had found sacrificed at the Nefari camp only a few days earlier. His horns were like the bark on the ancient trees in the Raven Wood, with intricate blue runes winding around them. Sorin was fascinated and had endless questions about the clan and its people, but they would have to wait.

Mavka had to stand on her tippy toes to whisper to the

curious man. "It is their way of greeting, Dadaí." She covered a smile with her hand.

"Ah." His voice was like gravel as he laughed. "Welcome, King Sorin. Forgive my confusion. It has been many a decade since I last met with a King of Asterion—a distant relative of yours if my memory serves me right." He paused before introducing himself. "I am Einar, Chief of the Highland Clan."

Sorin hid his shock at the realization of how old the man standing before him must be. He had known that the stronger Magi, and creatures who wielded similar powers, could live exceptionally long lives, but this man must have been hundreds of years old. Yet he did not look a day over thirty.

"It is an honor to be here, though I wish it were under better circumstances."

"Yes, the trees have kept us well informed of the events that have led us all here on this day. My daughter has been diligent in sending word of you all. She says that you are her friends. I have always trusted her judgment, so I will trust her now as she calls for help on your behalf."

"Thank you, sir, I will not forget this."

"See to it that you don't." Chief Einar gestured for them to enter the Highland village. Sorin had not yet had the chance to visit the different clans in the Raven Wood, but from his studies he knew that it was comprised of several territories. Each with its own chief.

Chief Einar's village was unlike any other Sorin had ever seen in Asterion: sturdy, moss-covered bungalows were built strategically around the clearing. Sorin was impressed with the Dwellers' resourcefulness, and he found himself wondering if one day he might be able to discuss more than war with the leader of this clan.

Once inside of a large vine-covered structure that centered the Dwellers' camp, Sorin and the others took up seats around a small fire. The bungalow was warm and sweat began to bead on

Sorin's brow. Mavka's father, Chief Einar, sat unphased by the stuffy air in the room. He passed Sorin a cup filled with a liquid Sorin did not recognize.

"King Sorin, if you will?"

Sorin took a sip of the bitter drink, and began to tell the Dwellers who had crowded into the room everything he and his friends had come to know up to this point. The men and women around the hut did not seem surprised by any of it. They nodded in silent understanding, some donning fierce expressions. It seemed that they were ready for a fight, and Sorin was glad of it.

"How many men... er... Forest Dwellers and creatures, do you think we can muster?"

Chief Einar thought for a moment and scratched at the base of his horns. The advisor sitting beside him leaned forward and whispered into his ear. Chief Einar nodded in response and spoke with confidence. "There are seven clans within this forest. We believe that, with some convincing, every one of them will stand with us. With them by your side, the magical creatures of the Raven Wood will follow as well." He took a deep breath, then blew it out onto the fire before them.

Smokey figures rose in the shapes of Naga, Fenrir, and even Fairies. They filled the air in the form of smoke and danced all around them. Chief Einar continued, "Ever since the Nefari entered the Raven Wood, they have fed on the magic of the land and the blood of its creatures." As Chief Einar spoke, new figures rose and morphed into tall, hooded men. Black smoke shot from the hooded figures' hands and into the defenseless smokey creatures who had risen first.

Chief Einar continued. "This has depleted Asterion's power and has created a dark curse—or as you refer to it, a blight. It has been driving prey from the woods, leaving predators with nothing to hunt. It has crept into the very soil of our lands, leaving us nothing to grow and nothing to gather for food. From here, it can only get worse."

Sorin remained quiet as he watched the smokey figures fade into the air, leaving only the smoldering fire in front of him. Chief Einar stood as he spoke again. "So, we will stand with you, Sorin, King of Asterion. We will give you our allegiance, but only if you do the same for us."

Sorin stood now too. "It would be my honor, sir."

Chief Einar eyed Sorin carefully. "Words come easily to mortal men. It will be your actions, once this is all over, that will prove whether you are as worthy as we hope you to be."

Sorin nodded, determined to prove his worthiness, no matter what it took.

Chief Einar sat back down in his seat and gestured for Sorin to do the same. He poured himself a drink. "Now, there is the matter of the girl."

Sorin's breath caught in his throat. "Shaye. The girl is named Shaye."

"She is dangerous. From what you have just told us, she has tapped into dark magic herself. She attacked you with that magic and yet you still wish to save her?"

"We *will* save her."

The atmosphere in the room grew tense. Forest Dwellers eyed Sorin and Bron, wary of the mortal men who sat armed in their presence. Sorin did not mean any disrespect, but he also would not waiver on this. Saving Shaye was non-negotiable.

"And if she is too far gone? Too consumed by the darkness she has allowed into her heart and soul... What then?"

"No one is beyond redemption." Sorin balled his hands into fists in his lap. He did not like what the Chief was insinuating.

"King Sorin, I have been around long enough to know that vengeance is a feeling not easily dealt with. They now have *both* pieces of the Stave, the relic that has the ability to enhance magical power. They will not make the mistake of parting with it again and risking it falling back into your hands. With the Stave whole again, and a Druid to wield it, they will be more powerful than ever before."

Mavka and Ingemar, the Ceasg who had stood by them since recovering their half of the Stave from the cave, looked at Sorin with sympathy.

The Chief, too, looked at him with pity. He spoke with more sympathy than before, "With the Stave and the girl, they will want to find the second relic. They will control the Sword."

"Sword?" Sorin furrowed his brow. He had not even considered that they would want to collect the other relics. So focused on finding the Stave, it never occurred to him that the other two relics of the three brothers were out there somewhere waiting to be found and used for nefarious purposes. "If they find the Sword of the second brother, what will happen?"

"With the Sword of the brother Roth, they will have the ability to cut down anything in their path. With the Stave and that girl you love, Shaye..." Sorin winced at the word, *love*. It was true, though he had not admitted it to himself until this moment. Chief Einar finished, "With the girl, I fear they will have the power to amplify the Sword's ability by using the Stave, spreading that power throughout their army until every Nefari wielding a sword has the magical strength to cut through their enemies. They will be unstoppable."

It felt as if the world was toppling over. Any hope that Sorin had clung to, began to fade away. He was so consumed with fear and doubt that he could barely register the rest of the conversation. Thankfully, Mavka took control, making plans with her father to gather the other clans for a vote. It would be then that they could proceed with their plans to save Shaye and stop the Nefari.

It had been only a matter of days before the other clans arrived in the Highlands. Sorin now found himself surrounded by strange creatures whose customs he was not yet familiar with. Men were shouting at one another in the large crowd; they had been carrying on like this all afternoon. A horn filled with sour ale slammed against the solid wood wall of the hall, and Sorin ducked as another horn shot past him as quickly as a loose arrow.

The clans were a rambunctious lot who seemed to have old rivalries with each other. Sorin leaned back in his moss-covered seat. Another headache was coming on and he was in desperate need of a bath. His hair had grown longer, curling at his ears, and he could not remember the last time he'd shaved. He scratched at the rough stubble on his face and let out a long groan as Chief Einar attempted to grab the attention of everyone in the small hall.

Mavka had been eager to get Sorin, Bron, and Ingemar settled, giving each of them their own private quarters. Sorin was grateful to her for it, but it still meant living amongst magical creatures who held a grudge against his father. King Allerick had taken magic from the land over a decade ago, leaving the Dwellers within the forest to fend for themselves as a band of dark Magi moved in.

Sorin kicked at a dead leaf that had found its way inside of the Great Hall. He snarled at the thought of the Nefari who had brought them nothing but pain and sorrow, rotting the land from within with their sacrificial magic. They had taken all they could from the earth and, when that wasn't enough, they took power from the life force of the magical creatures themselves, sacrificing them and using their blood as a payment for the dark magic they wielded. Even when they had nothing left to sacrifice, they gave a piece of themselves, resulting in the inky black marks that tainted their hands.

Even now, looking down at the rotten leaf, Sorin was reminded of all the ways the Nefari's blight had affected their home. His people could no longer farm the land and the trade strait to the east had been closed due to monstrous attacks in the Living Sea. Sorin had thought he could fix it all by putting the first relic back in place. The Stave of Leto. The damned thing that had started all this over twelve years ago and that had caused him nothing but grief since.

Ingemar caught Sorin's eye. She was sitting stoically on a nearby stump. It was a ridiculous sight, the elegant Ceasg sitting like a queen on a throne amidst all of this chaos. She adjusted her golden embroidered gown, and her dark skin shimmered with the hint of scales that glistened in the lantern light of the hall. The crown of golden stars upon her thick, black hair twinkled like the stars in the North Asterion sky. She noticed him staring at her helplessly as the clans bickered around them, and then nodded in understanding.

She rose, holding her hands out to call upon her powers. Water splashed from a barrel and onto the unwitting Forest Dwellers within its reach. Several angry shouts sounded out, but the rest of the hall went silent.

"Aye, what is the meanin' of this?" A gruff Dweller man pushed his soaked, bark-colored hair from his round, stout face.

Chief Einar laughed at the sight of one of the fiercest clan chiefs as wet as a cat caught in a storm. The rest of the hall followed suit, Dwellers from clans all over the Raven Wood bellowed in laughter.

Sorin did not find humor in the time they were wasting. He stood, adjusting the leathered jerkin he wore. "Now then. If you are all done arguing, I would like to get down to business."

"Of course, Your Majesty." Chief Einar bowed his head toward Sorin.

Sorin knew they saw him as a young and inexperienced king, but that did not make the situation any less urgent. Chief Einar set his drink down. "Please understand, friend, it has been nearly a decade since the clans have had to come together like this. We are strong here in the Raven Wood, and we've been successfully living in peace —"

"Aye, by staying out of each other's way." The stout chief dried his face with the woven plaid cloth at his waist.

Sorin suppressed a sigh. The Lowland's clan chief had been difficult to sway thus far and Sorin knew he would need to tread carefully where he was concerned. "I understand, Chief Herald, and I respect your laws and traditions here, I do." Sorin adjusted the scabbard he wore on his back, buying himself time so he could word this without starting another argument. These men were angry, and he didn't blame them, but he needed them to band together under his leadership if they were going to march on the Nefari forces that were gathering near the Norbrach valley as they spoke.

A hushed silence fell over the room as Sorin went on, "You already know the threat the Nefari pose to your people. You do not have the numbers to face them alone. Nor does my army possess the magical abilities to match them. Only *together* do we stand any sort of chance."

Chief Einar walked to the fire in the middle of the long hall. "We take it to a vote then. The seven clan chiefs of the Raven Wood will cast their gemstones into the fire, should they choose to stand with King Sorin of Asterion. To do so will mean setting aside any past grievances, to forge a new pact going forward." He held an emerald stone high above his head. "The Highland Clan will stand with King Sorin against the Nefari." He threw the precious stone into the fire, and it erupted with a bright green flame before dying down again to embers.

A beautiful woman stepped forward next. Her hair was so black it shimmered with purple like a raven's wing. It reminded Sorin of the crow that had called out to Shaye before she unleashed her dark magic on them in the abandoned Nefari camp. His heart ached at the thought.

She held up an amethyst stone. "The Eastern Clan will stand with King Sorin." The fire burst into purple flame as she dropped the stone into it. She winked at Sorin as she passed him to rejoin her sons in the crowd.

Following her lead, the Western, Central, Northern, and

Southern Clans stepped forward one by one, each declaring their allegiance to Sorin and throwing their gems into the fire. That left Chief Herald. Sorin could swear that the entire room held their breath as they waited for the stubborn, old chief to make his choice.

"For Mother's sake." He puffed his broad chest up as he finally gave in, "The Lowland Clan will stand with you, King Sorin, but I swear on our sacred gem, I will personally destroy you should you not live up to your word." He threw a jasper gemstone into the fire, bringing to life an orange-red flame like that of a tiger's coat.

That made seven—seven Raven Wood clans that would dedicate their men, magic, and strength to Sorin's cause. He turned to Mavka, who stood at his side jittering with excitement. "I will not let them down, Mavka. I can't."

She grabbed onto his sleeve and smiled warmly. "I know."

Chief Einar let out a jovial roar, cutting through the quiet, anticipating crowd. "Now we feast!"

Men and women, Forest Dwellers of all sizes and colors, began tittering around. They dragged in long tables and chairs made of uneven, raw wood. There were no servants here, so each clan member did their part in setting up for the feast. They brought in bowls of wild berries, smoked meats, and strange foods that Sorin had never seen. Sorin felt a twinge of guilt at the sight of such a magnificent feast. It must have taken the Dwellers days to accumulate such ripe and bountiful food when their stores were dwindling from the blight.

Now that the tension of the vote had begun to wear off, the room filled with laughter and good cheer. Dwellers from various clans mingled with one another in celebration of their newfound alliance. They filled their cups up and made toasts with wine that was strong enough to rival Rolland's brew. Sorin rubbed his temples. The thought of Shaye's family and the inn brought back the sting of losing her.

Sorin turned his attention back to the clan chiefs. Even they seemed to be enjoying themselves, talking eagerly with one another at the long table at the head of the hall. He supposed it was all worth it to give them any semblance of happiness before the inevitable battle that was to come.

Sorin found his seat beside Bron, and gladly accepted the drink that Ingemar offered him from across the table. She was sitting straight-backed as usual, taking in the sight of the celebration around her. Mavka sat on the other side of Bron and began explaining to him what the strange dishes on the table were. The massive Mortal Knight listened intently, hanging on her every word. Every once in a while, Mavka would say something to make him smile broadly at her, causing his dark eyes to crinkle at the corners. Sorin smiled at the sight of his best, and oldest, friend, next to the girl who adored him. He knew Bron returned Mavka's affections, even if he was too bull-headed to admit it.

Sorin watched the guests in the hall dance and laugh together. It seemed so easy for everyone to lose themselves in the festivities. Summer was fast approaching and Sorin felt himself sweating under his jerkin. He pulled at the collar of his shirt, wondering when he would be able to politely excuse himself to his private quarters. Since losing Shaye to Bastian, the dark Magi who had disguised himself as their ally, Sorin had not been in the mood for laughter and cheer, or much else for that matter.

"Here, Sorin, you must eat." Mavka pushed a dish his way; it was a plate of wild greens, and flowers that he had never seen before. Bron came to the rescue, piling a tender cut of venison on top of it. Sorin picked at it. He hadn't eaten since that morning, but he wasn't hungry.

The pit in his stomach had been growing since the moment Bastian had manipulated Shaye into using dark magic against them. There had been no sign of them or where they had gone, and Sorin had been forced to focus on other matters. He prayed to the Fates that this alliance would be enough—that organizing a force to go south to Norbrach would be enough to find her and to save her... To save them all.

Sorin asked, "Ingemar, has word come yet from your friend in the Nefari encampment?" After they arrived at the Highland village, they had sent word out to the other clans, as well as magical creatures on the coast. One noteworthy response had come from the Ceasg Lagoon to the east of them, where Ingemar had been taken by the Nefari; after which, they had sentenced her to guard the Stave in the Raven Wood cave.

The letter claimed that the Nefari had also taken a handful of young Ceasg, though they did not know why, or where they had taken them. Ingemar had spent the following days reaching out with her magic in search of them. She could not detect the Nefari because of their dark magic shields, but she *could* detect the magic that was linked to hers—to the magic of her people.

They were still waiting, in hopes that Ingemar's call would be enough to communicate with the Ceasg in Bastian's custody. She shook her head regretfully. "No, Your Majesty. However, I did sense them in the South, near the hunting village, like you suspected. If the Ceasg are with the Nefari, then it has to mean that Bastian has sent his forces there as you planned."

Sorin smiled in satisfaction and took a long drink from his cup. It was a small victory but one he would gladly drink to. Before Bastian had revealed himself for the monster he is, Sorin had given orders to Bron's second in command, Anik, to send Asterion troops to a hunting village north of Norbrach. What Bastian hadn't heard, however, were the new orders Sorin had given Anik in private: to send General Tyrell and his forces to surround the hill on either side of the valley, in which Bastian would no doubt station his troops for battle.

He stood to take his leave. "Please come find me if any word comes in."

"You're not going to stay and have a drink with us?" The deep concern in Bron's eyes made Sorin's chest tighten with guilt. He knew his friends were worried about him; he hadn't been eating or sleeping since they had lost Shaye. He also knew they were trying to understand why he was having so much trouble thinking clearly—they had grown to love the Druid girl too. But it wasn't the same. Sorin felt as if a piece of his own soul was missing, and he still could not forgive himself for letting her go... For not doing more to stop Bastian from worming his way into her mind.

"I'll see you all in the morning. Enjoy yourselves tonight. The real work starts tomorrow." He clapped Bron on the shoulder and found his way through the crowd. Dwellers stopped to bow to him as he walked to the door.

The show of respect did not go unnoticed by Sorin. He knew these people had suffered under his father's rule, yet they were here, putting their faith in him to set things right. He wasn't sure he could ever repay them for that trust, but he would do it. *Or die trying*, he thought harshly.

It was dark outside of the hall, the Dweller village sat still and peaceful in the silence. Sorin looked at the dim stars peeking through the dying treetops, and wondered if Shaye was looking at the same night sky. He ignored the pain in his chest at the thought of her, and at the memory of her long auburn hair and burning golden eyes.

Mavka, with the help of Chief Einar, had set up tents for him and the others, giving them privacy from the rest of the village. It was a modest set up, with a comfortable bed of furs and a simple desk. It reminded him of the tents he and his father had slept in when he was twelve, and they had marched north to Brenmar, ready to storm the Winter Palace.

Sorin removed his jerkin and leather boots; and, laying on the bed in his linen shirt and trousers, he put his hands behind his head and shut his eyes tight. He prayed to the Fates and The Mother that he and his allies would be successful in the weeks to come. He wanted nothing more than to be able to hold Shaye again, to never let her go. He wished desperately that he had told her how he felt about her—that he was in love with her and had been since the moment he had seen her standing helplessly in the ballroom when they were children. It didn't matter if she did not return the sentiment, he just needed her to know that she was loved. He needed her to know that it didn't matter what happened in the abandoned Nefari camp, he still cared about her and believed in her.

Before he drifted to sleep, he whispered into the night, praying that somehow the wind would carry his words to her, "Hold on a little while longer, Shaye, we're coming."

CHAPTER THREE

Shaye

Shaye tossed and turned in the large bed, throwing the furs off of her and onto the floor. She sat up with a start, sweat beading at her temples. She looked around frantically, trying to remember where she was, there were so many voices echoing in her mind. Bastian, ordering her to answer his call, and Sorin, pleading for her to stay strong. *Hold on.* He had said, but she couldn't decipher if it had been a dream or if it had really been him.

Bastian had assured her that her friends were alright. She grimaced, *No. They're not my friends. They only wanted me for the Stave and my magic.*

"That's right, my dear, and now that they no longer have the Stave, they have no use for you," Bastian cooed from the corner of the large tent. He was dressed immaculately, like a king in his own right. His black leather waistcoat glistened in the morning light that was peeking in through the tent's entrance. His dark hair was let loose down at his shoulders, only one simple braid at the side, and he no longer wore his gloves.

Instead, he showed his black hands off to the world as if it were a badge of honor. If only Shaye felt the same about her own fingertips, now tainted with the same mark of black magic—as was the price of wielding such power.

She sat up and wiped the sleep from her eyes. She wasn't sure how long she had been asleep, but it felt like she had spent a lifetime in the darkness. There had been no nightmares to plague her this time, only the safety and warmth of nothingness. Bastian sat on the bed at her feet, putting a hand boldly on her leg. This time she did not flinch away at his touch, as she'd done the day they had trained outside of the Winter Palace.

He smiled, flashing bright white teeth. "I know you were confused before, but everything is now as it should be. If you cooperate with us, then things will go much more smoothly. I can feel you fighting me still, but let me assure you, if you just give in to that primal part of you, then you will find happiness here." His hand slid further up her leg, hunger lingering in his eyes.

She thought for a long moment, her mind still felt clouded, like there wasn't enough room in there for anything, or anyone, but Bastian. She nodded but did not speak. It seemed to be enough for him as he stood abruptly and snapped his fingers. Guards appeared at the entrance of the tent, and with them, a very frightened girl, struggling to break free of their hold.

Shaye catapulted from the bed: *Brina*. Shaye ran to her, stopping short as the guards blocked her way. She looked pleadingly at Bastian and he signaled to the guards to let her pass. Shaye shoved them further aside, embracing the girl whom she had grown up with after her aunt and uncle had been slaughtered in the coup. Brina was breathing heavily and had a small cut on her lip from where she had been struck. Anger boiled inside of Shaye, overpowering the fog in her mind.

Bastian spoke as if sensing Shaye's fury, "From what my men tell me, she put up quite a fight on the way here."

Shaye turned on him, she could feel her magic pooling at her fingertips, begging for release. Brina cried out when she caught sight of Shaye's hands; she pulled back from Shaye's embrace. "Shaye, what have you done?"

The panic in her best friend's voice broke through Shaye's anger toward Bastian, but she ignored the question, turning back to the man who was now sitting casually in an armchair, like he didn't have a care in the world. "Why is she here Bastian? I've already given in, you *know* that."

"She's here as a simple gesture of good faith. A gift for your help; she is to be your lady-in-waiting on our journey to the Eastern Isles." He picked at his nails, not bothering to look up at the two horror-stricken girls standing before him. "And, if it helps to motivate you, to serve as a reminder of how merciful I can be and what is at stake should you fight against me... then all the better."

Shaye felt like her stomach was full of bricks. She couldn't stand the sight of him or the elaborately decorated war tent, with its obnoxious rugs and gilded vases. It was all a pretense, a show to distract from what this really was—what *he* really was. She pushed away the murderous thoughts she was feeling toward Bastian as she looked at her friend standing terrified between the guards. She needed to keep Brina safe, it was all that mattered right now.

Bastian smiled that all knowing smile; he knew he had won this round. He rose to leave, "Enjoy your reunion. After breakfast you will report to the general's tent. We have a trip to plan."

As soon as Bastian and the guards were gone, Shaye grabbed Brina by the arm; she ignored the way Brina flinched at her touch. Shaye pulled her over to the velvet settee, throwing its beaded, burgundy pillows to the ground. There were so many questions Shaye wanted to ask, but she started with, "Rolland and Rebecca —?"

"They're fine. I..." Brina let out a frustrated breath, trying to regain her composure. "I was on my way to Norbrach."

Shaye was puzzled. "Norbrach? Why would you go there?"

"Shaye, you were gone too long. When you did not send word, I started to get nervous. And then the rumors around the port began to pour in. They said there were dark magic users in the North, and that they were the ones causing the blight. I wanted to find you, to... I don't know, to warn you. Or to make sure you were alright?" She was breathing heavily again, and stood, swiping the untouched cup and plate of breakfast the guards had brought Shaye from the table.

The food scattered across the ground, the dark liquid from the cup poured onto the carpet. Shaye felt a little bit of pleasure at the sight of the mess, in this room that Bastian had so carefully curated for her. It was a small defiance, but a defiance all the same.

"Brina, is that where they grabbed you?"

"They came out of nowhere. Like Wraiths in the night. I fought them Shaye, I fought like hell." She laughed bitterly, gesturing to the tent. "Lotta good that did me."

"Brina, listen to me carefully. Sorin is coming. I know he is, we just have to stay safe until then; I need to stay in line."

"Look at yourself. Look at what he's doing to you. You look like you haven't eaten or slept in weeks, and your hands... By The Mother, your *hands*, Shaye."

Shaye looked down at the darkness that now marked her, a lifelong reminder of her shame. There was no way she could ever forgive herself for what she had done to Sorin and her friends. "Brina, I think Bastian is using his magic to manipulate me somehow. I—I get lost in this fog, it consumes me when I'm near him. It's like my own mind is betraying me... Turning Sorin and the people I care about into enemies." Angry tears streamed down her face and onto her lap, leaving droplets on her silk nightgown. "I'm afraid of what I might do—of what he might *make* me do."

She couldn't believe she had gotten herself into this mess. She was not the girl who allowed men to manipulate her. She was a fighter. She had survived a massacre, had paved her way in the world with her wit and her fists... But now, here she was, subjected to the whims of a madman.

"I'm here with you now. We will not let that son of a bitch win. I'll play my part, be the dutiful lady's maid, and I'll stay with you. Always." Brina grabbed Shaye's hands now, gripping them tightly.

Shaye was comforted by her friend's words, but she still chided herself for her foolishness. When Bastian had shown up at the palace, she had been so desperate to have someone who could understand her. She had thought that he would be the answer to all their problems. He had helped her tap into her magic, and she had thought that he wanted the same things as she did... But through it all, she had ultimately lost herself.

Shaye and Brina sat together for a while, hand in hand, as they had done so many times when they were young girls and Shaye had woken from a nightmare; the only problem was that this time, the nightmare never seemed to end.

Later, Bastian sent two Nefari guards to escort her to the generals' tent; too busy wreaking havoc to do it himself, she supposed. The camp was filled to the brim with Nefari, all looking at her as if she were a prized pig on her way to slaughter.

The tents seemed to be never ending, neat little rows of tanned canvas atop of the hill, overlooking a valley where a hunting village resided. An Orc with a particularly nasty grin winked at her as she passed. His fangs protruded from his mouth and a foul smell filled Shaye's nose. He wasn't the only magical creature in the Nefari ranks; she spotted Naga, Wraiths, Fenrir, and other fearsome beasts in the crowd. Sorin would find that he was fiercely outnumbered, and Shaye determined she would need to get word to him somehow.

A crow cawed from above her, flying in the direction that she and the guards walked. She wondered if it was the same crow from the abandoned camp, the one that had witnessed her fiery attack on her friends. One of the guards noticed her lingering and shoved her roughly.

The guards were an ugly pair, identical with their brassy red hair and scarred faces. Even the scars seemed to mimic each other. Their hands were what worried her the most—like all Nefari, they sported the mark of their dark magic. But on the twin brothers, the black ran from the tips of their fingers to their palms, proving that they had used more than just a little of the blood magic. Almost as much as Bastian had, with his stretching down to his wrists in inky tendrils.

She gave one of them a sideways glance, wondering if she could take them both in a fight, but one of the brothers caught her eye. His voice was gravelly as he said, "Don't even think about it." Fire sparked at his fingertips in warning and Shaye clenched her jaw in frustration.

They arrived at a large tent, not as large as the one she was residing in, but obvious in its importance. When she made her way inside, she was surprised by the group of men who bowed deeply to her. She looked to Bastian in confusion, but he ignored her; he continued speaking to the man beside him. A human man, Shaye realized with a start, one that she recognized from her childhood: Duke Brayham.

He had aged horribly. His fat rosy cheeks sagged, and he sported only a few awkward wisps of hair on his head. Bastian was speaking to him in an angry, hushed tone, reminding her faintly of when they were children and had watched Bastian's father arguing with the duke before the Winter Solstice. Bastian slammed a fist on the table, causing everyone in the room to cower. Everyone except for Shaye, who continued to stand tall with her stubborn chin held high.

Duke Brayham balked, "I assure you, sire, that is where the relic is being kept. My sources say—"

Bastian gritted his teeth, "Damn your sources to The Beyond. Why would I trust *humans* to do such a task?" He beckoned for someone to come forward. Shaye was surprised to see a Ceasg answer his call. The woman had an unearthly quality to her, much like Ingemar, with shimmering, golden scales glittering along her tanned arms and neck. Unlike Shaye's friend, however, her hair was shaved in a military style, and she was dressed modestly in a green cloak, much like the ones the Nefari guards wore.

"Yes, sire?" She bowed to him.

Shaye's jaw twitched at the respect Bastian was receiving. *So he thinks himself a king amongst these people.* She was disgusted by the sight of it.

Bastian looked at her as if she had spoken the words out loud, but said nothing. Instead, he addressed the Ceasg, "Signe, you will accompany us on our journey. I *wish* you to lead us to the Sword of Roth." At those words, the tent lit up in a golden light. When it ebbed away, a bronze, shimmering dust was left in its wake. Shaye realized then, that he was Signe's master—that he was the master of them all. Not only was he Nefari, but he was the Nefari leader.

Once they had mapped out the route to the relic, to the Sword of Roth, Bastian dismissed his generals. They bowed to him, and then to Shaye, as they took their leave.

Shaye was too stunned to speak right away, so Bastian helped himself, "Useless beasts, the lot of them. Thank the Fates I was able to capture several Ceasg to get the important work done." He sat, and motioned for Shaye to do the same. With a snap of his fingers, a human girl appeared from outside the tent. Her hands shook as she brought them two dinner plates and glasses to match. Anger surged through Shaye. He was kidnapping humans to act as servants to the dark Magi in his army. What else he was subjecting them to, she didn't want to imagine.

"Sit. Eat." He gestured to the plate sitting on top of the maps and papers littering the desk. Shaye obeyed, taking a few bites of the figs on her plate warily. He poured two glasses of wine and handed one to her. She took it reluctantly, noticing how it shimmered, unlike his own.

Bastian sat back casually, but there was malice in the way he looked at her. "I can feel you pulling away from me, you know. A shame, I thought we had come to an understanding this morning when I gave you such a touching gift."

She knew he was referring to Brina; this was a threat, a test of her allegiance to him. She crossed her arms over her chest as she spoke, "How can I be expected to trust you when you are playing with my mind?"

"I am only helping you to move past your silly feelings for that group of imbeciles."

"You do not need to read my thoughts and manipulate me to do so."

Bastian growled, "Don't I?" He motioned to the glass in front of her. "Drink."

She had no choice but to do as he directed. She downed the bitter liquid to the last drop, then slammed the glass on the table. Her throat burned in its wake, but she didn't let it show. She could not afford to show weakness when it came to Bastian.

He eyed her like a hawk, waiting for the warm liquid to settle in her stomach, before speaking again. "For this to work, I need you to use your full power. What we do here over the next few weeks will change the course of Asterion. Our people will finally take their rightful place. We were meant to rule, not to serve."

Shaye stared down at the knife beside Bastian's plate. It shined like a beacon of her salvation. She imagined what it would be like to stick the knife in the side of his neck. He cleared his throat, interrupting her daydream. She wanted to tell him that he was wrong. She wanted to demand that he stop this insane quest of his to conquer Asterion through dark magic, but she was having trouble finding the words that had been in her mind moments ago; every time she tried to speak, the words turned to ash on her tongue.

She looked down at her empty cup, there wasn't a drop left in the clear crystal glass. She wished she hadn't drunk it, that she had found another way to keep Bastian from thinking he needed to use his shadow abilities to control her mind. Shaye looked up at Bastian accusingly, "What—"

"Oh that? It was just a little something to relax you." He finished his own drink, the red liquid wet on his lips, like blood. Shaye shook her head, trying to snap out of the daze he had put her in.

"You don't need to drug me to get me to do as you say, Bastian." The room was growing dark, though it was midafternoon. Her breath was catching in her throat as she started to panic. Bastian made no move to help her; instead he sat by with those dark pools for eyes.

"Bass, please…" The last thing she saw was the vindictive smile on his face, as she drifted off into the void again.

She awoke later in her tent—the sky showing through the open flap at the entrance was pitch dark. She must have been out for hours; how had she lost an entire day?

"Here, drink this." There was a woman at her side, handing her a wooden cup. Shaye swatted it away.

"No, no more of that drink, please."

"It's me. It's Brina, and this is just water, I swear it, look." Brina took a small sip from the cup to prove to Shaye that there was no danger. She accepted the drink then; her mouth was dry, and her head was pounding.

"What happened?"

"You don't remember?" Brina's eyes were filled with dark concern.

Shaye shook her head. All she could recall was eating in the general's tent with Bastian. She remembered the bitter drink he had given her and the darkness that seemed to keep swallowing her whole.

"Shaye, they executed a Magi today. He was accused of being

one of King Allerick's sympathizers, all because the man had chosen to stay after the uprising and become a member of the Trade Guild."

Shaye sat up—there was no crime in that, in adapting to the new reign and to a world without magic. The Magi who had remained in Asterion after the death of the old king had had to move on, they had no choice. It wasn't like it had been easy on them, either; they faced disdain and mistrust from the humans they lived amongst.

Brina shared the sentiment, "They are weeding out expendable Magi, the ones who did not fight against King Allerick's rule. They're using them to frighten any remaining Magi into pledging their allegiance to Bastian and the Nefari... You really don't remember any of this?"

"No, I... I must have passed out after he drugged me. I don't remember anything between lunch and waking here with you."

Brina shook her head, tears pooling in her eyes. "Shaye, you were very much awake. You were there by Bastian's *side* as he made his judgment and bled the Magi dry."

"No." The word came as no more than a whisper, and she racked her brain trying to remember the events of the day. She would never have stood by for something like that. "Brina," her voice cracked, she couldn't hold back the tears anymore. "He's doing something to me... changing me. I try to fight him, but I don't know if I have the strength."

Brina cupped Shaye's face in her hands. "I don't know *anyone* stronger than you, Shaye. You are not alone in this, we will fight him together."

They fell asleep that night, side by side on Shaye's luxurious bed. As much as she hated Brina's being stuck in the midst of the danger, she was glad for the familiar presence. She stared up at the rough canvas ceiling, watching shadows dance from the lantern light.

She had spent the last few hours trying to remember the

events from the day. Not even a hint of memory was left behind —something she supposed she should be thankful for. The idea of taking part in such a heinous execution turned her stomach. She knew she needed to rest, to keep her strength for what awaited her in the morning, but she was afraid to close her eyes. The thought of what she would find in the darkness of her dreams terrified her.

CHAPTER FOUR

Shaye

The Nefari camp was bustling with excitement, and Shaye could feel the buzz of their magic alive in the warm morning air. They were nearing the summer season and the sun had been relentless over the last few days. She watched a small group of Nefari packing supplies for their voyage across the Living Sea.

Over the last week, Bastian had paraded Shaye around the camp, making grand speeches to his Nefari followers. He spent his days promising them the wealth and power that the Magi had enjoyed before King Allerick had taken his place on the throne— a throne that he had taken by the blood and tears of their people. Shaye could not blame the Nefari for taking so easily to his words. They roared in response to everything he said, hungry for what he was offering them.

Through it all, Shaye stood obediently by his side. The few times she had tried to disobey him, Bastian had presented her with the glittering red liquid, watching her drink every last drop. He had taken to giving her a weaker version of the potion than he had that first day. There were no more black outs; but, after each drink, she would spend the rest of the day in a fog, trailing along with him like a ghost. Nefari bowed to her as she passed, treating her like she was the queen to Bastian's king.

Shaye realized it was easier to play that part than to lose all control to the potion he would drug her with—even if it meant feeling like a traitor to Sorin and her friends. At the end of each day, Shaye would return to her quarters where Brina waited anxiously for her. They would eat and sleep in silence, with the ugliness of the day looming between them, then they would do it all over again the following day.

Shaye had also begun to practice placing a shield in her mind. It was not strong enough to fight against the magic in the potions, but the more she practiced, the more she was able to keep Bastian from her thoughts. Whenever he was able to slip into her mind, she was careful to focus on warm feelings toward him, however false those feelings might be.

"The ship is ready." Gorm, one of the red-headed twins, was waiting for her outside of her tent. He had forgone his cloak to sport clothes better for sailing. His large, muscled frame was visible now, without the bulk of the cloak to cover him. He was a mean-looking man, sneering at Shaye through a scar-covered face. She thought perhaps he had been handsome at one time in his life, before he had let hate overtake him.

"Let's not keep your commander waiting then." Shaye pulled a black hood over her head, covering her braided hair. Brina appeared at her side, dressed for a long journey in the same breeches and canvas doublet that Shaye wore.

"He's *your* commander too, Druid. Don't forget that." Gorm spat on the ground and nodded for them to start walking.

It would be a day's ride on horseback to the coast, where they would then hop a ship, sailing to the Eastern Isles. Gorm helped Brina to her horse, then moved to help Shaye. Not needing, or wanting, his help, she shrugged him off and mounted the white horse Bastian had gifted her with a few days before. He was a beautiful beast, but sitting atop his wide back brought a pang to her heart. She missed Finn, her loyal gelding, with his long silky mane. She hoped with all her heart that he was safe with Sorin. *Sorin, take care of my boy*, she thought quietly to herself, trying to keep the tears from starting again.

Sorin visited her thoughts often throughout her time with the Nefari. She was glad that he could not see her now, subjected to Bastian's whims. It was only on days when Bastian forced her to ingest the potion that she was unable to keep her thoughts straight enough to remember how much she cared for Sorin. Once the magic of the drink faded in the evenings, she would cry from the pain that accompanied her thoughts of Sorin and their friends, knowing they were out there without her.

She prayed to The Mother that they knew how sorry she was for what she had done. Hatred had flooded every one of her senses in the abandoned camp. She hadn't been able to stop the fiery magic that had risen from deep within her. It had erupted in a blast of dark magic, taking a piece of her soul in the process. She looked down at her hands, and the black leather gloves she wore to cover them, and her shame.

Six more Nefari joined them, riding to the coast where they would meet their master. Brina stayed close to Shaye—she had promised that she would not leave her side as they journeyed through the Living Sea. It had been a long time since Shaye had been on the water, and she was surprised at how much she missed it.

The smell of the salty air greeted her like an old friend as they rounded the hill toward the coast. She thought of the smuggler captain she had worked for before all of this began. She wished she had been able to get word to him and the crew, to warn them of what brewed so close to where they were docked. Captain Thorsten and his crew were survivors, though, and Shaye felt confident in their ability to sense anything amiss—to get themselves to safety before it was too late.

In the distance she could see the tall, dark masts of the ship that was to take them east. An obedient crew bustled on board, preparing them to set sail. Bastian was waiting for Shaye and the others on the deck in all his splendor. He was wearing a magnificent waistcoat—black, with the golden embroidery he seemed to like so much. It was an expensive jacket, and Shaye found herself wondering where he had gotten the coin to pay for it. *He probably forced some poor human into making it for him.* Shaye was disgusted at the thought.

They wasted no time, settling the horses below deck with the human servants they had brought with them. Shaye was relieved that Bastian had agreed to allow Brina to stay with her above deck—even if it was only so he could use the threat of her safety to his advantage, should Shaye decide to resist him again. There had been no glittering drink this morning and she was feeling clear headed. Another thing she was grateful for.

"Are you nervous?" Bastian slid beside Shaye, resting his arm on the smooth wood of the ship's side. They were alone on the quarterdeck, save for Brina who lingered nearby, keeping an eye on them both.

Shaye took control of her thoughts, focusing on the glistening water below and not the disdain she felt at Bastian's presence. When she didn't answer, he slid closer and put one of his hands on hers. "You needn't be. This will go exactly as I planned it: we will get the Sword, and with both it and the Stave you will power our army enough to destroy anything in our path." There was genuine happiness on his slender face. Shaye studied him, wondering how she had missed the ugliness that resided behind that handsome smile.

She felt sick to her stomach. As the last Druid of her line, she held the ability to amplify magic with the Stave of the first brother, Leto. They were on their way, now, to locate the relic of the second brother—a Sword, granted to him by The Mother, and powerful enough to cut through any shield or armor. By using the Stave to amplify the Sword's power, Shaye would be arming Bastian's entire Nefari army with the magic they needed to conquer Asterion.

She had to come up with a plan to stop him, to stop herself from being forced into obedience when the time came. When she was around him, he had power over her thoughts—the same way he had pulled the dark magic from her in the clearing with Sorin and the others. Bastian was the living epitome of every bad thought she had ever had, every hateful thing she had wished on the king who had slaughtered her people during the Winter Solstice.

Despite Bastian telling her that she didn't need to be nervous, she was—mostly she was worried that she would feel that hatred rise within her again, or that when the time came, she would *want* to power his army. She could not forgive the pain her people had felt, or the prejudice she had witnessed firsthand in the towns against the Magi, who had never harmed anyone, even when they still had their magic. Bastian knew it—he knew what was hiding deep within her soul, and he had the power to exploit it.

The ship's captain shouted something to the crew, cutting through her thoughts. There was a jolt as they set sail toward the endless horizon. Bastian whistled, meeting her eyes, "May The Mother guide us."

Shaye ignored the urge to give him a vulgar gesture before she left to join Brina on the other side of the deck. The girls made their leave to find some way to occupy their time. It would be days before they reached the small islands to the east, near Sagon. She had never been there, but she knew people who had. According to them, the waters could be dangerous, filled with magical creatures who lurked beneath the surface, waiting for vulnerable sailors to pass by.

She shivered at the memory of the blight she had passed through while on her way to Asterion. It had been several weeks since she had made that voyage home, but the memory of the dense, black fog laying on the water, filled with the screams of the sailors it had claimed, still lingered in her mind. Of course, now, she was sailing with the monster who had created the fog; Bastian had been behind all of it. She had just been too blinded by their shared past to see it.

Two sailors began arguing over a game of cards, drawing a crowd of laughing men around them. Brina nudged Shaye, "Wanna play?"

"Nah, I'm not in the mood."

Brina put a hand to her heart, feigning surprise. "*The* Shaye Wistari, world-renowned gambler, doesn't want to play cards? I am *shocked*." A laugh died in her throat when she looked at Shaye's solemn face.

Shaye turned her face away from Brina and back to the horizon. She knew she looked like hell. There were dark circles around her once vibrant golden eyes, which were now dulled like unpolished brass, and she'd lost weight. Bastian had given her a whole new wardrobe, in part, she knew, because he had wanted her in a style similar to his; but she also knew it was because her old clothes no longer fit her the same.

Brina got the hint. "Okay, how about a story then? That always cheered you up when—"

"When we were children and the nightmares only existed in my mind?"

"Shaye, you need to keep faith. If not in yourself, then in Sorin. I have to believe that the same man who showed up in our barnyard begging you to help him, is doing everything he can to find you now."

"He said he saved me, you know. That night at the Winter Solstice ball when we were children. But when he finally told me, I didn't believe him. Instead, I believed Bastian... I thought I knew him." She couldn't hold back the tears this time. The breeze pushed the hood off of her head, saltwater and tears stung her eyes. "I hurt Sorin. I hurt a man who believed in me. And in the process, I let the Stave fall into the hands of a madman. I would not blame Sorin for hating me for what I did, and he is better off without me. There is no coming back from this, from what I've become."

Brina stood in silence for a long moment. Shaye knew Brina well enough to know that she was searching for the words to help her friend. Brina squeezed Shaye's hand as she spoke, "You may not see it now, but we will find a way through this. And when it's over, you will find a way to forgive yourself. You *have* to."

Shaye shook her head and watched the horizon, hoping with all her heart that her friend was right. "Where are you, Sorin?" The heavy wind blew wisps of her hair from her braid as she spoke. Shaye closed her eyes tight and wished for the wind to carry her words away, like a bird taking flight.

CHAPTER FIVE

Sorin

It was dark when Sorin and the others reached the beach on the eastern coast of North Asterion, having traveled through the night to reach it as quickly as possible. Word had finally come from Ingemar's friend. She was in the Nefari camp, reporting directly to the commander... Bastian. That bastard had been their leader from the start, and Sorin had let him under the same roof as the people he cared about.

Bastian was the cause of the blight destroying the land, the man-eating fog that had taken Elijah, the monster attacks, all of it. Worst of all, he was using his dark magic on Shaye. He had been a step ahead of them the entire time.

Not anymore. Their Ceasg spy in the camp had told them everything—Sorin and his team now knew the exact number and configuration of the Nefari army, the location of the camp, and what their next move was. They knew on good authority that Bastian was headed to an island in the east to track down the Sword, but Sorin would beat him to it. Bastian underestimated Sorin, and he planned to use that to his advantage for as long as he could.

It had not taken long for him to find a crew to sail them to the Isles. Mavka found out about a group of smugglers from Sagon who had been stranded near Norbrach at the start of the blight; they had sailed up the coast when they noticed the trouble was spreading. Their captain, a man by the name of Thorsten, had been fruitlessly searching for a way across the Living Sea and back to their home port in Sagon.

When Sorin had first made contact, the man had brushed him off, having no interest in a journey that wouldn't benefit him or his crew. But when Mavka's moths whispered in her ear, she had giggled, "But it *will* benefit your crew, Captain. Is Shaye Wistari not a member of it?" At the mention of Shaye, the entire crew had looked stunned. These had been the very people she had sailed with before returning home for the spring festival. Sorin had to believe that it was destiny that had brought them together.

The crew had unanimously agreed to help Sorin, and now they found themselves nearing their destination, the Eastern Isles. In just a few hours, they would be within sight of the island that held their destiny. This could turn the tides in favor of Sorin's army.

"King Sorin." Captain Thorsten, the pirate-turned-smuggler, stood in front of him in a ridiculously flamboyant waistcoat. It was a gaudy thing that didn't quite match the scar on his cheek or the wild, thick, wavy hair at his shoulders. The captain wasn't the sort of person Sorin had spent a lot of time with in the past, but he had to admit, the man had a pleasant temperament and even better rum.

Captain Thorsten handed Sorin a dusty bottle and chuckled, "I was just thinking about the first time I met her. She was a wild thing, always up for a fight or a wager. When she came to us, it didn't take any time before she was a part of our family." He took the bottle from Sorin, pausing for a long drink. "But you know all about that, don't you? How easy it is to be around her, to love her."

Sorin raised an eyebrow at the man who was old enough to be Shaye's father. Thorsten laughed and took another swig of the rum. "Don't worry, lad, I love her like I love the rest of 'em." He nodded toward his crew who were sitting on the deck, laughing and telling stories. "Now, Haskell there... *him* you might worry about. He does love the ladies, though Shaye was always too wise to fall for his games."

Sorin chuckled, trying to imagine the warrior-like man fruitlessly flirting with the woman whom Sorin had come to know so well. Meeting the crew had been interesting. Haskell was a Skagan through and through. He carried himself like a warrior and was massive in size, even compared to Bron. His long, braided beard and hair to match was a dead giveaway to his Skagan roots. Sorin had recognized him from the day at the spring festival—the man who Shaye had danced with in the town square. Sorin had a hard time imagining Shaye with someone like Haskell, though he was easy to get along with, as were the others.

There were three more from their crew that had agreed to accompany their captain: Langley, a shy, gangly-looking man who they claimed was brilliant, even if he didn't look like it. And Ylva, a gifted sorceress who owned a club back in Sagon, famous for its exotic Magi women. Then there was Runa, the youngest of their crew. She was a mousey little thing with short hair, cut like a boy's.

Captain Thorsten had vouched for each of them, promising that they were all capable of such a high-stakes mission, and Sorin had decided from the start that if Shaye trusted them, then he did, too.

Laughter filled the air as Haskell taught Ingemar how to play blackjack. She was hesitant to be near Thorsten's crew, still unable to let herself trust human men, aside from Sorin, Bron, and Anik. Sorin thought that at least Ylva's presence was a comforting one for her—having another who wielded magic seemed to make Ingemar relax slightly.

Sorin and Thorsten stood in the shadows on the deck. A warm breeze swept through, showing signs of a hot summer ahead of them. Sorin was eager to reach the Isles and be back on land. He had loved fishing as a boy, but preferred the steadiness of a dock to the sway of a ship's deck.

"Captain, when we reach the Isles, it's imperative that we do this quietly. Our source in the Nefari camp tells us that Bastian knows the location of the second relic, so there is still the chance of a confrontation." They were in a race to retrieve the Sword before Bastian could get his hands on it.

Though Sorin did not relish the thought of going head-to-head with a group of Nefari, he secretly hoped that they would have a run in. He desperately wanted to see Shaye, and knowing how important she was to Bastian, Sorin was confident that he would not leave her behind. If Shaye was there, then they stood a chance of getting her back. He could bring her home and set things right.

Captain Thorsten nodded, "My crew knows the importance of discretion, Your Majesty. And I can assure you, we are ready for a fight if it comes down to it."

Sorin was counting on it. He was grateful for the experienced captain. They sailed the rest of the way, passing rum around, playing cards, and telling stories about Shaye. Sorin loved hearing about this side of her. A small part of him hoped that when all of this was over, she would tell him her side of these tales herself. Just as she had done that night in the caves.

Sorin excused himself from the others, wanting a moment alone. Finn found him, nuzzling his soft nose into Sorin's side. The other horses were safely below deck, but Sorin didn't have the heart to make Finn stay down there. The gelding had taken to Sorin over the last weeks and had whinnied when Sorin had ascended the steps to the upper deck. Overwhelmed, he had released Finn to wander the deck as the horse saw fit. He knew the loyal steed missed Shaye as much as he did, and somehow it made Sorin feel less alone.

Patting Finn's head, he looked out over the deck of the ship. The waters were quiet; normally Sorin would have been glad of it, but something seemed off about it. The others must have sensed it as well. Ylva and Ingemar appeared at his side, and the two Magi women wasted no time extending their magic out onto the water. Ylva's shimmering magic intertwined with Ingemar's golden dust. If Sorin hadn't been so nervous, he would have thought the sight beautiful.

"Captain," Sorin called for Thorsten. A hush fell over the deck as the others noticed something was wrong. Finn stomped his hoof on the deck and snorted. Sorin noticed Haskell picking up a bucket, and raising a hand to hit it. "Haskell, what are you doing?" he called out with a hushed tone.

"Sirens?" Haskell ignored Sorin and directed the question at Ylva. She shook her head and he set the bucket down quietly.

Something rumbled below them under the hull of the ship. There was a faint movement, but one that could only have come from something exceptionally large. Sorin drew his sword, and the others followed his lead. The ship shook as something hit it from below. Sorin reached out to Finn to catch himself. The horse stood firmly in place, but Sorin recognized the panic in his large eyes.

From the corner of his eye, he spotted a shadow rising from the water. Ylva and Ingemar noticed it, too, pulsing their magic in the shadow's direction. It rose high above them—it was monstrously large, with a body shaped like a human man, but towering twenty feet above the deck of the ship. Its long, dark body extended down below the sea.

Before anyone had a chance to react, the creature spoke, its voice like the distant rumble of thunder during a storm. "You sail where you are not welcome."

They were all too stunned to answer—all except Ingemar. Her dark skin shimmered in the wake of the magic she continued to extend outward in an attempt to protect the ship. "*Umibōzu*, we request safe passage." She was confident as she spoke, sounding nothing like how Sorin felt at the sight of the towering sea monster.

"There is a price for such a request—one you cannot afford, young Ceasg. The Eastern Isles are under my protection, and the punishment for trespassers is an eternity in a watery grave." The ship rocked with his words, and rain began to fall. A storm was brewing directly over the ship. To Sorin's dismay, it was over the ship only, and no other part of the water; it was coming from the sea spirit known as an Umibōzu. Sorin feared that under the Umibōzu's power, the sea would grow tremulous enough to sink them, as he had threatened.

Ingemar kept her composure, "Name your price."

The Umibōzu thought for a moment before answering. "I know your kind." He looked pointedly at Thorsten's crew. "Pirates carry the most beautiful bounty. Perhaps I will let you pass if you bestow your greatest treasure upon me."

Sorin's stomach dropped—the most valuable thing on this ship was a barrel of Thorsten's exceptionally potent rum. They had no jewels or gold to give this greedy beast.

It was Captain Thorsten who spoke next, "Of course. We would be happy to part with it in exchange for our lives."

Sorin nudged the captain and whispered, "What are you playing at?"

"Trust me," was his only response. He nodded to Ylva, who took his cue, even if Sorin did not. She disappeared below the deck, dragging a trembling Langley with her by his sleeve.

The storm continued to grow above them as the creature waited patiently for their return. Clouds circled, coming to life with the first signs of lightning. It felt like one of the longest moments of Sorin's life as he looked to his friends in reassurance.

There was no other way out of this, and trusting Thorsten was their only option.

Sorin could tell the Umibōzu was beginning to grow impatient, as it growled over the storm brewing in the sky and its shadowy form wavered. Sorin feared what the sea spirit would do when its patience ran out, and was relieved when Ylva and Langley returned with a large crate from below deck. They brought it confidently to the side of the ship where the Umibōzu waited. As they set it down with a heavy thud, the creature rumbled with pleasure.

Ingemar addressed the beast, "The deal is made and we have honored our side of the bargain."

Ylva lifted the crate with her magic, the shells in her wild, braided hair clinked together in the wind of the brewing storm. The Umibōzu took the crate in his shadowed hands, and Sorin could have sworn he spotted a smile in the dark abyss of the creature. The ship's crew held their breath in anticipation. Sorin knew there was no treasure awaiting the monster, they had left the beach with only the necessities; surely their measly food storage wouldn't please it enough to allow them to leave with their lives.

Before the Umibōzu had a chance to open the crate, Ylva spirited the ship away in a flurry of white-purple magic. They quickly left the beast behind. In the distance, Sorin could see the creature slinking back into the water, crate in hand. It seemed the creature planned to take it down in the depth of the sea before opening it to see what bounty he had taken for himself.

Soon the Umibōzu and the storm were no longer in sight and, instead, a dark, forested island lay ahead of them. Once they were a safe distance away, Langley let out a whoop. Ylva laughed, it was a deep velvety sound. "That is going to be one angry beast."

Thorsten stood, watching the island they were quickly approaching. There was no humor in his voice, "Let us be long gone before he realizes."

Langley addressed the confusion on the rest of the crew's faces as he shouted, "It's empty! Ylva enchanted it to show an endless supply of riches, all of which will disappear in just a few short hours—long enough for us to be a safe distance away."

It was a brilliant con, but Sorin couldn't help worrying about the wrath they would face when it was time to return through those waters.

CHAPTER SIX

Sorin

The island was desolate but beautiful, with a lush green canopy as far as the eye could see. Though it appeared to be nothing more than an abandoned land, Sorin could sense the power of the ancient islands, untouched and untainted by man. It was similar to how he had felt as a child when his father had taken him north to visit the old king's court.

The Magi, under King Idor's rule, had been out of control; they had torched human homes, let their magical creatures run wild outside of the Raven Wood, and endangered many Asterion lives. Magic had been strongest in North Asterion, and its power had radiated from the land. That is what he felt here on the Eastern Isles now.

Thorsten assured him that the creatures lurking beneath the canopy would be of no concern to them, but Sorin knew by now that a relic would not go unprotected. He'd learned that the hard way when they had retrieved the Stave from the caves. It had nearly cost him his life at the hands of Ingemar, who had been trapped there by the Nefari and forced to protect it from anyone who came looking.

Still, the goal was simple: follow the path that their spy had laid out for them in her message. They would venture into the heart of the island to find the second relic, the Sword of Roth. The crew readied themselves, strapping various weapons onto their persons. Even Runa packed on a large bow and an impressive quiver of arrows, looking out of place on her small frame.

Haskell bounced on the balls of his feet beside Sorin, like an eager hound ready for a hunt. The sun was relentless above them, even at this early hour, and sweat had already begun to bead at Sorin's temple. He wished that they had been able to bring the horses—riding would beat walking in this heat. But Thorsten had urged that it would be too difficult to get through the brush with them. Wordlessly, they began their journey on foot.

As of yet, there was no sign of Bastian and his men. The forest canopy was a harmony of birds and other creatures Sorin could not name. Every sense in Sorin's body was on high alert. With each flutter of a bird or rustle of grass, he prepared himself for an assault. Haskell led the way with his machete, Bron at his side with one of his own. The two large men forced their way through the brush, leading their team deep within the trees.

Mavka's moths fluttered rapidly around her, feeling the power within the jungle and eager to explore. Sorin had grown used to them by now, just as he had grown used to the small Forest Dweller whom he called "friend." Her father had assured him that they would continue gathering a force to face the Nefari army, so that when Sorin and the others returned, he and the rest of his forces would be ready for whatever came next.

After walking for quite some time, Sorin grew anxious. "Ingemar, are you sure your friend gave no other hint as to where exactly the Sword would be?"

She wiped the sweat from her brow and readjusted the shell-enameled headpiece on her head. "She only said that it would be within the heart of the mainland."

Mavka held a hand up, stopping Sorin from responding with

his complaint. As she did so, Sorin noted a small ghost light ahead in a clearing. It glowed in the shadows of the trees like a small lantern beckoning them. She whispered, "Hello, friend."

Sorin knew better than to question Mavka's connection to the magical elements of the land and, instead, took her cue as she followed the little light through the trees. They lost sight of her for a moment as she squirmed her way through the brush, until Bron and Haskell could cut their way after her.

When they found her again, she was standing amongst a cluster of tiny blue lights. They danced around just as her moths usually did, their luminescent light flickering in excitement. Mavka whispered something to them and giggled at their response. She turned to Sorin and the others with glee on her face, "They will take us to the Sword."

"Who are 'they'?" Langley looked frightened, clutching his pack to his chest.

"The Will-o'-Wisps, of course." Mavka laughed as one fluttered past her vine-covered hair. "They know who we are and why we have come. And they wish to help you, King Sorin."

Sorin did not wish to question the generosity of these ghostly creatures, so he simply bowed to them. "I am honored."

The Will-o'-Wisps proceeded, this time with fierce determination. Sorin felt a seed of hope growing within him. This had to be the break that they had been waiting for. They would get the Sword, keep it from Bastian's dark grasp, and stop the battle before it began.

They neared a small pool of water, glistening softly within a clearing. Across the pool, a small cliff led up to the top of a waterfall, the sound of its running water was peaceful. Sorin looked around for any sign of the Sword. A strong burst of light erupted, blinding Sorin temporarily. The crew shielded their eyes and Mavka ducked behind Bron's broad back. The Will-o'-Wisps were flooding the clearing with their bright, blue light, then directed it to a bare patch of dirt. Sorin wasted no time, pushing his way through the crowd. He knelt, feeling the cold, hard ground beneath his fingers.

The land responded to his touch, sending a jolt through him. He looked up at the others. "It's here! The sword is here. Help me." He began to dig with his hands, scrambling to get to the relic he believed lurked beneath. The others joined him, using whatever they had on them to burrow into the ground. It took a great deal of effort, but soon they hit something solid. Sorin dusted the remaining dirt away to reveal the golden hilt of a sword. He gripped it, pulling with all his strength to reveal a magnificent blade. Its hilt was gilded in gold with an emerald jewel in the center of it. As he held the Sword up in the dim light of the jungle, the blade glistened, as clean and sharp as freshly made steel, as if it hadn't spent centuries buried in the dirt of an ancient island.

His friends stood in silent awe of the beauty of it. Sorin looked around at the dense trees—they needed to get the Sword to the ship before anyone found them. He stood, quickly removing his own sword from its scabbard, and replacing it with the relic. The crew took his lead, ready to head back the way that they had come, when a familiar voice came from the cliff near the waterfall.

The soft voice carried down over the trickling sound of the water, "Sorin."

It felt like his heart had stopped in his chest. It was as if the entire world melted away at the sound of that voice, the voice he had dreamed of since the day she had been taken away from him. *Shaye.*

She stepped from behind the shadows of the jungle. Sorin's eyes searched for any sign of abuse, but she was the same Shaye that he remembered: beautiful, with her golden eyes and long, auburn hair. Only now, her once-bright eyes were dimmed, and her full frame had thinned slightly. She was dressed in all black, with a red embroidered flame on her jacket, over her heart—just like the flame that had burst from her that day in the abandoned camp.

He wanted to go to her, to scale his way up the cliff, but the fear in her eyes gave him pause. "No," she urged, just as she was joined by Bastian and a handful of others. They came from the trees like creatures appearing from the night, just as quickly and silently as the Umibōzu had come from the sea. Bastian's eyes glistened in delight at the look of hurt and rage on Sorin's face.

He said with a mocking tone, "We meet again, *King* Sorin, and it seems you have done the grunt work for us." He gestured toward the Sword strapped to Sorin's side. "Now, if you'll just hand it over, perhaps I will be merciful and allow you to walk out of here in one piece."

Shaye had a look of utter horror on her face as Bastian addressed Sorin. He must have noticed it as well because he put a hand on her shoulder and said through gritted teeth, "Shaye, if you would, ask your friends to hand over what is rightfully ours."

"Sorin, please." She took a step forward, nearing the rocky ledge, but Bastian held her in place. Sorin could see Bastian's grip on her shoulder tighten.

Sorin's blood rose at the sight of that monster's hands on her. Sorin could see Bron draw his sword beside him, and he could feel Ingemar's power rising behind, ready to fire at his order. Sorin looked at Shaye, wishing he could read her mind, wishing she could tell him what to do to get them all out of this mess.

Captain Thorsten warned him quietly, "Easy now, Your Majesty."

Sorin shrugged off the warning. He could not give up the Sword so easily, but he also would not risk losing Shaye a second time. "If you want it, Bastian, come and get it."

Bastian leaned into Shaye, still holding her with one sickly black hand, and brushing the hair off her neck with the other. He whispered something in her ear, and she shut her eyes tightly in response; tears escaped, falling down her flushed cheeks. The hair on Sorin's arms rose as Bastian snapped his fingers. Shaye opened her eyes, only this time there was no regret, only anger.

She lifted her hands, calling on her magic, and Bastian smiled like a feral cat. The ground shook beneath their feet, and the water from the pool lifted in response to her call. There was no recognition in Shaye's eyes as she released the water onto Sorin and his crew. They turned to run but the water caught Sorin in its grasp. It lifted him off the ground and into the air like a giant's hand, pulling him within reach of Bastian and his men.

"Shaye, you have to fight him." Sorin struggled under the grip of the water. When she did not respond he shouted at her, "Do you *hear me? Fight!*"

One of Bastian's thugs stepped forward and tore the Sword from Sorin's scabbard. Shaye kept her hold on the water, suspending Sorin at the mercy of Bastian. The man who had taken the Sword handed it to his master. Bastian took it eagerly like a greedy child. He rotated it before him, smiling in admiration of the craftsmanship of the magical object, reveling in its power before pointing it at Sorin.

Sorin ignored the sharp point of the blade at his throat and kept his focus on Shaye. Nothing else mattered at this moment. Bastian had already taken the Sword, but Sorin had to get through to Shaye. "He does not own you, Shaye. Claim your power for yourself, not for him and this ridiculous vengeance he is after. This can only end in a river of blood, just as the brothers' story foretold."

Bastian stepped closer, but the water shifted Sorin away slightly as Shaye's magic buckled beneath her hold. Sorin could not help but notice the fleeting look of terror in her eye. Bastian must have noticed it, too, as he turned on her. "Shaye. Hold His Royal Majesty in place. Things will go much more smoothly in Asterion with him out of our way."

Shaye regarded Bastian with a stone-like look. "I am trying, sire, but my magic... it has its limits..." And with that, she dropped Sorin. He plummeted toward the empty pool, but before he could hit the exposed ground beneath, a gold, glittering magic swept him up and in the opposite direction of the Nefari.

Ingemar pulled him to them with her magic. Sorin ran back to the water and shouted at Bastian, "I will kill you, you son of a bitch!"

Bastian sneered down at Sorin and the others. "You have nothing left to fight for. I have the relics." He paused to hold the Sword up in the light with one hand, while he tapped a black obsidian pendant hanging around his neck with the other. "And, I have *her*."

Shaye stood by his side with tears pooling in her eyes. Sorin could see that she was trying to hold her composure. Bastian nodded to his men, and they obeyed the silent order, raising their hands to hit Sorin and the others with their black magic.

Ylva shouted to Sorin, "We are not strong enough to take them! We must finish this later."

Sorin's friends did not give him the chance to argue before tearing him away and through the brush. Bastian shouted to his men to follow, but instead, the Nefari were met with a wall of bright blue magic, the work of the Will-o'-Wisps. Sorin turned back to see the sparks of their ancient magic holding against the Nefari. He took one last look at Shaye, and then ran as quickly as he could toward the ship on the other side of the island. He and his friends did not stop until they reached the shore and boarded the small boat they had taken to the island.

There was no sign of the Nefari as they left the shore. Sorin sat in the boat, watching the island fade from view as Ylva guided them further into the sea and away from the Eastern Isles. Away from Shaye. A tear found its way down his cheek as he tried to accept everything they had just lost.

CHAPTER SEVEN

Shaye

Shaye could barely see through the bitter tears welling in her eyes as their ship left the island—she wiped them away before anyone could notice. The Eastern Isles were mere spots on the horizon now, but she could not escape the memory of Sorin suspended at her mercy, locked in the cool water of the pool. He had pleaded with her, but he didn't understand. Bastian's power had crept into her mind like a parasite, it was all she could do just to release him against Bastian's order. And now she worried about who would pay the price for her insolence.

One thing she was grateful for was the sight of her friends, Ingemar, Bron, and Mavka, safe and unharmed from her attack on them in the camp. Between the drink Bastian was drugging her with, and the darkness that had crept into her soul that day, she hadn't trusted that they had all walked away from the attack unscathed. It was as if a large weight had been lifted from her chest after seeing them there. More so, she was shocked to see Thorsten and his crew there with them. Fates only knew how they had all been thrown together...but if anyone was going to make things difficult for Bastian, it would be that lot.

Brina had embraced her when they returned to the ship, but the look on Shaye's face gave her pause. Before Shaye could tell her what had happened on the island, Bastian appeared in a fury. He grabbed Brina by the hair, tearing her away from Shaye's grasp. Both girls yelped as he threw Brina onto the splintered deck of the ship. Bastian raised a hand to strike her in the face, but before he had a chance, Shaye felt a flood of cold darkness wash over her. She welcomed the feeling, pulsing it into Bastian, and throwing him from her friend and into the stairs leading to the upper deck. His body made a horrible crunching noise as he slumped to the ground.

Shaye ran to Brina to help her up, checking her for injury. Brina turned her stunned gaze to Shaye's hands which were holding her. "Oh Fates, Shaye, what have you done?"

When Shaye looked down, she saw what had her friend so rattled. The inky blackness that had overtaken her fingertips had now spread to the midpoint of her knuckles—a sign that she had once again tapped into the black magic that the Nefari used. She began to panic. "No. No. Brina, I didn't mean to, I..."

Bastian laughed from where he had been thrown, propping himself up on the railing. Shaye could hear the crackling of his bones popping back into place; he was using his magic to heal himself. The act of healing himself so easily told Shaye just how much power he had. It was uncommon for Magi to heal by sheer willpower, without the help of potions and incantations.

He groaned and then said, "It feels good, doesn't it? The power coursing through your veins. How easily it answers your call, Shaye Wistari."

Shaye backed away, shaking her head in denial, but he was right. It had felt too easy, she had not called on the magic; instead, it had come to her, offering its power in response to the fear and anger she had felt at the thought of Bastian hurting Brina.

Bastian approached her with a slight limp. "It lives inside of you now. Just as the Druid magic lives in your blood. Each time will become easier, until you no longer feel the weight and guilt of it."

"I am nothing like you, Bastian. I am not so weak as to let darkness taint my soul." She pushed Brina behind her, determined to protect her friend at all costs.

"I know of your nightmares. You think I haven't felt them, too? Sorin's father took everything from us that night at the Winter Solstice ball—our wealth, our power…" He trailed off as he closed the gap between them. Brina pulled on Shaye's sleeve, trying to get her to step away from him, but Shaye could not move. She was locked in on his eyes, on the words that rang true. "I know it was easy for you to let Sorin into your heart, to believe that he was different from that bastard father of his. But you know deep down, that the only way to set things right is to *take* what is ours."

"You know nothing of my nightmares." Shaye sounded more confident than she felt. The black magic was still strumming through her veins, and she hated to admit it, but it felt good.

A storm brewed over them, dark and powerful, just like the dark magic that was calling to her. Bastian did not stop advancing on her as he said, "You do not owe them your forgiveness, nor your mercy. I know you have dreamt of revenge. You know that vengeance is the only cure to the nightmares that have plagued you for so long."

Shaye's heart was racing, but the impulse to run from him was no longer there. Heat flooded her cheeks as he touched her hair and spoke, "Harness your nightmares, Shaye. Take control and make others *feel* the fear that you have endured all these years."

She touched his hand as it caressed her cheek, and pulled it from her face, but did not let go of it. Power beckoned to her—

the power within herself, the power that was coming from his touch, and the power of the Sword radiating from his side. It was like a beacon, impossible to turn from. She felt like one of Mavka's moths, unable to resist the call of a lantern light.

She followed Bastian's gaze to his hand in hers, the black mark of dark magic had crept further down her fingers toward her palm, only now it was accompanied by the faint glistening of the power that was radiating from her, *between* her and Bastian. Brina faded into the background, along with the crew and the very ship on which they stood.

She could think of nothing else but the powerlessness she had felt all her life. She thought of the Master Mages who had punished her for not being strong enough, of her aunt and uncle who had looked down on her because of her weakened bloodline. She sneered at the thought of the men who had slaughtered her people, and the poor treatment of Magi she had witnessed since then.

Bastian was right: with the Stave and the Sword, she could harness power beyond anyone's wildest dreams. She could set things the way she saw fit, she could protect the ones that she cared about. Even if it meant working alongside the Nefari for the time being. She was done feeling like that scared little girl in the palace with dirt on her new dress, waiting for someone to rescue her and lead her to safety. She was finished with the nightmares that had haunted her for so long.

She removed her hand from Bastian's. She felt cold and distant as she decided at that moment that she would no longer take orders from the honeyed tongues of men. Bastian had the good sense to look surprised as she raised a hand to his face and tore at him with her nails. The deep marks dripped with blood, and she swore she saw fear in his eyes as she made her decision. "You are right, Bastian. I am done being haunted by nightmares—so I will become one, instead."

CHAPTER EIGHT

Shaye

When they returned, the Nefari camp was buzzing with the news that Bastian had succeeded in his quest to capture the second brother's relic. With it, Shaye would be able to power their army with enough magic to cut down anything in their path. Now it was a matter of waiting for Sorin's army to arrive in the valley below. The Nefari had the upper hand in every way: in weapons, in numbers, and in holding the high ground.

Shaye had been stuck in the generals' tent for hours listening to them gloat about their predetermined victory. She sat silently at Bastian's side, lighting small fires at her fingertips. She watched the flames dance along her fingers, obeying her every command. She was bored with these men, these Nefari who talked too much. She desperately wanted to leave the stuffy air of the tent and she craved a strong drink of ale.

She noticed the sudden pause in conversation and looked up to see all eyes on her. Bastian looked at her expectantly. He tapped his fingers on the table impatiently. "Shaye. Are you listening?"

"No, not really." She looked around in boredom, still allowing the fire to dance on her fingers as she sat slumped in the hard wooden chair. The high-ranking officers in the tent shifted their gaze between Shaye and Bastian, waiting to see what would happen as a result of her blatant disobedience.

Bastian shifted uncomfortably in his seat. "Duke Brayham was asking if you would be ready to activate the Sword's power under the blood moon. Sorin's army has been spotted a few days' ride from the valley."

"I'll be ready. Will you?" She sat forward giving the traitorous duke a pointed look.

The ruddy man puffed up his chest at her insinuation. "Listen here, *girl*—"

He did not have a chance to finish his sentence before Shaye blew at her fingertips, sending the flames onto the man's expensive waistcoat. He shouted as he patted out the fire that was now trying to engulf his clothes. The smell of burned hair and fabric filled the tent.

No one moved to help him as Bastian let out a roar of laughter. Duke Brayham threw the coat from himself and onto the ground, stomping out the rapidly growing flames. The Nefari in the room bowed their heads in obedience to Shaye. That sort of show of power was well respected within their ranks.

Shaye sat, still as a statue with her head cocked to the side. There was no amusement in her eyes when she stood. The generals parted in her wake, allowing her to pass by them, leaving the tent and the shocked duke behind.

As she left the tent, the sunlight was beating down. Shaye put a hand up to shield her eyes, her black fingers bare for all the camp to see. She no longer hid what she had become under gloves. There was no point. She *wanted* them to fear her, to know what she was capable of.

She strolled confidently through the camp, accepting the presence of the twin brothers who still guarded her movements throughout the encampment. She didn't mind anymore; if she really wanted to escape them, she could.

Gorm was looking up at the murder of crows in the sky and stumbled into her. She shoved him back and kept walking. The crows had been following her relentlessly lately, and she had grown used to their presence.

Gorm, however, appeared nervous as he asked, "What's with them?"

"They're friends of mine," Shaye replied, picking up her pace so that the guards were forced to fall in line behind her.

Though she hadn't tested the true strength of her new power, she had often wondered if she could call on the crows to do her bidding if she so chose. She smiled at the thought of the Nefari guards' smug, scarred faces being pecked from their skulls.

An Orc paused at her passing, laying the axe he was sharpening down so that he could bow to her. She stopped to admire the beast in all its brute strength. She wondered if she was powerful enough to crush its skull with the wave of her hand. Before she could test her theory, Brina appeared. She looked as if she had not slept in days, since they had returned from their journey. There were dark circles around her eyes, and her beautiful honey-blonde hair, which was usually pulled back neatly, was now down and disheveled.

They had hardly spoken a word since that day on the ship. Brina had even taken to sleeping in a separate bed, rolled in for her by one of the human servants. Something deep within Shaye tugged at the thought of her friend's suffering. She knew she should try to comfort her, but the words would not come. Shaye needed to focus on destroying Bastian's force from within. Even if that meant shutting herself off from the one person there whom she cared for.

Brina offered Shaye a flask of water, and as she accepted it, she searched for something to say. Brina spoke first, "Are you alright?"

"Fine. Just tired of the ramblings of those fools in the tent." Shaye noted that the camp had cleared out around them. The Nefari army had taken to giving Shaye her space since they had returned with the Sword. She knew they had heard about the confrontation between her and Bastian on the ship, and that they could sense the power Shaye had finally claimed. When she strolled through the camp or entered a meeting, eyes would lower to the ground, as if they did not want to draw her attention to them.

In the distance, she could see the altar Bastian's servants were erecting for the ceremony that would take place under the blood moon. At his command, it would consist of a platform for both him and Shaye to stand on. They would be raised above the crowd so that the endless Nefari army could see them claim the ancient power of the relics. When the full moon rose in the sky, Shaye would activate the Stave's power, connecting it to the Sword and thereby amplifying the army's own weapons. Anything with a blade would become unbeatable.

Shaye stood a moment longer, thinking about how much of a waste it was to use supplies to build the altar, when she could just perform the ceremony on the ground. But Bastian loved a good show and that is what he planned to give them. She was feeling irritated, which was strange, because she had not been feeling much of anything lately.

A group of women rounding the corner caught her attention. They were pretty little things in expensive gowns that looked out of place in the grim camp. They were chattering and giggling to one another, their cheeks flushed with the heat of the early summer day. When they noticed Shaye, they stopped and curtseyed to her. Shaye made no movement in return, not even a smile in their direction.

The woman leading the group beamed at Shaye brightly, she had a pinched face and pale blonde hair. "Shaye, it's so lovely to see you again." She stepped toward Shaye, but the rest of the women stayed in place, keeping their distance from the Druid girl they had heard whispers about in the camp—the one who could wield magic powerful enough to hurt their leader. A few of them tried not to look at her black hands, laying idly at her side.

Shaye did not respond, though she did recognize the girl. Adella, she had been a spoiled and spiteful child. She and Shaye had grown up together in the Winter Palace before the uprising, and though Shaye's uncle had been a well-respected Magi of the court, Duchess Adella had teased and tormented Shaye.

Once, Adella had broken an expensive vase belonging to the Queen. But when her father, Duke Brayham, asked her about it, she accused Shaye of having done it. Shaye had been forced to put the vase back together piece by piece, the jagged edges making her fingers bleed—but Nanny Jin hadn't cared. She had stood and watched as Shaye glued the shards back into place, tears streaming down her face and blood trickling down her hands.

Adella was as bad as her father. Both were traitors for working with Bastian to betray their own king, to betray Sorin. Adella may have had sway with Bastian's court of Nefari, but she held no power over Shaye, not anymore. No one did.

When Shaye stood silent, Adella's smile wavered and Shaye caught the hateful gleam in her eye, the same one she'd had when they were children. The other women shifted uncomfortably where they stood. Adella glanced back at them. Shaye knew that it would embarrass the duchess to be snubbed by someone who was as favored by Bastian as Shaye was. She had seen Adella fawn over him in the camp, finding ways to touch his arm or to bring a smile to his handsome face.

Adella broke the silence, "We were just headed to midmorning tea with Bastian. He requested my presence personally, which is really quite an honor." This time there was malice in her smile.

Shaye felt no jealousy at the thought of Bastian courting the young human girl, but the smug look on Adella's face was irritating her. Flames flickered to life on Shaye's fingertips, surprising even her, as she had not called on them. It was as if they were appearing in response to what she was feeling. The group of women stepped back in alarm by the sudden appearance of Shaye's magic.

She thought of how easily she could singe that pretty dress Adella had so carefully picked out to impress Bastian, and she smiled at the thought. Brina put a hand on Shaye's arm, drawing her attention away from the dark thoughts. One of the twin guards, Ulf, chuckled at the display. He had witnessed her attack on Bastian when they had been on the ship and, since that moment, since Shaye had taken to the dark magic, he and his brother Gorm had been friendlier toward her. It seemed they found delight in seeing this side of her.

Adella held a hand to her chest but did not step away. Instead, her long nose flared in anger. "If only Sorin could see you now." She turned on a heel to leave, but Shaye blocked her with a hard wall of magic, separating the duchess from her friends.

"You have not yet been dismissed." It was the first time Shaye had spoken and she saw the tension in Adella's shoulders at the coldness of her tone. "If I recall, Sorin said he did not much care for you and your desperate passes at him." Adella turned back, staring at her with wide eyes as Shaye went on, "Oh yes, I know all about it. You thought you could bag yourself a king and now you find yourself gaining favor with Bastian. It's a shame, really, that neither man is as enchanted with your charms as your friends here. Actually, it seems they *both* prefer *my* company. Perhaps your friends would as well. Should we see?" She smiled brightly.

Shaye addressed the group of women before her, "I would very much like to extend an invitation for drinks before the festivities tomorrow. Will you accept?"

Each woman nodded nervously at the request. She smiled

triumphantly. "Fabulous. I will see you all then." She walked to Adella, who flinched as Shaye patted her on the shoulder. "Don't worry, dear, you are welcome to come as well." Adella bowed her head slightly, though Shaye could feel the anger radiating from her. "You are *dismissed*." With a lazy wave of her hand, Shaye dropped the magical shield and walked away from the stunned group of women.

Brina accompanied Shaye back to their quarters. Shaye kicked off her black leather boots as soon as she entered the tent. She tore at the buttons on her jacket, removing it and feeling free from the weight of the outfit that matched Bastian's. She hated that he still controlled what she wore. As soon as this was over, she would burn all the clothes he had given her while here in the camp.

"That wasn't like you, Shaye. What you did back there."

"She's an insufferable brat and always has been." Shaye sat, propping her feet up on the red velvet stool in front of her.

"Of course she is. But you have enough enemies, you don't need to declare war with another." Brina removed her dirt-brown jacket, the one that all humans in the camp wore. Bastian had wasted no time in making it known what the new order of things would be when he took power. It didn't matter anymore—he had the army, but Shaye had the strength. He underestimated her, and without the drink used to drug her before, she was clear headed enough to make him believe that he was the one controlling her.

There was no going back to the girl she was, no matter how much Brina and Sorin prayed. She could never forgive herself for the darkness she had welcomed into her soul, but she also would not forgive Bastian for turning their world upside down. She wasn't sure how yet, but she would make him pay.

They sat in silence the rest of the day, reading and eating beneath the cool shade of the tent. Shaye called on a light breeze to cool them down until evening, until the night air would grow cooler on its own. It was nearly dinner time and, as usual, Bastian would be arriving to dine with them. Shaye changed into a modest red dress; the light fabric clung to what remained of her curves, but it was more comfortable than the others that filled the large bureau.

Bastian arrived with his servants, several plates in hand. He took the liberty of placing a basket of sweet rolls in front of Shaye. She took one and bit into it without a word of thanks. It was dry and made her miss the citrus cinnamon glaze that Rolland topped his with. She missed Brina's parents and the comforts of their home in Aramoor. She lost her appetite and set the roll down on the table.

Bastian moved his chair closer to her and sat with his arm up against her own. "Adella had quite the story to tell today at tea. She is demanding that you be punished for such insolent behavior." He smiled at her playfully; then, in a serious tone, "You know, Lord Brayham is one of my greatest advisors. His support is essential to a smooth transition with the human populace in Asterion. We wouldn't want any... unrest. I would hate to shed more blood than necessary as I take the throne."

Shaye choked on the piece of the roll in her mouth. "We both know that's a lie. Are we lying to each other now, Bass?" She raised an eyebrow as she turned to him.

"No, my love, of course not." He tossed a grape in the air, catching it gracefully in his mouth.

Brina eyed their exchange warily from across the table. She hadn't touched her food, moving it around her plate every so often. Shaye knew this was difficult for her to watch; but it was necessary if Shaye wanted to keep Bastian from trying to cloud his way into her mind. If he trusted her, then he would let her be, and eventually he would let his guard down.

"Did your lady tell you that I invited her and her friends here for drinks tomorrow before the celebration?"

"Ah, yes, she did mention that. You are free to do as you

please, so long as you are ready when I come to escort you to the ball."

The ball. Shaye suppressed the urge to roll her eyes. Bastian had spent every moment since their return making preparations for the ritual, and the celebration that would take place beforehand. It was to be a grand affair, Bastian's tribute to the Winter Solstice. It would be a reception marking the moment of the Magi uprising that he would lead soon after. Sorin's forces would arrive within days and a battle like Asterion had never seen would surely follow when they faced the Nefari army.

"With you by my side, the entire court will be in awe." He brushed her hair from her shoulder, running a finger along her collarbone. She fought a shiver in response, refusing to show him the revulsion she felt at his touch.

She took his hand, removing it from her, and smiled sweetly at him. "Of course. I would love nothing more."

CHAPTER NINE

Sorin

Sorin shoved another dagger into his pack and let out a low growl. Bron grunted in response from the corner of the small tent. "Slow down, Sorin. We're going to get her back."

"Not soon enough." He threw the overstuffed bag to the floor. "You were there, Bron, you saw her. He had his filthy hands all over her. I can't stand the thought of her being held prisoner for one more second."

Bron scratched at his closely shaven head and took a swig from his flask. "I don't know Sorin, she didn't look like a damsel in distress to me."

Sorin shot a glare in his friend's direction. He was about to say something he knew he would regret, when Mavka popped her head through the entrance. She looked between the two men with her strange, mossy eyes, pushing her vine-entwined hair from her face. "She has arrived."

Bron gave Sorin a sympathetic look as they stood to greet their guest. Outside, the sun was beating down, bringing the heat of summer. The crews looked exhausted, both his own and

Thorsten's. Sorin had been grateful when the captain and his crew agreed to stay and see this through. They had been just as shocked as the rest of them at the sight of Shaye standing with the Nefari. When she had been with Sorin and his men, she had struggled to drum up even a hint of her magic. Now it seemed she had claimed her power, and then some.

They were still on the beach, just south of the Ceasg Lagoon. It had taken longer than he would have liked to make their way across the Living Sea; they had gone the long way around to avoid a run-in with the shadow monster, who by now must have realized he'd been duped. Though they were successful in avoiding the Umibōzu, the seas had been tremulous. Ylva had speculated that it was due to the anger of the beast dwelling below on the ocean floor. Still, Sorin was grateful that they had not had to face it again, even if it meant braving a stormy sea.

Since returning to Asterion, Mavka had sent word to her father and the clans, explaining that Sorin and the others would meet them in the forest north of the battlefield. Sorin's team would arrive there first, giving them the opportunity to scout the area and set eyes on the Nefari army for themselves.

Ingemar was waiting for them patiently, dressed even more extravagantly than usual, though Sorin would not have thought it possible. She had on her best gown, with her thick black hair piled gracefully on top of her head, which was adorned with a sparkling crown of blue-green sea glass. A woman stood beside her, her sun-kissed skin glistening with water, evidence that she had swam there. She was wearing a silk wrap, deep blue like the sea. Sorin gave a rushed bow to both women. Time was of the essence, and he was eager to speak with their spy from the Nefari camp.

"Signe, thank you for coming."

Her accent was thick like Ingemar's as she replied, "It is an honor, King Sorin. I want to thank you for showing such kindness to my friend. If only the rest of us were so lucky."

"When this is all over, you will be. I will see to it personally that each of you is released from the magic that forces you to grant wishes and given the freedom you so deserve. That we all deserve."

She smiled a dazzling white smile at him, and he noted the golden scales along her neck and arms. It still caught him off guard that such magical beings existed. It was times like this, when faced with such courageous and caring Magi, that he could not fathom what his father had been thinking when he stripped the entire land of power. *A desperate act of fear-driven people*, Sorin thought to himself. He knew now that there would be no going back to the way things were when his father was alive. He had been through too much with these magic wielders and knew what it would mean for them to have their power back.

Signe interrupted his musings, "Thank you. Unfortunately, we must make this quick. I do not have much time. Bastian allows us only a short time in the water each day. I swam as fast as I could up the coast, but if I am not back soon, he will suspect something." It was clear that Signe feared Bastian's wrath. Sorin could never thank her enough for taking such a great risk in meeting them face to face.

"Of course, please, sit if you'd like." He gestured to the logs they had placed around their makeshift fire pit on the beach.

She accepted the offer. "As you know, Bastian now holds all three relics. He has the Stave, the Sword, and he wears the Obsidian stone in a pendant around his neck at all times. With these, and your friend Shaye's help, he will tap into that power, making his army unstoppable. We cannot allow this to happen."

"When?" It was Thorsten who asked. He was sitting forward with his elbows resting on his legs, hanging on Signe's every word. They all were.

"Under the blood moon. Now, Bastian is nothing if not extravagant... He is throwing a ball before the ceremony. I think I can get Captain Thorsten's men into the celebration undetected.

It is likely that Bastian will not notice them in the crowd, or remember their faces from the confrontation in the Eastern Isles. If you can get to the relics, then we will turn the tides in the war that is brewing."

The plan wasn't foolproof, but it would do for now. Sorin did not want to waste another moment. Signe rose to take her leave, but Sorin stopped her. "Signe, please, how is she?"

She was thoughtful before she answered, "She has been… different, since her return from the isles. Bastian no longer drugs her with his magic concoction, nor does he use his magic to enter her mind as much as he once did…" Sorin gave a sigh of relief, but she held up a hand. "Because he no longer *needs* to. She is using her dark magic more readily now. I believe she is up to something. I have noticed, on several occasions, her interactions with the guards when Bastian is not watching. They are entertained by her mischievousness. She may not be an ally to the Nefari, but she *does* risk losing herself to the power she wields. I am afraid if you do not succeed in your mission to steal the relics, if she is in that camp for much longer, you will have lost her for good."

There was sympathy in her eyes as she bowed to him. Ingemar walked her to the edge of the water, taking Signe's hand in hers. Sorin watched them from the fire; the way they held one another reminded him of the moment in the library he had shared with Shaye. He looked away, feeling this was a private moment, not meant for his eyes.

When Ingemar returned, there was immense sadness in her eyes. She sat beside Sorin on the log, and looked longingly at the sea. Sorin put a hand on her shoulder giving it a light squeeze. "You'll go home soon enough, Ingemar. We all will."

"I hope with all my heart that you are right, Your Majesty. I am not sure what awaits us in that valley, but I fear the price we will all pay."

"You love her." It was more an observation than a question.

She smiled to herself—he knew the look, she was lost in

memories. "I think I always have. Though it seems I waited too long to tell her." The pointed look she gave Sorin made him chuckle.

"I suppose that's something we'll all need to work on when this is over. Perhaps we'll all find the courage to be bolder."

"Bold like Shaye."

"Yes, like Shaye."

They sat there a while longer, lost in their own thoughts, and comforted by one another's presence. When lunchtime approached, Bron and the others came down from the camp, fresh fish in hand. They roasted it over a spit on the fire, and passed the rum around. There was a quiet unrest, unusual for this group. Sorin suspected they were all preparing themselves for the trials ahead.

Everything was packed and ready to go. They were to leave when they finished eating, giving them enough time to travel quietly down to the Nefari camp. Ingemar and Ylva would be tasked with cloaking their movements against any scouts Bastian had circling. The two women had been cloaking them since their return to Asterion, and as far as they could tell, it was working.

Once they finished eating, they put the fire out, and gathered the horses. Finn danced around, pounding the ground with his hooves. Sorin patted the restless gelding on his neck. "I know boy, you'll see her soon."

Sorin mounted his own horse and tied Finn's reins to his saddle. At his signal, they set off. Signe had given Ingemar a location where they would be safe to set up camp. She promised to have provisions waiting for them, along with clothing for Thorsten and his men. Thorsten, Haskell, Langley, and Runa, all being human, would have to wear servant's clothing, while Ylva would be given a gown with gloves to hide her untainted hands—without them, it would be a dead giveaway that she was not Nefari.

By the time they reached Signe's secret camp, they were

exhausted, and the horses were grateful for the reprieve. Though the group desperately needed the rest, they had made it just in time for the celebration—which meant they would be going headfirst into the Nefari camp that evening.

Runa sat with Mavka, watching the moths flutter in different patterns. They were forming the shapes of various magical creatures when Bron arrived from a quick perimeter check. At his presence the moths abandoned their show and fluttered over to him. It seemed they had taken a liking to the knight just as Mavka had. The girls giggled together as Bron shifted around in his seat, trying to get away from the attention. Sorin did not miss the smirk on his face, though.

Ylva and Ingemar sat huddled together; Ingemar was trying to prepare her for the ball with information Signe had given her. Thorsten and Haskell were sharpening their swords near where Sorin sat. Sorin drew his own sword with a halfhearted intent to do the same.

"Ready when you are, King Sorin." Thorsten gave him a wink.

"Then let's not waste another minute." Sorin feigned confidence as he stood.

They strapped on their weapons, and bid each other farewell. Thorsten and his crew were dressed and ready for the ball. The sun was setting, and the festivities would begin soon. They needed to wait until the Nefari were gathered for the ball so they could slip in undetected.

Sorin, Bron, Mavka, and Ingemar were headed to the outskirts of the camp. Signe would meet them and take them to the Stave and the Sword. She insisted that they would not be able to get to the third relic, the Obsidian stone, since Bastian never took it off. Two out of three would need to be good enough for now.

He pulled Thorsten aside. "Promise me. Promise me, that you will not leave that ball without her."

"I give you my word that Shaye will not be left behind. Not this time."

Sorin nodded, confident in the captain and his crew's love for Shaye.

They parted ways, wishing one another the luck of the Fates. Sorin could hear the Nefari camp before he could see it. Signe had not been exaggerating when she spoke of Bastian's need for a big show. A large tent had been constructed in the middle of the encampment. Light and laughter flowed from it. The Nefari were already celebrating their victory, and it only made Sorin more determined than ever to prove them wrong.

Signe appeared silently from the camp. She was dressed in a deep blue gown that shined under the moonlight, stunning in its simplicity. She held a finger to her lips, and led them down into the enemy camp. They moved wordlessly past the endless rows of tents. Bastian's numbers were far greater than Sorin had believed, and he prayed they would not have to resort to a battle. The pressure of retrieving the relics weighed on him heavily.

The guards monitoring the camp were sparse with everyone else at the ball. Signe motioned for them to follow her quickly behind a small tent where two ugly guards stood. They were laughing about an incident they had witnessed in one of Bastian's meetings with his generals.

"She's really a sight to behold! Setting fire to the duke like that. It was the highlight of my day." The shorter guard waved his black hands wildly.

The taller guard picked at his teeth with a small, thin dagger. Pulling it from his mouth he sneered, "Lord Bastian has his hands full with that one."

The excited guard, a chunky man with buck teeth, agreed, "He'd better be careful. If she gets it in her mind to challenge him, I think she'd give him a run for his money."

The tall guard grunted in agreement. They were talking about Shaye, and Sorin felt a small sense of pride. It seemed she had been creating her own sort of havoc in the camp. Just like the Shaye he remembered.

Signe and Ingemar linked hands and chanted something under their breath. Their magic ebbed steadily from them, flowing over to the Nefari guards. When it reached the men, they raised their hands to block it with their own magic, but they were too late. Their eyes drifted shut, and their bodies hit the ground simultaneously with a hard thud. Sorin smiled, *that's going to hurt in the morning.*

He followed the others into the tent where the relics sat, side by side. The Ceasg women used their magic to disable the protective spell locked around the relics. Sorin wasted no time, strapping them both to his back. His heart raced as the power of the ancient objects drummed into him. It was magic not meant for mortal hands, and he wanted nothing more than to get back to the camp, to get the relics off of him.

They left the tent, still unnoticed by the Nefari making their rounds. When they reached the clearing that led from the camp to the tree line, they heard a crow call out. Mavka held up a hand to stop them. "No," she whispered faintly, and Sorin looked at her in confusion.

Bron shouted something to him, but it was too late. It wasn't until something hit Sorin from behind that he realized the crow's caw had been a warning to them. His vision went black as he hit the ground.

Once Sorin came to from the blow to the head, Bastian was standing over him with a smug look on his face. This was not the same hurt and frightened man that had begged for help at the palace door weeks ago. Now he revealed his true self. The signs of black magic ran up his arms in inky tendrils, and his eyes were pooled with black, drowning out the whites that had once been there.

Sorin felt such hatred at his presence, that he attacked without a second thought. It caught Bastian off guard, not giving him enough time to call on his magic. Sorin was on top of him in an instant, pummeling his face relentlessly. One of the guards stepped in, pulling Sorin off their master and throwing him into the dirt. He rolled and stood again.

Bastian was standing now with the help of his men, licking the blood from his busted lip. He hissed in pain, then said, "King Sorin, brawling like a common man. Why am I not surprised? All of you mortals are the same, savage and *pathetic*."

Sorin looked around, remembering his friends who had been with him during the ambush. Bron was slumped on the ground, his face a bloody mess, but Ingemar and Mavka were nowhere to be seen. Sorin prayed that they had escaped in time. To his relief, the relics were still strapped to him. He would not let them go without a fight.

Bastian knew it, too—he held out a hand and squeezed it shut. Sorin felt his throat close, and he panicked trying to get a breath in. Bastian held tight to the power, and Sorin fell to his knees once again, his vision going white. He felt the guards roughly remove his baldric. *No*, he thought, *it can't end this easily. Not like this.*

Bastian released his fist, and the grip on Sorin's throat loosened. He gasped for air, choking, and waiting for his vision to return. He could hear Bastian's laughter in the distance as he walked away. By the time Sorin's vision cleared, Bastian was gone. In his place, stood a group of Nefari, black hands strumming with magic. Both Sorin and Bron pushed to their feet and drew their swords; they would not make this easy for the traitorous Magi standing before them.

CHAPTER TEN

Shaye

Bastian sure could throw a party, Shaye had to admit that. The enormous tent had been transformed into a wonderland. It was alive with light and music; lanterns floated overhead, charmed by the magic of the Nefari Sorcerers. Grand ice sculptures lined the tables in the shapes of magical creatures; Sea Dragons, Unicorns, and a Phoenix winked at her under the warm lantern light, expertly crafted from the ice. Best of all was the glorious spread of food laid out around them.

Shaye had no idea where they had gathered such a beautiful fare when the country was in such turmoil from the blight. Seeds were no longer sprouting from the land, and the game that was left in the forest was thin and sickly. She ran a hand along the lace tablecloth, lost in thought when Brina appeared at her side. Shaye knew Brina was always within view, she had not left Shaye's side since she had arrived, unless forced to.

Brina snorted, "This is such a joke; celebrating his victory before anything has even happened."

Shaye agreed, though she did not say so out loud. Too many ears were constantly listening for her to slip up. She had to be careful not to reveal her deceitful intent toward Bastian and his army. She tugged at the bodice of the gown Bastian had picked out for her. It had long sheer sleeves with black embroidered details. There was a plunging neckline, accenting her breasts. The shimmering black detail ran down the length of her torso, stopping just at her thighs, where the sheer fabric began again and continued down to the floor. It had a tulle train that flowed down around her, trailing behind like a thin veil of shadows. As beautiful as it was, she was incredibly uncomfortable.

Adella and her fawning ladies acknowledged her with curtsies as they passed by with attractive Nefari officers, on their way to the makeshift marble dance floor that had been placed in the middle of the tent. They had shown up to Shaye's quarters earlier that evening, as she had suggested they do. There, Shaye had played the gracious hostess, listening politely to their gossip —whom they thought would show up in the most beautiful dresses, and whom they each hoped to dance with. It was all trivial... These women had no clue what horrors awaited them all.

Shaye fed them hors d'oeuvres, and kept their glasses filled with the finest wine from Bastian's stash. They genuinely seemed to have enjoyed themselves, and by the end, Shaye had to admit that she didn't mind their company. They were vain and spoiled, but it was only a result of their upbringing. Adella, on the other hand, had sat quietly with a sour look on her face the entire time. Shaye had known her long enough to see that she was a hateful, jealous creature, and something like that ran much deeper than rotten parents.

When Bastian had arrived, the women were still in Shaye's tent. They fawned over him, dressed gallantly in his black jacket and tailored black pants. The pocket of his jacket was embellished with the same design that made up Shaye's dress. It was yet another way for him to show the world that she belonged to him. She had fought the urge to sneer at him, instead smiling brightly as she bid farewell to the tittering women so she could prepare herself for the ball.

Bastian and Shaye had then walked arm in arm into the celebration, greeted with cheers and deep bows befitting royalty. Shaye played her part, standing silent at his side, as noblemen and officers vied for a small acknowledgment or favor from their would-be king.

He had parted ways with her to speak with men whom he had taken the liberty of appointing as high-ranking officials, leaving her alone to sample the food laid out on the table. It had been a while now since she had last spotted him. Shaye and Brina wandered aimlessly through the drunken crowd. She was grateful for Brina's presence, but Bastian's absence made her nervous. It was odd that he was nowhere to be found, when he could typically be seen basking in the attention.

Shaye decided to worry about Bastian later and joined a group of Nefari guards who were enjoying a game of cards. She helped herself to a seat between Gorm and Ulf. Gorm chuckled and dealt her into the game. It was getting easier to tell the twins apart after having spent so much time with them. She often found herself wondering where they had come from. Any time she had pried, they avoided the questions entirely. Perhaps tonight they would be drunk enough to give something away that she could use to her advantage...

Ulf kicked at her playfully under the table. "Heard you gave that fat imbecile a little heat the other day."

Shaye feigned innocence, holding her cards to her chest. "Oh, the duke? An accident, I assure you." She winked at them and played her hand.

Gorm bellowed out a laugh. "I always knew you had a little fire inside of you!"

You have no idea, she thought. Instead, when she spoke, she chose her words carefully, "I can't fathom how a man like that made it so high on the totem."

A guard she did not recognize took the bait and scoffed, "Seems to be given a title, you gotta be fat and stupid."

Gorm piped in, "Shit, if that were the criteria, then you'd have been crowned King of Asterion long ago!"

Everyone at the table laughed, even Shaye. She was trying to think of a way to plant seeds of doubt in these men's heads. Bastian relied on the adoration of his followers, and if she could bring light to his faults, then she stood a chance of weakening his hold on these men.

She threw a card onto the deck and drew another. "King Idor really only ever gave favor to the Magi who benefited him. It left many of the less powerful Magi throughout the land at the bottom of the food chain, along with the humans. It always bothered me, even as a young girl."

The table was silent as they continued to play cards—gone was the good cheer they had shared only moments ago. These men surely had no love for the old king, who had not only oppressed less powerful Magi, but who had failed when King Allerick staged a coup, suppressing magic throughout the entire land. It was a long shot, but perhaps if she could make them draw a comparison between Bastian and King Idor, then they would realize that they would never hold as much power as Bastian had promised them.

The foul mood lingered into the next round of cards. Shaye took the opportunity to excuse herself, hoping that once she was gone, the men would discuss the matter she had brought up to them. *Let them stew and see through Bastian's facade,* Shaye thought bitterly.

She went back to the long table to fill a plate with food. A servant rushed to her side, handing her a plate filled with sweet rolls and cakes. She had to hold back a yelp when she saw the familiar face of the man. He was smiling, his hair slicked back neatly, not like the messy ponytail he usually sported. She grabbed his sleeve roughly, dragging him into a dark corner, and away from the distracted crowd. Brina followed silently, standing in front of them to block any wandering eyes.

Shaye looked around for anyone who might be listening to them, then whispered furiously, "Thorsten, what in The Mother's name are you doing here? Do you have any idea what Bastian will do to you if he finds you—"

"Lookin' good, kid," he interrupted, letting his gaze slide playfully over the revealing dress. His eyes found Brina next, and he winked at her. "Who's your beautiful friend?"

"We don't have time for this." She grabbed his hand, trying to pull him toward the servants' entrance of the tent. But he held firmly in place.

"You're right, we do not have time. You need to come with us. Sorin will be waiting for you with Finn at the tree line."

Shaye's heart dropped. "*Sorin*? You brought the *King* of Asterion to the edge of his enemy's camp? You've really lost it this time, you pompous ass!"

Thorsten looked around uncomfortably, not meeting her eyes. "Actually, I brought him into the *heart* of the camp. Which is why we really should be going."

"I'm not going anywhere. I'm not finished here."

"Finished? There is nothing to be done here. Sorin and his friends are retrieving the relics as we speak. This thing is over, as of tonight."

Shaye was reeling. She could not believe they had been so reckless. She needed to get Thorsten out of there before anyone found him. "I mean it. You need to leave, *now*." Her magic flared, and Thorsten drew his hand back quickly, as if he had been burned by her touch. She did not miss the flicker of fear in his eye.

Good, she thought, *fear me. Run from me, far from here.*

A woman's voice interrupted them, husky and seductive. Shaye knew immediately who it was. She rounded on Ylva, who stood dressed in a beautiful gown of burgundy and purple. "You, too? Have you all lost your minds? I suppose Runa and Haskell are nearby? Langley too?"

Thorsten laughed, "Don't be ridiculous. Langley is waiting by the explosives."

"By the Fates, *explosives?*"

"Well, if things go south here, we thought he could give us a distraction long enough to grab you and go."

"I *told you*, I'm not going anywhere," Shaye said through gritted teeth.

Ylva moved between Shaye and the captain in an attempt to diffuse the situation. "Shaye, please. I know things are..." She glanced down at Shaye's hands. "Complicated. But we are still your friends. We are on your side, and we want to bring you home."

"Home? What does that even mean? I don't have a home. I haven't had a home for a long time."

Her words struck a blow, and she knew it. The hurt in her friends' eyes made her heart ache, but she ignored it. Every moment they wasted here put them further in harm's way. If she needed to break their hearts to get them to leave, then that is what she would do.

Footsteps interrupted the confrontation, and Shaye locked eyes with the eavesdropper. Adella. *Dammit.* Shaye's stomach lurched at the sight of her standing there. Adella's eyes darted between Shaye and her friends. Adella smirked then took off, getting lost in the crowd.

"*Go. Now.*" Shaye shoved Thorsten and Ylva back roughly with her magic. They stumbled, but hesitated.

Thorsten shook his head in protest. "I promised him I would not return without you."

Shaye felt her face flush at the panic she was feeling. Adella was surely running straight to Bastian. "T-tell Sorin I remember. Tell him I know it was him that night at the Winter Solstice, and that it is my turn to save *him*." Shaye heard guards shout from across the room. Her magic flared to life with the adrenaline that coursed through her now. She growled at Thorsten and Ylva, "*Go.*"

They obeyed, escaping through a flap at the back of the tent, and out into the night. Bastian's guests began to look up at the commotion, watching the guards search the room. They rounded up all the servants, corralling them to one corner of the tent. Shaye searched their human faces in alarm, looking for any sign of Runa. The mousey girl was smart and quick... She must have slipped out before the alarm had been sounded.

One of the humans cried out as a Nefari lifted him into the air with his power; black fog encircled the man, squeezing him like a boa constrictor. A woman in the crowd of human servants fell to her knees, begging the Nefari to let him go. He was her husband, and he had done nothing wrong. Shaye balled her hands into fists at the sight of the guards roughly questioning the humans. Thorsten and the others would be long gone by now, but the servants left here would be severely punished for allowing spies within their ranks.

Before Shaye could stop the guards, Bastian's voice rang loud above the crowd, "Enough."

Without hesitation, the Nefari released the human—the man who had been dangling within the foggy grip fell to the ground. Shaye waited for him to stir, but he was not moving. His wife crawled to his side and let out a sob. Shaye ignored the crowd, who now bowed at their master's presence. She rushed to the unconscious man's side. His wife and the other humans recoiled at her presence, afraid that she was there to finish what the guard had started. She shut her eyes, trying to drown out what was happening around her in the tent.

Her hands tingled as she called on her magic; not the black magic that had begun to seep into her soul, but the magic that had been born in her veins. She was calling on her Druid power. She dug deep down and whispered words she did not recognize.

It was an ancient spell from before her time, but the words came to her as easily as breathing. When she used the black magic it felt like lightning, a shocking and powerful feeling. This was different: it felt warm and safe, like the world itself was embracing her, and sharing its power with her. The man was cold at first touch, but as her magic flowed into him, warmth returned, and he stirred awake.

Shaye opened her eyes to find the humans in front of her standing in awe. There was no more fear in their eyes as they watched her heal the man. He sat up unsteadily, Shaye and the man's wife offering him a hand to help him. The man and woman embraced, crying into each other's shoulders. Someone stood behind her clapping, loud and slow. She turned to find Bastian there. There was a bruise on his cheek, and his lip had been split open; but there was a wicked grin spread across his face. She knew that look—he was displeased with her, but saving his wrath for when they were alone.

He turned toward the Nefari who stood as still as statues in a courtyard, unsure of what they should do. "Isn't she marvelous?" He gestured widely to Shaye, as if she were an act in a show. "Milady demonstrates for us both the immense power she possesses, as well as her mercy." He clapped once more, his Nefari court joining in with him this time. Some of them smiled, but others looked around nervously; if any one of them had healed the mortal man, they knew they would have paid for it with their life.

"The intruders are of no threat to us. Let us resume our celebration." Bastian signaled for the band to play, and they obeyed, playing a beautiful melody. Bastian held out a hand to Shaye and she took it obediently. She knew this was an act and that he expected her to resume her part.

He pulled her onto the marble dance floor, spinning her once, then drawing her in close to him. The dream she'd had back at the Winter Palace flashed in her mind—the dream in which

Bastian had stolen a kiss, the one where they had danced, and she had craved his touch. This time, she felt no desire rise within her.

No, this was much different than the magical night she had dreamt about. Nefari stood to the side, trying to appear as if they were still enjoying the fabulous party their master had thrown for them. The servants stood in the corner, eyes to the ground, doing their best to appear demure and invisible. Bastian pulled Shaye closer to him, gripping her waist so tightly with his fingers, she was sure it would leave a mark. She shifted uncomfortably under his touch, but he did not release her.

"Did you have a nice little reunion?" He spoke in a hushed tone so only Shaye could hear.

There was no use in lying to him, but she had to be smart about it. She put a hand on his chest, running her fingers along the delicate detail on the pocket. "They were only here for me, Bass, and I told them I would not leave. I told them that this is where I belong now, here with you."

He laughed bitterly, but she could see in his eyes that he wanted to believe her. "It does not matter now. They will be taken care of soon enough. My Black Shuck is hunting them as we speak."

He dipped her low as the song came to its end. Once the dance floor cleared, he loosened his grip on her. "As for His Royal Majesty…" Shaye's heart sank at the mention of Sorin, but she was careful not to show it on her face. "He is *exactly* where he should be. Having a reunion of his own."

"A reunion? What do you mean Bastian?"

"I've been holding onto a little something for him. A gift." As he smiled, an inhuman screech came from the night, drowning Shaye in dread.

CHAPTER ELEVEN

Sorin

Sorin looked down at his hand—purple bruises were already forming from where it had connected with Bastian's face. A piercing scream bellowed from the darkness of the night causing Sorin to look up in alarm. It was a blood curdling sound that made the hair on Sorin's arms stand on end.

Sorin and Bron readied themselves for the Nefari guards to advance on them; but, instead of attacking, the Nefari parted down the middle, allowing a nightmarish creature to pass through. The monster was dripping in a dense, black fog—like the man-eating fog they had encountered in the forest. There was something human-like about it in the way that it moved, but the low growl that sounded from its chest was anything but. The creature moved toward them slowly, allowing Sorin enough time to raise his sword.

The fog shifted around the creature, revealing pieces of rotting flesh underneath. Bron realized before Sorin did, and cursed under his breath. "Elijah."

He was right—the man, or whatever was left of him, was their fallen friend. There was no mistaking the face that Sorin had known since childhood. The face that had laughed over drinks and fought side by side with them. Sorin lowered his sword. This had to be a trick, like in the caves when he had heard Elijah calling for him. They had lost him to the man-eating fog, and there was no way he could have survived after all this time.

Unless the fog hadn't been deadly... If Bastian had enchanted it with blood magic to transform anything caught within its grasp, then it was possible that the monster standing before him was what was left of one of his closest friends.

"Elijah, what have they done to you?"

The Nefari snickered at the shock on Sorin's and Bron's faces. Elijah, if they could still call him that, let out another earth-shattering screech. Sorin and Bron dropped their swords to cover their ears—the sound was painful as it pierced through their thoughts. It felt like a thousand pins digging into Sorin's mind.

Elijah took the opportunity to strike, bounding on Sorin in a savage rage. They went down to the ground, Sorin choking on the thick black fog as Elijah clawed at him. Sorin had bested Elijah in a fight many times, but this was different; there was a rabid strength to Elijah now, as if he felt no pain as Sorin threw blow after blow into him.

Bron joined the fight, trying to pull Elijah off Sorin. Elijah threw Bron off him and Sorin as if he were no more than a fly buzzing around his ear. Sorin could smell the putrid scent of black magic on Elijah. He struggled under Elijah's brute strength, but it was no use. Sorin could hear bones cracking as he hit Elijah, but it did not stop him.

A blast of magic erupted from the trees as Ingemar slammed into the Nefari guards, who were too distracted by the fight to see her coming. Mavka whistled, and an enormous murder of crows barreled down on the dark Magi, drawing blood with each peck of their razor-sharp beaks. Ingemar did not let up as she continued to slam her magic into them. It took only minutes for the Nefari to be overtaken; between Ingemar's magic, and the crows obeying Mavka's command, they were left dead in a heap.

Sorin was still going hand to hand with Elijah, as Bron continued to jump in to aid him. Ingemar blasted her magic into the three of them, throwing them apart, and giving Sorin and Bron a moment of reprieve. Elijah shook his head, the fog clearing from his face for a moment to reveal that half of it had been eaten off—nothing but skull was showing beneath. The skin on the other side of his face was rotting, and Sorin could see pain in his remaining eye.

Elijah was still in there somewhere, he realized with a start. Elijah let out a crackling hiss, ready to lunge again, but Sorin spoke: "Elijah, I know you're in there. Please, fight it."

Something flickered in Elijah's eye, and he looked between Sorin and Bron helplessly. The fog tried to close in again around his face, but Elijah shut his eye tightly; he was fighting it. He fell to the ground, crying out in pain. The black magic would not let up, it was not going to let Elijah go.

He looked at Sorin hopelessly, and spoke in a pained voice, "Make it stop. Kill me."

"No, Elijah, you have to fight it. That's an order, soldier."

Elijah shook his head. "Look at me." He choked as the fog tried to worm its way into his mouth. "Please, Sorin. Kill me."

Sorin looked at Bron, his hands shaking as he picked up his sword. Bron nodded to him. They both knew what needed to be done. Elijah was too far gone. Sorin stepped up to where Elijah knelt on the ground. He made a promise to his friend: "I will destroy the ones who did this to you, brother. Your work here is done... May The Mother keep you." Sorin took a deep, steadying breath, and plunged his sword through the heart of his friend.

Elijah looked relieved as the fog faded away, leaving him lying on the ground, free in death. Sorin dropped to his knees as blood pooled around his friend's body. Bron let out an anguished shout. Ingemar and Mavka stood silently by the trees.

Ingemar spoke first, cutting through the grief Sorin was feeling. "We need to go, Your Majesty. It is not safe here."

"No, it most certainly is not." A woman appeared out of the shadows. She was shrouded in black, so they could not see her face clearly. "Such a sweet display of mercy, King Sorin. I am quite impressed. Bastian had doubted your capacity to kill a man who had been raised alongside you like a brother. It seems we were both wrong." Magic slithered from her in long, black shadows, it was like she had extra arms.

Ingemar shot out a shield of her own magic to protect them from whatever this woman was. It was clear that the shadow woman was not human by the way that she moved, almost as if she were floating above the solid ground. Ingemar tried to hold her off with her Ceasg magic, but it was not enough. Sorin knew he was too far away from Ingemar, and she had stretched her power thin to defeat the guards. The black magic extended from the shadow woman, and grabbed hold of Sorin, dragging him through the dirt, and toward her. She was like a Kraken, with a thick tendril holding him while others still reached for his friends.

She had him, but it was not too late for his friends. "Run!" He ordered them, desperately wanting them to obey. They hesitated, just long enough for an enormous blast to sound from across the camp, near the valley.

Sorin suspected he had Langley to thank for the distraction. His friends took the opportunity to do as he commanded, disappearing into the tree line. Vines appeared, building a wall between the shadow woman's magic and his friends. They were safe, but he was not so lucky. He caught a glimpse of the woman's face shifting beneath the veil, as if it was having trouble holding a solid form.

She smiled wickedly. "Allow me to introduce myself—they call me Umbra. I am your new keeper, King Sorin, and I believe you and I are going to have the time of our lives."

The camp was buzzing with excitement as Umbra dragged Sorin past the tents. Her black shadowy tendrils had snaked around his wrists, holding onto him with a tight grip. Nefari, still dressed in their finery from the ball, shouted bitter, hateful words at him. Sorin spotted a few humans scattered amongst the crowd, high-ranking men he recognized from the Summer Palace.

Signe had warned him that some of the noblemen had turned to Bastian's side, but seeing it with his own eyes now broke a small piece inside of him. Had they really been so miserable that they would choose a world of dark magic over the world his father had created? Anger boiled inside of him, those men were cowards. He wondered what riches and power Bastian had promised them.

There were other magical creatures mixed into the crowd: Orcs who foamed at the mouth, and Wraiths floating aimlessly beneath the moonlight. Bastian had built himself an impressive force. Sorin grimaced at the camp, the dark Magi, and the people who were flocked around them. He scanned the crowd for Shaye, but there was no sign of her.

Umbra led him like a dog into a small tent, surrounded by aggressive-looking guards. They spat at his feet as he passed by, entering the dark tent. A gust of wind followed them in, lighting the candles in the small space. There was no furniture in the tent, save for a small table and a chair sitting in the middle of the room. Umbra pushed him into the chair, and nodded to the guards to secure his arms and legs with an enchanted rope—the rough, brown twine shimmered with the magic.

Umbra leaned casually against the table, the light casting a glow through her veil. It was still impossible to make out her full face, but he could see the shadow of it, wavering as if she were struggling to keep hold of the human form. Though he had never encountered a creature like her, he knew for certain that she was not of this world.

She began to hum a slow, eerie tune. She was watching Sorin and smiling. "You are an interesting mortal. A man raised to hate all magic, yet the thing you love most in this world is a girl engulfed in it. Right down to her very soul." She approached Sorin where he sat helpless. She reached out a shadow-covered hand—it was as if the fog he had seen in the forest had taken human form.

"It was you. You are the black fog from the forest." His nostrils flared as she ran her shadowy hand up his neck and into his hair. He wanted nothing more than to escape her touch. He could feel the sharpness of her nails, long like the claws of a hellhound.

She sat on his lap, running her hands through his overgrown blonde hair, a deep contrast to the darkness of her. "Clever boy. Yes, though that is just one of my many talents." She leaned forward to whisper into his ear. There was no breath coming from her, no heat; instead, all he felt was a deep void. "Would you like to see my others?"

"I would prefer to take your word for it."

Umbra let out a wicked laugh. "Bastian has agreed that, for tonight, you belong to me." She sighed and kissed him on the cheek through her veil. "Though kings hold no magic, they do contain a great deal of power... Power that I hunger for; a life force that is of great use to someone like me. You won't mind if I take a bit of yours, will you?"

Before he could respond, he was overtaken by shadows. They consumed him so that he could no longer see the tent or Umbra, but he could feel her bony body on his still. He thrashed against his restraints, trying desperately to escape the suffocating void that she was trapping him in. It felt as if everything, the very breath and life of him, was being drained away. The pain of it was agonizing, and he prayed for it to end. There was no way to fight it... To fight her.

A force struck them suddenly, throwing Umbra from his lap, and onto the floor. His vision returned and he gasped, trying to catch his breath—his entire body ached. Umbra screeched from the floor, "You *bitch*."

"Easy now, Umbra, you forget who you are speaking to." Bastian stood at the tent's entrance beside Shaye. Shaye's hands were engulfed in flame and there was a fury in her eyes. Sorin did not know if it was the light of the flames, but her eyes were no longer the golden color of a sunset; instead, it was as if the flame itself was shining through them. She looked every bit the fierce Sorceress that Signe had warned him she now was. He had not been able to accept it, to let himself believe that she had been tapping into dark magic, but it was true; she had used it to stop Umbra from hurting him, and now the dark lines of blood magic snaked from her fingertips to her wrists.

"Master..." Umbra was still on the dirt floor of the tent. She bowed to Bastian, touching her head to the ground. "You said he would be mine for the night."

Bastian stood at Shaye's side, looking down in disgust at Umbra. "You need not remind me of what I said. Rather, it is *you* who needs to be reminded of who is in charge here." He used his magic to drag Umbra across the ground to his feet. She shook her head violently, bowing once again to him in obedience.

Bastian turned to Shaye. "You see, he is alive and well. Just as I promised. Now enough of these theatrics." He clapped his hands and the tent opened up to reveal a fat, ruddy man, wringing his hands nervously, and a young woman Sorin recognized all too well: Duke Brayham and his daughter, Adella.

Adella strode in, more confident than her traitorous father, and stood at Bastian's other side. She placed herself as close to him as she could, her arm brushing up against his, as she smiled down on Sorin, triumphantly. The duke lingered back; he looked as if he would rather be anywhere else. Sorin spat at them, wishing he could run his sword through their greedy hearts.

"Bass..." Shaye's flames had ebbed, and she placed a hand on Bastian's dark jacket. Sorin did not like the way she called him by his childhood nickname. Bastian, however, seemed to enjoy it. He smirked at Sorin as Shaye continued, "You do not need to kill him, you could keep him and use his shame as a display of your power. Perhaps with the king captured, his men will yield. There will be no need for a war at all and—"

Adella interrupted her, "You would say anything to keep your lover alive. Lord Bastian does not answer to *you*." She stuck her too-thin nose in the air, arrogantly.

Shaye snapped a graceful finger and Adella's dress caught fire. The hateful girl let out a loud yelp and stomped the flame out. She turned to Bastian in disbelief. "Sire, surely you know I speak the truth. She has been deceiving you this entire time. The moment those thugs of hers showed up at the ball, she did everything she could to protect them."

Bastian held a hand up to silence her. "Adella, although you have a point, you are out of line. You are not the mistress of this camp." He didn't deign to look at her as he spoke, keeping his eyes on Sorin. "Shaye is. Isn't that right, my dear?" He held a hand out to Shaye and she took it. Bastian turned to the side, steering Shaye to face him, and then he kissed her. It was not the passionate kiss of a lover, there was no tenderness there. This was a display of ownership. Bastian wanted Sorin to know exactly how much control he had over the woman that Sorin loved.

Sorin felt sick at the sight of it, and he fought fruitlessly against the restraints. He could not understand why Shaye wasn't fighting back, why she was allowing herself to be treated like a plaything. She moaned in pain as Bastian bit her lip, drawing blood on her pale lips. Bastian pulled back, and looked Sorin in the eye again, smiling. Every instinct in Sorin's body screamed. He wanted to tear Bastian's black eyes from his face, to cut his heart from his chest, and hold it up for all of the Nefari to see.

Bastian signaled again to his guards, and they pushed their way into the cramped room. With them, they held Signe and the two guards that Ingemar and Ylva had knocked unconscious earlier that night. They were forced to their knees where Umbra had been moments ago. Signe's face was bloodied and swollen; someone had done a number on her. The two men beside her looked as if they had just come out of a daze, a result of the magic they had been hit with.

Bastian looked down on the three of them in disgust. Shaye stood silently at his side with blood still on her lip. Her face gave nothing away as she looked down at the ground, refusing to meet Sorin's eyes.

"Signe, you are charged with treasonous acts against the new regime. For this you will be sentenced to death after the battle. Once I have claimed my last wish from you, you will meet your end." He turned his attention to the guards next. "As for you two imbeciles... You allowed *women* to get the best of you and nearly cost us our victory. What shall be done with you?"

The men looked up defiantly at their leader, neither said a word. Shaye interrupted this time, "I know these men from the camp, they have been faithful servants to you, Bastian. They could not have known that we would be infiltrated with people who wield magic. If it pleases you, I would ask that you spare them."

The men looked at Shaye in blatant shock. Bastian seemed surprised at her defense of them as well. Her mercy seemed to confuse everyone in the room, but Bastian was far too vain to allow his power to be questioned. "I will spare their lives to please you, my dear, but they will not go unpunished." Bastian snapped his fingers, and in a slash of his dark magic, the men were struck on the face. The Nefari guards fell over, but did not cry out at the attack.

When they rose, each had an identical gash running from their brow to their cheek, cutting right through their right eyes. They glared at Bastian as if the hatred they felt in that moment would cut through his own unblemished face. Bastian ignored them, no longer concerned with the men or the wounds he had just inflicted on them. He turned to take his leave, whispering to Shaye before he disappeared into the night.

Shaye helped the wounded men to their feet as blood spilled from the wounds on their faces. She held a hand over each of their eyes, summoning her magic. Sorin could see that she was struggling; she furrowed her brow in concentration, and the light of her healing magic ebbed. She could not hold it. The open skin on their faces struggled to close together. Shaye stepped back. "I am sorry, I cannot save the eye."

One of the men nodded in understanding, and patted her on the shoulder. The other grunted in thanks for her efforts, and led his friend from the tent. Sorin could sense Umbra's unwanted presence still in the room with them. Her darkness was suffocating. Shaye ignored her as she stood, staring at Sorin. He wanted nothing more than to go to her, struggling under the ropes that held him to his seat.

Shaye looked back at Umbra. The two meeting one another with glares of hatred. Shaye's breath was rising and falling like she was in a panic. Sorin was going to have to say his peace with an audience—Umbra was not going anywhere.

"Shaye, you need to release me."

"You know I cannot do that." She stood firmly in place with a stoic look on her face; but there was true sadness in her eyes, and Sorin felt a seed of hope that she was not yet too far gone.

He needed her to give into her emotions, to tap into her humanity. So he said the one thing he knew would strike a chord with her: "I killed Elijah."

It worked. She gasped. "W-what happened? No, the fog took Elijah."

"Bastian turned him into a monster. He tried to destroy his soul with the darkness, but Shaye, it didn't work. Don't you see, Bastian is not infallible. We can still defeat him."

Umbra interrupted, smacking Sorin in the face with one of her shadows. "Silence."

Sorin shook his head, trying to get rid of the sting of the blow. Shaye kept her composure; her face was a mask of indifference once again. She raised her chin before addressing Umbra, every bit the picture of Nefari royalty in her black gown. "Your presence is no longer needed here. Bastian and I will be discussing the fate of the prisoner tonight. You are dismissed."

Umbra seethed at the dismissal, but did as Shaye commanded. Sorin could not imagine how Shaye had risen so high in stature here in the Nefari camp. Bastian trusted her, and that frightened Sorin more than anything Umbra could do to him. Shaye turned to leave, but Sorin could not let her leave without telling her one last thing. It could be the last chance he had to speak with her, and he would use it to be bolder than he had been in his entire life.

"I love you, Shaye. I have loved you for a long time, and nothing that has happened here in this Mother forsaken camp is going to change that." Tears filled his eyes, and he fought against the restraints that were burning his arms with the rough rope.

Shaye did not say a word as she took the lantern Bastian's men had brought in with them and walked from the tent, out of his sight. A swift wind swept in, blowing out the candles, leaving him and a battered Signe alone in the darkness.

CHAPTER TWELVE

Shaye

Shaye's hands were shaking uncontrollably by the time she reached her tent. She stood before the entrance, trying to calm herself before going in to face Bastian. She could not show him how rattled she was by the encounter with Sorin. If he saw her like this then he would surely take it as a sign of weakness—and to Bastian, weakness meant him losing control. He would make her drink the enchanted amber wine to cloud her mind, and would take control of it again. She could not afford that sort of setback. Not when Sorin's life was on the line.

She shook her hands out at her sides and bounced on her feet, but before she could enter the tent, Gorm and Ulf appeared from the darkness. Gorm held a large finger to his mouth, and gestured for her to meet them in the shadows beside the tent. Curiosity got the better of her and she went to them.

Ulf spoke, his gruff voice was no more than a whisper, "We know what you did."

Shaye was unsure of what they were referring to. She feared that perhaps they had seen her talking to Thorsten and Ylva at the ball. She wracked her brain for a believable lie, but Gorm said, "The guards you tried to heal... They grew up with us in the mountains after we went into hiding. We've known them since we were boys. Why did you do it? Why did you speak up on their behalf?"

Shaye was shocked by the question. Were these men really so jaded and full of hate that they could not comprehend the idea of an outsider showing mercy to one of their own? She bit her lip anxiously, hissing as she reopened the wound that Bastian had left behind.

Gorm and Ulf did not appear to be much older than her. She had never heard about their upbringing, but it did not come as a shock that it would have been as traumatic for them as it had been for her. Had they lost their family the night of the Winter Solstice, as she had?

They waited silently for her to respond. Finally, she found her words. "I know in my heart what is right." She took a deep breath. Her next words could be her death sentence, but she was willing to risk it—to see if it was truly possible to turn these men to her side. "Bastian is a shell of false promises. You both know deep down that he will never allow all of you to rise in stature. He will only allow you all to pillage this country until there is nothing left; and once he has control, he will discard you like the dogs he believes you to be."

The men shifted on their feet and Shaye braced herself for a fight. But none came. Instead, the brothers looked to one another as if sharing thoughts only the two of them could hear. Shaye waited. Wordlessly they drew their swords. Shaye held her hands up ready to call on her magic, but instead of attacking her, or taking her to Bastian to out her as a traitor, they dropped to one knee.

Holding their swords out to her, Ulf spoke. "Life for life. You have saved our friends, and for that you have our protection."

Shaye wanted to yelp with joy. If these two malicious men could offer her their protection, then perhaps there was still hope to turn more of Bastian's men to her side. Or, at the very least, to turn them away from Bastian himself. She motioned for them to rise. With nothing left to say, the brothers turned away, disappearing into the darkness of the night.

Shaye was willing to celebrate any victory, no matter how small. She took a deep breath, having found reprieve from the fear she had felt only moments ago. With her nerves settled, she entered the tent, suppressing a smile and instead looking indifferent. Bastian was laid out on her bed, while Brina sat silently in the corner with her hands folded on her lap. The Black Shuck was there too, gnawing on a large, bloody bone. It stained the expensive carpet underneath the beast's massive paws, and Shaye felt disgusted at the sight.

When Bastian noticed her presence, he sat up eagerly. "What did he say to you?"

Shaye held tight to her power as she answered, keeping him shut out of her mind so that he would not know the truth. "Nothing much. Just that I'm making a mistake." She sat down on the edge of the bed, picking at her nails.

"And what did you say to that?"

"I said that he should save his breath. I would rather be on the winning side."

Bastian laughed, delighted by her words. "Good girl." He inched closer to her on the bed. "Once we dispose of him and that traitorous Ceasg, we will be free of distractions." He ran a finger down her spine and she suppressed a shiver. She hated the way his touch felt; even more, she hated that she had to endure it to make him believe that she was his.

"Would it be wise to dispose of them when they can still be of use to you?" Shaye could not let him sentence Sorin to death. She was risking everything to trick Bastian until she could make a move against him, but she would not risk Sorin's life. *I love you.* She savored the memory of Sorin's words ringing in her ears. It had taken every ounce of strength in her to walk away from him in that moment; to not say the words back, for fear of who may hear.

Bastian's soft touch on her back moved to a tight grip on her arm. He pulled her in close, turning her face to his with his other hand. "I do not need that mortal for anything. Nor do *you*. Do you understand?"

Brina bristled in her seat, looking up with a fury that could destroy mountains—but Shaye held out a finger down low, out of Bastian's sight. Brina sat back again, regaining her composure. Shaye needed to get a grasp on this before things got out of hand. She batted her lashes and caressed his angular face. Staring deep into his black-pooled eyes, she kissed him. Bastian grew hungry the moment their lips touched. He was on top of her before she could stop him.

She pulled back—this was not what she wanted, but she could not say so without risking his wrath. She smiled sweetly at him as she said, "Bass, not like this, please." She shifted from under his weight, and he rolled away from her with a raised eyebrow. Shaye was relieved not to see any signs of anger, but the amusement on his face made her breath quicken in anticipation.

She continued, "It's just... I would like it to be more meaningful between us. I wouldn't want the camp to get the wrong idea about me. If I were to become your mistress, they would not respect me." She was on dangerous ground here and needed to tread carefully.

He was thoughtful before he spoke, "I've been thinking about that as well. That is why, when this is all over, we will wed." He said it matter-of-factly, as if it were another mundane task to be checked off his list. He had not even asked her if it was what she had wanted, but she could not reveal her true feelings.

Instead, she told him exactly what he wanted to hear, "I would love nothing more. But if I can make one request...? Think of it as a betrothal gift..." Shaye nuzzled her nose to his neck, keeping her breath even and steady.

Bastian moaned, "Anything."

"Keep Sorin alive until after the battle. Allow him to witness the fall of his kingdom. It will be a mighty blow to his army to see their leader in Nefari chains." Shaye kissed Bastian's neck, and prayed to The Mother that it would be enough. She needed to keep Sorin alive long enough to figure out a way to save him.

"That is a big request." He kissed her, then breathlessly whispered, "I will grant it. I will spare him until the battle is over."

Relief washed over her, but before she could thank him, he grabbed her by the throat. His fingers dug into her soft flesh. "But do not forget, I hold the power here. The ritual to activate the Sword will go as I plan, or it will be *your* friends who suffer the consequences." He released her throat, grabbing her chin and pointing her in Brina's direction. Shaye fought back angry tears as her dear friend stared back at her with fear-filled eyes. He hissed into Shaye's ear, "Do we have a deal?"

She nodded, and he released her. Bastian rose to take his leave. When his Black Shuck stood to follow him, Bastian gave the command, "Stay. Make sure she does not make any late-night visits to our prisoner."

The canine bowed in answer, laying back down on the rug. Once Bastian was gone, Shaye gave the beast a vulgar gesture. "I could kill you, you know."

The Black Shuck bared his teeth in a challenge, but he did not move against her. She got under the furs on the bed, still dressed in the gown from earlier. She did not have the energy, or the heart, to change. The night had taken its toll, and all she could think about was how worried she was for Sorin. Umbra was a vicious and terrifying creature, and Shaye didn't want to entertain the thought of what she might do to him, if given the opportunity.

She heard Brina find her way to her own bed, and was relieved knowing that at least one of her friends was safe tonight. "Goodnight, Brina."

"Goodnight, Shaye."

Shaye regarded the Black Shuck with a sarcastic tone, "Goodnight, *beast.*" He rumbled in response.

Shaye looked up into the shadows of the tent, then closed her eyes. In a hushed whisper, she said the words she had so desperately wanted to say earlier that night: "I love you too, Sorin."

CHAPTER THIRTEEN

Shaye

Shaye awoke to shouts in the camp. She tumbled out of her bed, only to be met with the Black Shuck. He was staring at her with suspicious eyes. For a moment, he reminded her of Finn with his fiery attitude. There was intelligence behind his eyes, and, if he were not a hound from the depths of hell itself, then she thought she might have enjoyed having him around. As she dressed, she felt her curiosity about the shadowy beast peak. "Did he even bother to name you when he called you up from the gates of hell?"

The hound snuffed at her. She removed her gown from the night before and put on a pair of fitted pants and a red blouse that had a deep V down the front. She rolled her eyes at the style that Bastian had chosen for her. Brina was dressing as well, and noticed Shaye talking to the beast.

"Are you seriously *talking* to that monster?"

"It's not his fault that his master is a horse's arse."

Brina laughed at that. It was the first time Shaye had heard her laugh in a long time. Things had been strained between the two of them since Shaye decided to play the role of Bastian's pet.

She knew it could not be easy for Brina to hold her tongue in the camp, and was actually quite impressed that she had been able to control her temper for as long as she had—particularly when faced with the poor treatment of the human servants. A few of the nastier Nefari soldiers had taken to bedding the unwed women, and using dark magic on the weaker men as entertainment.

Shaye knelt in front of the Shuck. "We're a lot alike, you know. Both trapped here, and forced to play a role in this nightmare... Both thought of as nightmares ourselves." She reached out a hand, but the hound made no move to meet her touch. "Perhaps I will give you a name."

At that, she swore she saw a glimmer in his eye. Bastian was feared by his followers, and she saw it in the hound, just as she saw it in his men. She had been clever the night before, taking the side of the guards; they were not likely to forget her mercy. If she could turn even a few of Bastian's followers toward her favor, then it could make a big difference.

"No need." Signe spoke from the tent's entrance. Her face was bruised and swollen; a long cut ran from her shoulder to her chest. It had been healed by magic but still left a scar. She carried two plates of food over to the table. "He is called Erebus. It means 'deep shadow,' or 'covered,' in the ancient tongue."

Shaye walked to the plate of food, taking a scrap of meat from it and handing it to the hound. He accepted it gratefully, laying at her feet while he ate. She took a chance and patted his head. His shadows danced away from her touch, but he accepted the gesture.

"Erebus. It's fitting." Shaye rose and dusted her hands off. Regarding Signe she asked, "He released you?"

"On the condition that I stay by your side throughout the ritual. He still has use for me since he still has a wish to use." She sat across from Shaye and Brina, who now dug into their breakfast. Shaye knew it would be a long day, and she wanted to be at full strength.

"The blood moon rises tonight."

Brina spilled her drink along the table. "Tonight? So soon?"

"Yes. We must prepare you for the ritual, Shaye. Bastian has demanded that you stay in your quarters until it is time." Signe poured herself a cup of tea and looked at Shaye as if waiting for her reaction.

Shaye gaped at her, "That's absurd."

Signe smiled knowingly. "You put on an impressive show, but he will not take any chances. Not when the stakes are so high."

Shaye threw her napkin down in frustration.

Adella's high pitched voice cut in cheerfully from the tent's entrance, "Poor dear, confined and forced to miss all of the festivities of the day." She walked into the tent as if she owned it, taking a moment to admire herself in the floor-length mirror. She smoothed out her pale hair piled high on her head, and straightened the skirts of her obnoxious gown. Lace and frills had no place in a war camp, nor did she.

"What are you doing here, Adella?" Shaye did not bother to use her title, knowing the slight would irritate her.

It worked. Adella bristled and turned to Shaye, her face as red as the apple sitting on Shaye's plate. "Bastian is with my father right now, you know. They are making preparations for after the battle."

"Why would I care what Bastian and your father discuss?"

Adella sat beside Signe, helping herself to the cup of tea in front of Brina. She did not acknowledge the two women, only Shaye. "You should care. He won't need you after tonight. Once he has used you, and your power, to get what he needs, he will throw you away."

Shaye laughed, and sat back in her seat. She held her hand out below, and Erebus came to her. He nuzzled his pointed snout at her hand and she stroked his rough fur, never taking her eyes off of Adella.

The arrogant woman shifted in her seat, uncomfortable in the presence of the hellhound, but she did not leave the topic alone. "It's true. My father is making plans for our betrothal as we speak."

Brina let out a loud bark of laughter, "Bastian is going to marry *you*? You're crazier than you look."

Adella looked as if she would claw Brina's eyes from her face. She snapped, "Servants should be seen, not heard. I could have you whipped for your insolence."

Shaye's anger flared, and through gritted teeth she said, "You do not address her, Adella. You do not come in here, and insult me, or my friends." Erebus growled by her side, eyeing Adella's throat.

Brina did not back down at Adella's threat. "You are *mortal*. Do you not see how he treats us? You honestly think that you will have a place in his court when all of this is over? You will be lucky if he even allows you to shine his shoes. Mortals, *all of us*, will be enslaved the moment he has full power over the kingdom. Surely you are not so vain as to believe you will be treated any differently."

Adella shook her head violently and stood. "You know *nothing*—and when I am queen, sitting by our lord's side, you will be sorry." She left the tent with a swish of her ugly gown.

Shaye rolled her eyes. "That was fun. Now how will we occupy the rest of our day?"

Brina smiled wickedly, "Let's start by making our own plans."

The day passed by fairly quickly. Shaye, Brina, and Signe spent the day lounging in the tent, relishing in the cool shade. The days were growing warmer as the Summer Solstice neared.

Brina hummed to herself across from Shaye. She was in better spirits than Shaye had seen her in since being at the camp. Shaye was relieved to see her friend back to her fierce self. Shaye found her spirits rising as well. She was feeling better than she had in weeks, and even took a moment to tap into her natural magic. It had been a challenge to use it since she had accessed the dark magic of the Nefari. Even now, as she tried to raise the droplets of water from her glass, she struggled. It felt as if her Druid power was resisting her.

She took a sip of her lemon water as they plotted against Bastian. They were careful to speak in whispers so that the guards outside would not be able to hear them. New guards were assigned to her for the day, and Shaye hoped it was because Gorm and Ulf had been needed elsewhere—not because someone had overheard their declaration to her the night before.

As she continued to try to raise water from the pitcher in front of her, she said, "I need to speak to the twins."

"Gorm and Ulf? Why in the world would you want to speak to them?" Brina bit into a plum.

Shaye released the droplets. She was out of breath from the strain of holding them. "Because Bastian messed up last night. He humiliated and brutalized his men like they meant nothing to him. By saving their friends, I earned their respect."

"Life for life," Signe whispered.

"Exactly." Shaye sat forward. "We target the powerful Nefari, closest to Bastian. When the time comes, they will hesitate to help him." She smiled wickedly. Holding her hand out to a bare patch of dirt, she called on the land to sprout life. She closed her eyes, feeling the resistance again. Nothing came.

Signe put a hand on hers. "Give it time, Shaye. Your magic will return to its full strength, you just have to be patient."

Shaye wanted to believe her. "What if losing my divine magic is the cost of the black magic I have used?" It was something she had feared more of as of late. When she had not been able to fully heal the punished guards, she had been terrified. "What if each time I use black magic, it eats away more of my natural magic?"

Signe shook her head. "I cannot say for certain. I fear I do not know much of Druid magic. But I know you. I have seen you these last weeks and Ingemar has told me of your strength. If anyone can overcome this and heal from it, it is you."

Shaye appreciated the sentiment, but deep down grieved for her magic, and for her soul. Shouting came from outside of the tent again. It sounded as if the camp was readying for battle, and it was driving Shaye crazy being confined to the tent. She needed to have eyes on Bastian and his men.

A whistle cut through the noise—it was coming from the back of her tent. She held a finger up to Brina and Signe and said, "Stay here."

"Shaye, you don't know—"

"I would know that whistle anywhere." She grinned, hurrying to the back of the tent and lifting the canvas off the ground. A mousy teenage girl was peeking from underneath. She was dressed in Nefari garb, gloves on her hands. Gloves to cover her untainted pink hands. Runa smiled up at her mischievously. Shaye helped her crawl inside of the tent, and the two of them embraced.

"Runa, what are you doing?"

"Cap'n was worried. He heard you had been placed under house arrest, so he sent me. The Nefari are too distracted to notice someone like me." She smiled proudly. Her hair was longer than Shaye had remembered, brushing past her ears. She had no words for how happy she was to see her friend.

"Tell him I am fine. I'm more concerned about all of you. Is everyone okay?"

"Yes, the crew is with King Sorin's people... Your people. When the king was taken, Ingemar and Mavka escaped with Bron. They are all awaiting word."

"Word from Sorin will not come. He is under heavy guard, not even I can get to him."

"No, Shaye... They're awaiting word from *you*."

Shaye was surprised. She had been worried that Bron and the others had not forgiven her for the attack on them. And after how she had ignored them all on the island, doing as Bastian had bid, she thought they would all have believed the worst of her. Shaye put her head in her hands and then brushed her long hair back away from her face. She needed to think. Knowing that the others were depending on her was a weight she did not want to carry. Not when she still had to figure out a way to stop the ceremony tonight.

"Okay, look, we're vastly outnumbered here. And with Sorin captured, there is no one to lead the army. Runa, I need you to tell Bron that I have convinced Bastian to stay Sorin's execution. If we cannot free Sorin before tomorrow, then Bron will need to lead the army."

"The clans are awaiting his orders as well. When they arrive, their forces will level the playing field." Runa looked hopeful.

"Not if the Sword is activated." Shaye scrambled to keep her thoughts straight. She was trying to think of what Sorin would do in this situation. "Mavka and Ingemar will lead the clans. With them and Bron occupied, it will be up to you and the rest of the crew to bide your time. Keep your eyes on Sorin, and the moment you see an opening, take it. Get him far from here, and keep him there, no matter what happens to me."

"What are you going to do?"

"I'm going to kill Bastian."

CHAPTER FOURTEEN

Shaye

When night fell, Bastian sent his men in to retrieve Shaye. Signe had dressed her in fine silk; the color was remarkable, a deep purple that shimmered when she moved. It reminded her of the Northern Lights she longed to see again. The silk wrapped around her body with a cinch at her waist. Signe clasped it together with a black, jeweled brooch. The dress was unlike anything she had ever seen, and she marveled at it in the mirror as Brina pinned her hair back neatly.

Signe caught Shaye's eye, noticing her admiration of the dress. "It is a style that was common in early Asterion, centuries ago."

Shaye blushed. "It is lovely." It was the first thing she had worn since coming to the Nefari camp that did not remind her of Bastian.

"I chose it for you. It is the style of your ancestors. I told Bastian it would be best if you performed the ceremony under their blessing... Not that a dress would ever make a true difference, but he bought the lie just the same."

Shaye turned to Signe, embracing the Ceasg who had become

her friend in the last weeks. It gave her courage to know that she had so many to stand behind her. No matter what came next, she knew that there were people out there who cared for her, no matter how broken she was.

Brina smiled at her from across the room, "Beautiful... There's just one thing missing." She pulled something from her jacket and Shaye caught the flash of steel. "I believe this belongs to you."

Shaye took the jeweled dagger that Brina held in her hands. She ran a tainted black finger over the Asterion crest: a stave and sword, surrounded by florals. It was the same dagger that Sorin had given her right before they found the Stave. She gripped the small hilt tightly to her chest. As a tear rolled down her face, accompanied by the memories of Sorin and the freedom she no longer had, she embraced Brina, whispering in her ear, "Thank you."

Bastian interrupted, breaking through the heartfelt moment, and Shaye's heart leapt from her chest. He could not catch her with the dagger he had taken from her on the night she had arrived in the camp as his prisoner. Brina slipped the dagger from Shaye's hands and tucked it into her own jacket.

Shaye turned to Bastian and fought the urge to sneer at him. He beamed at her, "Perfect." The mere sound of his voice made her sick to her stomach. He held his hands out for her to come to him. Shaye took one hand, and he spun her, admiring his prized pet.

Shaye motioned to the tent's entrance, "Shall we?"

He offered his arm and escorted her out into the dark night. There were no stars out tonight, though the skies were clear. The blood moon loomed high above them. It was massive in size, and Shaye thought of the crows that had been following her. The moon seemed close enough for them to fly up and touch. The camp glowed under its red-orange light.

Bastian steered her through the bustling crowd of Nefari and other magical creatures. A group of Orc grunted in acknowledgment as she passed, and Nefari soldiers bowed to their royal couple. Bastian did not release her until they were on the wooden platform. They were surrounded by native Asterion flowers in full bloom, and there was a flat, sleek rock centering the altar.

On the altar, with Shaye and Bastian, stood Duke Brayham and his smug daughter. She was dressed in a gown befitting a queen, and for a moment Shaye wondered if Adella had spoken true—if Bastian had agreed to marry her when all was said and done. Shaye wanted to scoff, *He's all yours, I don't want him.*

Brina and Signe also joined them. The guards escorting them shoved them into their place behind Shaye. Bastian had not told her what she was supposed to do once she was in place, so she stood wringing her hands together nervously. She looked around for any sign of Sorin or the others in the crowd, but they were nowhere to be found. She did, however, spot Gorm and Ulf standing at the edge of the altar—they glared at the guards who had handled her friends roughly.

Bastian raised his hand, and a hush fell over the crowd. "We stand here tonight, unified." His voice rose, sounding every bit the king that he fancied himself to be. "Our people have been met with persecution and slaughter. Magi were once powerful and revered throughout this land. Now we squander our lives away on the docks of our oppressors, or are forced to hide away."

The Nefari in the crowd nodded in agreement, and a few shouted in anger. Bastian was in his element, and Shaye was hating every second of it. He reveled in the crowd's response, growing more intense in his words as he shouted, "But no more! Tonight we take back our birthright... Tonight we take back our power!"

The crowd went wild, stomping their feet and cheering. Bastian waited until they were silent again before continuing. "Once we harness the power of Roth's Sword, we will be unstoppable. At dawn, we *destroy* our oppressors. We will take Asterion back through bloodshed."

Shaye flinched at the familiar words. It was just as *The Final Judgment* had read. The three brothers had been given a test. One that the last brother, Pris, had failed in his need for vengeance. The Fate, Atropani, had been right: Sorin, Shaye, and Bastian were facing their own tests, and Bastian was about to fail his.

The crowd erupted in a roar of applause. Bastian turned to Adella, who proudly presented him with the Sword. Signe took that as her signal and presented him with the Stave. Bastian nodded, and the women took the relics to the smooth stone, placing them gently on the sleek surface. He gestured for Shaye, and she came to him. She eyed the Sword; the emerald stone in its golden hilt glimmered under the moonlight. She could feel the power of it calling to her. She wondered if she would be quick enough to run it through Bastian. He was close enough, and once he placed it in her hands, he would be at her mercy.

She did not care about the consequences. With him dead, her friends stood a fighting chance of getting out of there. Even if she lost her own life in the process, it would be worth it to end all of this now. Her fingers itched to feel the cold steel of the Sword in her hand. She fought to steady her breathing and kept her hands still at her side. She had to strike at the right moment, or risk failure.

Bastian turned to her; his pale face was flushed with excitement. Shaye held her hands out, expecting him to place the relics in them. He reached down to grab the Sword, then paused. "Signe."

Signe stepped forward obediently, her eyes shifting between Shaye and Bastian. "Yes, my lord."

"I believe this would be a good time to use my last wish."

Shaye's stomach dropped as Signe bowed. If he was using a wish, then Signe would be powerless against it. She would have to do anything he asked.

His lip curled as he spoke, "I wish for Shaye to obey my every word."

Shaye's stomach lurched. "Surely by now you must know that you can trust me, Bass. Please, this is not necessary."

He ignored Shaye's plea, grabbing Signe roughly by the arm. "Would you defy your master?"

Signe looked helplessly to Shaye. "I am sorry." Tears filled her eyes as her magic bloomed around them. Golden dust blinded Shaye from the roaring crowd. They cheered, loving the show that their master was putting on for them.

Shaye felt as if she were on fire. Signe's magic burned as it coursed through her, down to her very soul. She fought the urge to cry out—she would not satisfy Bastian with her despair as he took the last ounce of freedom away from her.

When the magic faded away, the burning stopped. Shaye collapsed onto the altar, but she refused to show him her defeat. She stood carefully, raising her chin as she pushed her shoulders back, feigning confidence that she no longer had. She looked him directly in the eyes, and heard the crowd gasp. Looking around to see what had caused the shock, she realized it was her. When she looked down at herself, she saw black lines running along her arms and chest. Her body was covered in the thin black marks.

Brina let out a sob as Shaye turned to her in a panic. "Your eyes, Shaye. They...they're like *his*."

Shaye raised a hand to her face, and looked into Bastian's endlessly black eyes, as dark as the Obsidian stone hanging around his neck. Her despair was replaced with a wild fury as he tested his hold on her: "Pick up the relics."

The magic connecting them rocked her body, as she did as he commanded—shocked at how her body obeyed, even as her mind screamed not to. Bastian smiled, pleased with Signe's work. "Now call on the darkness."

Shaye fought it; inside she was screaming at herself to stop, but it was no use. She felt the lightning rising within her, demanding to be released. Bastian goaded her, he was enjoying every minute of this.

Images of pain and death flashed in her mind. She could no longer see the power-hungry Nefari, or the beasts that stood with them. Instead, she saw her parents, lying dead before her, with lifeless, empty eyes. She saw King Allerick, slaughtering her people in the ballroom. Hatred bloomed inside of her, Bastian's pull was growing, and she could not fight it.

Sorin. I need to think of Sorin. She tried to picture his handsome face and the dimple when he smiled, but the vision did not come. Instead, visions of his father, King Allerick, danced in her mind. He grinned at her as he cut her aunt down, sticking his sword into her breast. He grabbed Shaye's uncle next, but it was no longer Allerick looking at her. Sorin's deep blue eyes stared back at her now, as he cut her uncle's head from his body.

Shaye knew these were false memories—Sorin had been a child when the Winter Solstice coup occurred. But it was too late, she could not deny the fear and anger fueling her magic, pushing it to the surface for Bastian to use. A fiery pain shot through her as Bastian stepped closer.

Again, she saw her parents. They were alive this time. She watched as her father was beaten by Allerick's men, as her mother was ravaged by them. It was too much, she needed it to stop.

"Please..." She could not get out more than a whisper, "Please, Bastian, stop."

She knelt down on the altar, dropping the relics beside her. She dug her fingers into the rough wood beneath her. Bastian knelt down in front of her, raising her chin so that she had to look into his soulless eyes. His smile was like venom in her veins as he spoke, "Power the Sword, Shaye. Do you feel it? Do you feel me in your magic? We are one now." He snapped his fingers, and Adella came forward, smiling down at Shaye's pain.

"My lord." She bowed deeply to him as he stood, leaving Shaye to writhe in pain.

Bastian took Adella's dainty hands into his own. He caressed her cheek, before kissing her deeply. "You have been a faithful servant to me, and for that you will reap a great reward." He bowed to her, and the crowd followed suit.

Adella reveled in the attention, looking at Shaye triumphantly. Bastian lifted the Sword from where it laid, and Shaye moved to get up. She needed to get to that Sword while she still had an ounce of free will left. Bastian noticed her before she could rise, "Stay down."

Shaye's body betrayed her, and she sank back down to her knees. It felt as if she was trapped under stones. She looked to Signe and Brina, knowing they could not help. They stood to the side, shaking in horror at what they were witnessing. Adella giggled, and stood proudly beside Bastian.

The crowd waited in anticipation, unsure of what would happen next. Bastian had been secretive in his preparations; they did not know what the ceremony would entail. Even his personal guards looked to one another, not knowing what they were supposed to do.

Bastian held the Sword up for all to see. It gleaned in the light of the blood moon, its power flashing on the steel. Shaye wasn't sure if the others could see it, but she could. Bastian put an arm around Adella, pulling her close and running his fingers down her bare skin, as he held the Sword up with his other hand. Shaye watched Adella's face, shining with glee at the attention she was getting.

Shaye heard gasps from the crowd, and Adella's smile was replaced with a grimace. Adella groaned, brow furrowing, as she looked down at her chest. Shaye followed her gaze to find Roth's Sword plunged into her heart.

Adella cried out as Bastian tore the Sword out of her. Blood poured from the wound it had left. She looked at Bastian with confusion and betrayal before falling to the ground. Shaye looked around, waiting for someone to run to the girl, to help her, but no one moved. Even the duke stood uselessly as his daughter bled out before him.

Shaye tried to go to her, but her body still would not cooperate. She was trapped, helpless to watch this innocent mortal die before her. "Bastian. What have you done?"

He held the Sword up; a bright glow was now emanating from it as it dripped in Adella's blood. He announced, loud enough for all to hear him, "Blood for power. With this mortal sacrifice, we power our army. Raise your weapons." The Nefari army silently unsheathed their swords. They held them up, pointing them at the altar.

Bastian released Shaye from the magical restraint that was keeping her on the ground. "Rise. Power our army and take your place as my queen."

Shaye could not shake her desperation. She was not strong enough to fight him. This was the end. She stepped over the stream of blood that was flowing along the altar. Adella's blood. Her body laid untouched on the platform, her lifeless eyes staring up at the moon. Shaye stood at the stone, looking down at the Sword where Bastian had placed it. He handed her the Stave, and she gripped it tightly in her hands. Its wood felt smooth and powerful under her touch—it was hard to believe that this was the same piece of wood they had found broken in the cave. It felt so long ago... Shaye could not believe their actions had led to this.

Bastian was close to her, and she felt the strength of his power, dragging dark and hateful thoughts from the hidden depths of her heart. She saw the massacre of the Magi again. She saw Witches being punished by the people of Asterion, for simply existing. She saw herself, running away to Sagon, leaving her people to fend for themselves in a society that did not trust them. Her vision clouded as he whispered to her, "Harness your nightmares. Make *them* feel the fear that you have endured."

Her magic answered his call, erupting from her as it had in the abandoned camp. She closed her eyes as dark magic flooded her senses—the smell of sulfur filled the air, and she burned from within. All she could think of was releasing it out into the world, of making them hurt just as she was hurting.

She gave in as he commanded. When she opened her eyes, she unleashed her power into the Stave. The moon glowed brighter in response to her call, a blood red light flowing from it, through the Stave and into the Sword. It flowed simultaneously with her power from the Stave. The darkness of night was drowned out by the magic, lighting the camp in its wake.

When the light winked out, the camp was once again left in darkness. Even the moon seemed to have dimmed from the drain on its power. Shaye stumbled back, strained from the magic she had used. Guards began to light lanterns and under its light Shaye was able to see the inky black lines still snaking along her body.

Bastian took his own sword then. Spinning on his heel, he slashed through Duke Brayham, cutting the man's torso clean in half. The duke fell to the ground, now in two, gory pieces. The crowd cheered wildly. The Nefari and the magical creatures in their ranks let out whoops of triumph. The ceremony had worked. The Nefari now held the power to cut through anyone, and anything, in their path. Shaye fought back the vomit rising in her throat.

Bastian grabbed her hand, wordlessly leading her down the stairs, and away from the horrific scene on the altar. Brina and Signe did not follow, as guards blocked their path, keeping them in place. Shaye struggled as Bastian dragged her back to her tent. He pulled her into the dark room and threw her onto the bed. "Stay." With a snap of his fingers, he lit the candles throughout the tent.

No matter how much she struggled against the command, she could not move. Bastian removed his jacket; his movements were wild with adrenaline. He was the picture of pure glee as he turned back to her. "That was marvelous. And you..." He ran to her, kneeling before the bed. "You were *remarkable*."

Shaye looked away in disgust. "You're a monster."

"We are the same, you and me. We are connected now. And we will stay that way. There is no use in fighting it." His mood shifted to something more ominous as he stood, stalking to the table to pour himself a drink.

"Bastian, please. This is too much."

"No Shaye, I am just getting started." He leaned against the table. His words were bitter as he spoke, "You will not fight me ever again. You think I did not know you were plotting against me. Playing the demure woman... It was a nice touch, but I know you better than that."

"I..."

"Silence. You answer to me, and you speak when I allow it. We could have done this the easy way. If you would have cooperated, then it would not have come to this."

He made his way back to the bed. Sitting beside Shaye, he unpinned the brooch that held her dress in place. The silk fell from her body, exposing her bare breasts beneath. Shaye's blood boiled as she sat helpless against his whims.

"You may speak now."

She thought of the jeweled dagger that Brina had tucked away in her things. "I could kill myself, you know."

"No. You cannot. Here is what happens next. You will obey me. You will not resist. It is not just you who is under my control. Do not forget that I hold Brina's life in my powerful palm, as well." He ran a finger along her collarbone, and added, too casually, "As we speak, my guards are forcing poison down her throat."

Shaye's heart dropped. "Bastian—"

"The poison will work its way slowly into her system. It will take days to kill her. You will play your role tomorrow, and when we have destroyed Sorin's sorry army, I will give her the antidote."

Shaye nodded, she would do anything to keep Brina safe. Even if it meant destroying their country. Bastian leaned in and kissed her neck. He smelled of sulfur and honeysuckle. It was a disgusting mix, and Shaye resisted the feeling of bile rising in her throat. He kissed lower, making his way to her breast before he stopped. She let out a heavy breath in relief when he rose to look at her.

"Don't worry, love, I will honor your wish to wait until our victory before I take you as my own." He kissed her lips before he rose to leave her. Tears of relief streamed down her cheeks. She could still feel his mouth on her and it made her skin crawl. He was nearly to the tent's entrance before he turned to deliver the final blow to her spirits. "In one day's time, we ride into battle; and after we have destroyed them in body and in spirit, I would like to give Sorin's army a little show." He flashed his teeth in a vengeful smile. "Once we have achieved victory, *you*, will execute King Sorin."

Bastian threw the canvas flap open and disappeared into the night. Shaye let out a sob once he was gone. She felt as helpless as she had the night of the Winter Solstice. She hated herself for her own weakness. If Bastian gave the command, then she would have no choice but to obey. She would have to kill the man she loves.

CHAPTER FIFTEEN

Sorin

Sorin felt weak as he tried to find the strength to keep his head up. His throat ached from the need for water, and his lips were cracked. His body was stiff from lack of movement, and his head throbbed from the work Umbra had been putting in on him. She had been digging her shadowy claws into his mind for the better part of the day, until Bastian had called her to his quarters. Sorin was thankful for the reprieve.

He was alone in the prisoner's tent, and the air was suffocating and hot. His eyes had finally adjusted to the darkness, and he feared that he might never see the light of day again. He hung his head and tried to find the strength to go on. Umbra was truly a monster from The Beyond. She delighted in torment and excelled at entering one's mind. She had spent the day filling Sorin's head with scenes of gore.

It was becoming difficult for him to tell what was real and what wasn't. She had started off slow, taking him back to the Winter Solstice, drudging up memories of Magi being massacred at his father's hand. But as the day had progressed, she grew more malicious. She delved deeper into his mind, and his heart, presenting him with the deaths of each person he cared for.

He was helpless, watching Elijah being consumed and mutated by the fog. Then Bron being eaten alive by the Black Shuck. The beast's mouth was red and dripping with Sorin's best friend's blood, as he watched the light in his eyes go out. The worst, and final, vision was of Shaye. It had been too much for Sorin to take and had nearly broken him.

Umbra created a scene that felt like torture, as he watched Bastian strip Shaye naked in front of the Nefari army. Then he was forced to watch as Bastian ripped her very soul from inside her body, and devoured it. Sorin wanted to die at the sight of it. Only when he begged for Umbra to stop, did she relent.

Now he sat in the darkness, alone and praying to anyone who would listen, that the people he loved did not meet the ends that Umbra had shown him. She had not revealed much about herself throughout their time together, but he had gathered that Bastian had some sort of hold on her. She was immensely powerful, and not of their world. Sorin knew Bastian's magic was powerful, but he could not fathom that it would be strong enough to control a dark magical being like Umbra.

He himself could not escape her clutches without help, and he was praying now for a miracle. He had not eaten or drank anything all day and he felt sick. Every time he tried to picture Shaye, he could only conjure the image of her on the altar the night before. Her attempts at fighting Bastian had been fruitless, and Sorin knew her well enough to know that she was blaming herself for not being able to fight against the magic that Signe linked them with.

Umbra had cackled by Sorin's side that night, as she forced him to watch the entire thing. Had it not been for Umbra's hold on his mind, he would have ripped the world apart to get to Shaye. To stop her from becoming Bastian's slave. A sob escaped him now, in the darkness of the tent, thinking about the moment of Shaye's defeat. His heart was broken, and he hated himself for being too weak to save her.

A laugh interrupted Sorin's grief—it was Bastian. He stood in the shadows, but Sorin knew it was him by the bitter laughter. Sorin was not sure Bastian could feel amusement or joy enough to really laugh. The dark magic had eaten away so much of him that hardly any humanity remained.

"Bastian, finally decided to grace me with your presence?" Sorin spat on the ground.

"I just came to see how you were holding up. Umbra said she'd done quite a number on you today. I was curious to see if there was anything left of you."

"Ah, well I do have to admit, your friend Umbra's company leaves something to be desired." He coughed. His throat burned from speaking.

Bastian ignored the quip and pulled a chair over so that he was facing Sorin. "I'm not here for games. I simply want to give you an update. Your army has arrived in the valley. Sorry numbers, I must say. I expected something far more challenging from your famous General Tyrell. Nevertheless, we will destroy them tomorrow."

Sorin glared at Bastian, and imagined what it would feel like to rip his throat out with his bare hands. His breath quickened at the thought of Bastian's hot blood running down his hands, and onto the dead Asterion earth. Bastian shifted under Sorin's intense gaze.

Bastian cleared his throat, and continued to taunt him. "It is too bad you will not be there to see my victory. I had considered keeping you around as entertainment at court, but I could not have you distracting Shaye with your presence."

Sorin bristled at the mention of Shaye. "Where is she, Bastian? If you've laid a hand on her I—"

"Shaye is no longer your concern. And I will lay my hands on whichever part of her I see fit."

Sorin felt a growl rise from within him, and he lunged for Bastian, but the restraints on his arms held him firmly in place. Bastian laughed at his efforts. "Don't worry, you will have a chance to say your goodbyes to her at dawn. Right before I order her to execute you."

"She would never—"

"Oh, but she would. Thanks to Signe's magic, I *own* her. Mind, body, and spirit. She *will* dole out your execution—and when she does, there will be nothing to hold her back from her true potential. We will wed, and she will rule Asterion by my side." He rose, looking down at Sorin in disdain. "Sleep well, *King* Sorin."

Once he was gone, Sorin hung his head in despair. Bastian was right, Shaye would not be able to resist a direct command from him. The Ceasg's magic was too powerful and binding. Sorin wanted to scream, but he held back; he would not give Bastian the satisfaction of knowing that he had given up.

Umbra returned shortly after Bastian's visit. She stalked around the room, circling Sorin where he sat. His instincts went on high alert at the sight of her, but there was no use fighting his restraints. He needed to save his energy to fight her in his mind instead.

Umbra closed the gap between them. She smelled of rotten earth, like a cold, sulphureous place. It made him shiver. He gritted his teeth as she put her cold, veiled hands to his face, forcing him to look up at her. Her claws dug into his skin, drawing blood; it trickled down to his jaw.

She purred like a feline, "Now where did we leave off? I'm feeling *much* more refreshed now."

Sorin struggled to pull his face away from her grip. "Perhaps someone else would appreciate your attention more. I think you and I could use a break." He hissed between his teeth when she grabbed him by the throat. She dug her long, sharp claws into his skin once more. This time, dangerously close to an artery; one wrong move, and Sorin would be dead.

"Unfortunately, this is our last night together. Let's make it count, shall we?" She released his throat and sat in his lap. She was surprisingly light, almost as if her body were suspended in the air, but her shadows enveloped Sorin with a heavy weight on his mind. His vision went black as she took hold of his thoughts. It was an excruciating feeling—Sorin felt as if he and Umbra were physically in his mind together.

It always began the same, in a small dark room. When Sorin was rested he was able to put up a fight before allowing her through the doors to his innermost thoughts. But each time, no matter how hard he tried, he could not fight against her strength. This time was no exception; he was at his weakest point now, and the doors were already opened for her.

She pulled the two of them through to the chamber of his mind that she enjoyed visiting the most—his fears. Sorin could not deny that there was plenty for her to work with there. They had spent hours in that dark corridor of his mind, as she used the fear of losing his friends to torture him. She had even tapped into his fears about taking his rightful place as King of Asterion. Making him live through all the ways he could fail.

Umbra spoke, her voice echoing in his mind, "It is interesting, you know... That you do not fear bodily harm to yourself. Bastian was right to enlist my assistance in breaking you. Had he sent in one of his thugs to physically torture you, I suspect it would not have done much good."

Sorin ignored her. "Let's just get this over with. What will it be this time? Watching my friends stretched on a rack? Watching my mother drown in the harbour again? This is getting old, don't you think?"

"Oh, I'm just getting started. Let us revisit your fears about being king. Or, should I say, of becoming your father."

"My father was a great man who tried to be a fair king."

"*Tried,*" Umbra spat the word out. "I've seen a great many kings in my time, each one claiming they 'tried.' Sorry excuses for failure." She paused for a thoughtful moment, and Sorin braced himself for what she was planning.

The chamber of his mind flared to life as she threw them into a vision. They were at the Summer Palace. It was just as he remembered it, warm and inviting. Sunlight drifted through the floor-to-ceiling windows, illuminating the king's private rooms. Sorin searched anxiously for anything that was out of place. Umbra's visions were always dark and full of anguish. This one was different.

The door opened and Shaye came fluttering into the room. She was dressed in light, airy fabric, perfect for the summer heat. Her hair shined and her eyes were the bright gold that had mesmerized him since the first time they met. Her cheeks were flushed as she came face to face with him. She beamed brightly at him, and his gaze dropped to her full belly—she was pregnant.

He stuttered, "W—what is this?"

The vision of Shaye grabbed his hands and placed them on her round stomach. He felt a small flutter as the baby kicked. Shaye giggled, "He's growing strong, like his dad."

Before Sorin could speak, Shaye kissed his cheek and bounded to the other side of the room to pour herself a glass of water. Lost in the sight of her standing before him, beautiful and healthy, Sorin forgot about Umbra's presence. He approached Shaye, who had walked gracefully to the terrace overlooking the capital. He could see Aramoor in the distance; the colorful buildings towered high, and the water by the docks sparkled under the summer sun.

Shaye rested her head on his shoulder as they looked out on their kingdom. There was no blight. No sign of war, or of Bastian's Nefari. Shaye sighed and leaned into him, "It is wonderful, isn't it? I am so proud of you, my sweet husband."

Sorin's heart ached. He knew this could not be real, no matter how much his heart longed for it to be. He shut his eyes tight. "That's enough, Umbra."

Umbra's voice came from behind, "But you haven't seen the best part." She clapped her hands and the palace rocked. The floor beneath Sorin's feet rumbled and he reached out to steady Shaye, but her fingers slipped through his like a ghost. She vanished before his eyes, as the room around them morphed into something ugly and horrible.

Gone was the sunlight that had flowed through the windows. It was replaced with a dark gloom. The king's private chamber was now a shell of its former self. The curtains at the terrace door were shredded, and broken glass lay scattered across the floor. Furniture was overturned, as if there had been a confrontation. Sorin ventured back to the terrace, knowing that he would not like what he would find.

Aramoor, which had stood proud and prosperous in the distance, was now in piles of rubble. Smoke drifted from the city and into the dark, cloudy sky. Skeletal creatures screeched from above, circling the remnants of the harbour. Even from this distance, Sorin could hear the cries of his people, begging for mercy.

Soft crying came from behind him, and he turned to find Shaye staring beyond him, to Aramoor. He tried to go to her, but when his hand reached for hers, it slipped through his grasp. He couldn't touch her, and she could not see him. She limped toward the balcony. He could see bruises peeking through her elegant black gown, as if someone had injured her badly. There were bluish-purple marks along her arms and around her throat. Sorin's anger flared, and he clenched his fists. *Bastian, you son of a bitch.* Sorin did not need to see Bastian to know that this was all his doing.

Sorin stood beside Shaye, studying her. He wanted so badly to be able to reach out and comfort her. He looked down to see her hands on her round belly. She was pregnant in this vision as well, but he knew this time, it was not his child she carried. Shaye choked out a sob and spoke to the wind, "I am so sorry I could not be stronger, Sorin."

In this vision he had failed, lost the battle, and his life. This is what would become of Asterion if Bastian succeeded on that battlefield. This is what would become of the woman he loved.

The vision of Shaye sucked in a breath; when she released it, she spoke again, "If I could kill myself I would, Sorin. I would join you in the afterlife and be free of Bastian. But I can't do it, you see—I need to protect this innocent child. I have to be strong... I have to let you go."

When she turned to leave the terrace, Sorin watched the change in her. Her face became hard and determined, no sign of the despair that was there only seconds ago. Sorin understood what she was doing. She was turning away from her humanity, and the memory of the people she had lost, so she could survive this nightmare she was being forced to live through. Sorin felt it deep within his heart at that moment that the Shaye he knew and loved was gone.

Umbra laughed gleefully from behind him, "Marvelous, just *marvelous*! The utter anguish you're feeling right now is absolutely delicious. Interesting how the vision of you no longer being of this world did not drive you into hopelessness; but rather, it was the idea of the woman you love being forced to carry on in the world that Bastian will create." The vision faded away, and Sorin opened his eyes to find that they were back in the tent... Back in reality.

Umbra was still settled into his lap with her arms around his neck. She lifted her veil slightly to lick a tear that streamed down his face at the pain and anger he was feeling. Sorin pulled back and slammed his head into Umbra's face, knocking her off of him and into the dirt. She let out a venomous hiss and screeched in frustration. Though he knew it did not harm her nearly as much as he had wanted it to, it was still satisfying to have caught her off guard.

Umbra dusted herself off indignantly. "I will never understand you mortals. Horrible little *pests*. I look forward to watching your execution. And more than that, I look forward to the moment that Shaye is unprotected. When given the chance, I will *gut* her. Ohh, but not before I shatter her mind. What I have shown you, is only a fraction of my power. Pity I could not show you what I can really do. Bastian insisted that I not break you entirely. He would like you to be coherent for your army's defeat, and your execution that will come after." Sorin watched her with hate-filled eyes—he could feel the rage rising in him.

She bowed to him, startling him with the odd show of respect after she had spent all this time torturing him. He could see the shadow of a smile beneath her thin black veil. "Thank you, King Sorin. Thank you for feeding me with your fear. It has been too long since I have tasted a king's power, especially one as strong and noble as yourself. I have quite enjoyed myself. I need to rest now, see you in a bit."

Before Sorin could spit a retort, she vanished through the flap of the tent. He struggled to rest in her absence, haunted by the vision of what would become of his country if Bastian succeeded on the battlefield. Worse was the lingering memory of what *could be* if the Asterion army emerged victorious tomorrow. Of what his life would be like, reunited with Shaye and able to start a life together... If that's what she wanted. It had not escaped him that she had not said she loved him too, when he had declared his feelings for her the night before.

Shouting interrupted his thoughts, and two new guards arrived with a prisoner. They dragged the woman in by her arms, her feet leaving a trail behind them as they pulled her roughly through the dirt. She lay in a heap where they had discarded her, and did not move for several minutes. Sorin feared that she was dead, until she let out a gasp.

"Are you alright?" he whispered to her, not wanting the guards to punish them for talking.

The small woman struggled to rise from the ground. Her clothes were filthy and brown—the color assigned to the mortals Bastian had enslaved in the camp. Bastian's way of 'putting them in their place.' There wasn't a doubt in Sorin's mind that Bastian would undo all the good King Allerick had done. Though Sorin knew his father had made mistakes as a ruler, he believed that his heart had been in the right place. If Sorin got out of this, he would build on what his father had started. Except, this time, he would raise *all* of Asterion up. No mortal and no Magi would be revered over the other; they were all equals and deserved to be treated as such.

The mortal woman choked, trying to catch her breath, and pushed her disheveled hair from her face—revealing the familiar, fierce woman that had once held an axe to him and his men in defense of Shaye.

"Brina?" Sorin was shocked to see her here, and in this state. "What did he do to you?"

She began to cry, before falling into a fit of coughing. She covered her mouth with her sleeve, as she struggled to settle herself. When she took her arm away, the sleeve was coated in blood. As she spoke, her voice cracked, "His guards... They forced a black liquid down my throat. They've poisoned me. I could not fight them, Sorin, I tried. I swear I tried."

"I know, Brina. I know you did."

"And Shaye, oh Fates, did you see what they did to her? It's my fault. I just stood there like a stunned fool."

Sorin spoke with all the sincerity he was feeling, "It wasn't your fault. Look at me." She looked up at him with wounded eyes. "It is not our fault. It is *his*."

"Shaye thinks she can handle things on her own, but she can't." Brina looked around for anyone who may be lurking in the shadows as she spoke.

"No one is here—the guards will not enter the tent without

Bastian or Umbra. And I believe both are done with me for the time being." He had to ask, "Is Shaye alright?"

"I don't know how to answer that anymore." She coughed again.

Sorin was concerned—her skin was pale, and sweat was beading rapidly on her brow. *We'll be lucky if she even lasts the night,* Sorin thought with despair. He would need to keep her awake.

"Shaye is stronger than she wants to admit."

Brina laughed weakly, "You've got that right." Her eyes began to flutter shut. The poison was taking its toll on her.

"Listen to me, Brina—I need you to believe in your own strength right now. Shaye needs us... She needs you. We're going to get you help. Do you understand me?"

Her face hardened, and she sat up straighter now. "Yes, Your Majesty. I understand. Just tell me what you need me to do. But make haste, I am not sure how long I have."

CHAPTER SIXTEEN

Shaye

Shaye was struggling to fall asleep. She feared what she would once again find in the dark corners of her mind, especially now that she and Bastian were magically connected. The tether between them was a constant ebb of power, like a leash. Shaye squeezed her eyes shut in the darkness, willing herself to forget Bastian; to dream of better things.

Erebus shifted beside her, his large body splaying across half of the bed. The hound had wandered in sometime in the night, helping himself to a spot at her side. With Brina missing, Shaye welcomed the familiar presence of the Black Shuck. He nuzzled his sharply pointed snout under her arm, and she relaxed enough to drift back to sleep.

She had expected to find herself in a nightmare, but this time her mind took her back to the library in the Winter Palace. It was startling to be in the dimly lit comfort of the room, rather than in the ballroom full of bad memories, downstairs. Shaye tiptoed through the library; it was profoundly quiet, and she reveled in the peacefulness of it. It was a welcomed change from the usual settings of her dreams, which consisted of a bloody ballroom and the screams of the old king's court. She breathed in the scent of the dust-covered books. The last time she had felt this sort of peace was when she had danced with Sorin in this very room.

She was aware she was still in her dream as she closed her eyes, trying to recapture how she had felt that night with Sorin holding her in his arms; she thought of the way his lips had felt on hers when she had kissed him. It had been the first time she had let herself act on the feelings that had been slowly building between them. Now she couldn't stand the thought of a life without him.

When she opened her eyes again, she was still in her dream, but she was no longer alone. A woman stood before her, with long hair, the color of leaves in the fall. Her eyes were warm and wrinkled softly at the edges with the first signs of age. Shaye recognized her, though she could not believe what she was seeing.

"Mom..." Shaye took a step toward the woman slowly, worried that if she moved too quickly then the mirage would vanish. It had been a long time since she had last dreamt of her mother—other than in the malicious visions Bastian had given her of her parents' deaths.

"*M'lo.*" She used the term of endearment that Shaye had forgotten until now. Yrlissa Wistari held her arms out for her daughter.

Shaye was frozen in shock and confusion. "This is a dream. You aren't really here." Shaye was afraid if she blinked her mother would disappear, and she desperately did not want that to happen.

"I am not part of your dream, Shaye. I am here because you need me now, more than ever."

"You can't be here. You're dead."

"I am gone, Shaye, but the ways of The Mother are mysterious. I am here because of the power you hold."

Shaye hung her head in shame. "The black magic."

"No, M'lo, not the black magic." Yrlissa closed the gap between them, taking hold of Shaye's inky black hands. "You hold power greater than sacrificial blood magic. The magic of Asterion courses through your veins always and forever. Nothing you do will ever change that. I am proof of it."

"I don't understand."

"From the land you are born, and to the land you return." Yrlissa spoke the words that Mavka had prayed over the body of the sacrificed Forest Dweller. Shaye's mother spoke gently, "You are able to see me now because of your connection to the land; but we do not have long, and there is much to show you."

The air around them shimmered and the old library faded away. It was replaced with a white stone temple. It was unlike anything Shaye had ever seen—held up by shining columns grooved with carvings of leaves and vines. The aroma of mint and blossoms filled the air, and the sun shone down through the columns, illuminating the statue standing high above the altar.

More stunning than the architecture of the temple, was that statue. It towered above, sculpted of the finest marble in the shape of a woman of immense beauty. There was a soft smile on her marble lips, and her gaze peered down below to where Shaye and her mother stood. Magic shimmered all around them, and Shaye turned to her mother, stunned, "Where are we?"

"We are in The Mother's temple. This is where our people once came to worship her. It has long since been replaced with the forest you know as the Raven Wood." Yrlissa sat on a white stone bench and gestured for Shaye to join her.

The women sat side by side. Shaye had never noticed how much she looked like her mother, with the same autumn-colored hair and feminine features. She had been a child when her parents had been taken from her, and all she had been left with were faded memories. Shaye was terrified that this dream would slip away from her at any moment, and she clung tight to the magic she felt encircling them.

Yrlissa was thoughtful as she spoke, as if reciting from a tale that had been told to her many times: "Long ago, the Magi were split into three clans; they were believed to be descendants of the brothers Leto, Roth, and Pris. Pris and Leto's clans held the land in North Asterion, but there was tension between the two. The children of Pris wanted to find and control the relics left behind by their ancestors, but it was too great a risk for one entity to hold that much power. Their greed tore them apart, ultimately leading to their own downfall. Innocent people were hurt and the clan of Pris was forced to disband."

Shaye scoffed, "Seems Bastian could take a lesson or two."

Her mother laughed—it was a warm sound, just as Shaye had remembered. She took Shaye's hands again, unphased by the ugliness of her marks. "Bastian would do well to heed the mistakes of his ancestors."

"He comes from the clan of Pris?"

"Yes. He hails from one of the prominent families of that time. They were Shadow Dancers as well. The Obsidian stone they held was once meant to be used as a means of protection, but once Pris chose vengeance it was cursed with the dark blood magic you have witnessed these last weeks. Bastian's family is deeply rooted in that darkness, and it gives him the ability to harm, rather than protect. As you have experienced firsthand, he is able to poison the mind." There was sadness in the way she spoke of Bastian. Shaye squeezed her hands in reassurance, and Yrlissa continued, "I know that you cared for the boy."

"That was a long time ago."

"It is alright for you to grieve the friendship you lost." Shaye could sense regret in her mother's next words. "What I am about to show you will bring you pain—please know that I do not relish the thought. I had hoped it would not come to this."

She waved a delicate hand, and bright magic closed in around them. When the light faded, they were in a village. Shaye recognized it as the Druid village she had been born in, where she had lived until her parents met their end. Smoke billowed from the houses around them, and there was distant shouting. Shaye could see Druids in the distance, being pushed to their knees before men in sickly green cloaks—Shaye would have known those cloaks anywhere. They were the same uniforms that the Nefari army now favored.

Shaye looked at her mother, bewildered, "Nefari? I do not understand. It was Allerick's men who destroyed the village. It was he and his men who killed you and father."

Yrlissa placed a warm hand on Shaye's cheek. "M'lo, Bastian has manipulated your memories. It is the power of the Obsidian... The curse of his bloodline." Her eyes were filled with sympathy. "Shaye, what I have to show you... It will not be easy. But you need the whole truth for what is to come tomorrow, when you wake."

Shaye followed her mother into a small house. It was one of the few left standing in the small village, and Shaye paused at the little garden, which had been trampled in the assault. She could remember playing in that garden as a girl; teasing the Fairies who made their home there, as her mother tended to the flowers and vegetables.

Her mother led her silently inside the house. Shaye looked around at her childhood home. The walls were adorned with small paintings of flowers and stars—paintings that they had done together. Some of the flowers were crooked and smeared, the work of a five-year-old Shaye. Books were piled all around on the small hand-woven rug her father had gifted her mother with as a wedding present.

Her father's pleas drew Shaye's attention to the back of the room, near the table where her family had shared their meals. "You are too late. Please, Baal, leave us be." He was on his knees in front of a familiar man, who was flanked by Nefari guards. Bastian's father, Baal, sneered as he looked down at her father.

"Tell us where it is, Caldor, and I will leave you and yours to live out the rest of your wretched existence."

"I have already told you, we do not know where it is. It has been missing for decades."

Baal struck her father in the face. Caldor did not move from where he knelt, his strong body holding steady under the force of the blow. He spat blood at Baal's feet, and stared defiantly up at the evil man. To Shaye's horror, Baal waved a hand lazily in the air, snapping her father's neck with his magic. It happened so suddenly she did not have time to react.

Yrlissa placed a hand on her shoulder. "It is all in the past, Shaye. There is nothing you can do."

Shaye's eyes welled with tears. "He killed him like it was nothing. Like *he* was *nothing*."

"I am sorry to do this, Shaye, but there is more I must show you."

Shaye held a hand to her heart as she looked at her father one last time before the room faded from view. The shift in scenes was disorienting, and Shaye gripped her mother's arm to steady herself. They stood in a field, the Druid village within sight, and Shaye could see her childhood home burning in the distance. The sturdy roof gave in to the flames, burying her father's body in the rubble. Yrlissa grabbed her hand and squeezed it tightly. Shaye turned her gaze to where the memory of her mother stood face to face with Baal and a young version of Bastian. Shaye would have recognized his thick, dark hair and warm brown eyes anywhere.

Yrlissa turned to Shaye, "I am here with you. Hold onto that; this is a memory, but I am here, beside you now."

"Mom, I don't understand. Bastian already showed me what happened."

"He showed you what he wanted you to see. It was the only way to fuel your anger so that he could control you. *This* is the truth." She nodded to where the memory was taking place.

Baal tapped his foot, impatient and brooding. "Yrlissa, your husband is dead and my men are hunting your daughter as we speak. Tell me where the Stave of Leto is."

Yrlissa, or rather, the memory of her, spat at his feet and held her hands out to call on her magic. "You will not succeed. It is already in Allerick's hands. Your reign of terror is over, here in Asterion." She smiled as the ground quaked beneath them.

Baal had the good sense to look nervous at the power Yrlissa was calling upon—the same power of the land that had answered Shaye's call before. Only, her mother had mastered that power. The ground opened between them, revealing the rocks and dirt deep in the earth, and Baal stumbled back, pulling Bastian with him by his collar.

Bastian bared his teeth at her from across the broken land. He looked to his father, awaiting orders. Before Yrlissa had a chance to run, Baal gave a nod to Bastian. He stepped to the edge of the crevice, raised his hands, and began to chant, *"Ble-her, ble-her..."* His magic reached out, closing the gap between him and Yrlissa, who stood frozen in place.

Blood began to drip from Yrlissa's eyes and nose. She gasped for air, unable to catch her breath as blood bubbled up through her throat. It pooled from her mouth, and she fell to the ground. Yrlissa was dying, though she did not give them the satisfaction of looking defeated. She looked up at the evil Sorcerers standing before her and smiled, before drowning in her own blood. They may have beat her, but they were walking away without the relic they had come for. Still, to Shaye's horror, Bastian looked satisfied with his work as his father patted him on the back. Baal then led him away from Yrlissa, and away from the Druid village they had slaughtered.

Shaye wept at the scene of her mother's death. She had known that Bastian was a monster, that he had let darkness consume him... But she had never fathomed that it was his hand, his magic, that had ended her mother's life so brutally and mercilessly. Anger surged through her, and she tore her hand away from her mother's.

"I will destroy them all."

"M'lo, no." Yrlissa pulled Shaye into a warm embrace, whispering into her hair, "Hatred and anger are not the way. Greed is a powerful thing. It makes men do things they never thought themselves to be capable of." She pulled back and looked into Shaye's red-rimmed eyes. "Baal allowed that greed and hate to swallow him whole. He passed that onto his son—an innocent boy who never knew any better. You are different. You were born a protector; and like your ancestor Leto, you must *forgive* if you are to succeed."

"How can I forgive that *beast*? After what I have just seen, how can I forget? I have spent my entire life surrounded by men who use violence and call it a means to an end. Baal, Allerick... Bastian. They have all spilled innocent blood in the name of their own beliefs. How can I be expected to forgive them all, when it seems that there is no one in this damned world who chooses to take the righteous path?"

Yrlissa smiled sadly and the field faded away, replaced with the ballroom on the night of the massacre. Shaye watched herself, standing helpless in the middle of the chaos. Her small hands were shaking, and tears were streaming down her face as she watched the massacre taking place. A boy ran to her. He grabbed her hand and pulled her away. As the memory of the children passed her, she saw his eyes. They were deep blue, like Sorin's; no, they *were* Sorin's. Shaye held a hand to her mouth as the memory played out.

"It was him. It was him all this time. I knew it. Deep down, I always knew."

"Yes, M'lo. It was the mortal boy who heeded The Mother's call and saved you that night; but, you already knew that. I need you to look again." The vision began again, this time from the beginning, before the slaughter had started. "*This* is what both you and King Sorin need to know." Yrlissa pointed a graceful finger toward the main doors of the ballroom.

Shaye focused this time, not on her childhood self, but on the men who were congregated by the doors. Allerick's men burst into the ballroom, plowing through the party goers. The rebels filed into the room, without striking a single person. Shaye was shocked to see that their weapons were not even drawn. Allerick stood at the head of them, the resemblance between him and Sorin was striking. His dark blue eyes surveyed the crowd, until they found the old king. King Idor was sprawled out on his throne, drunk with wine, and a half-naked Magi woman was fawning over him on his lap.

Allerick shouted to the slothful old king, "King Idor! You have abused your power, and worse, you have abused your people. You sit here on your gilded throne, far removed from the suffering of the mortals throughout your kingdom. Your favored Magi are free to terrorize innocent men, women, and children. It ends tonight. You are now under arrest." Allerick gave the signal for his men to move on King Idor.

Shaye did not remember any of this. Her nightmares always began in the midst of the attack. She watched intently, scanning the crowd. Her eyes fell on the doors, seeing what her mother had intended all along. The doors were being locked, but not by Allerick's men. Two *mortal* men, men she recognized as lords of the court, slipped through the crowd, and clicked the locks into place.

"By The Mother..." Shaye whispered in horror.

"There is more to be seen." Her mother gestured to Duke Brayham, who stood meekly in the corner. Baal stood behind him, dressed in all his finery. He leaned in to whisper into the duke's ear, and the rosy-cheeked man nodded, dabbing his sweaty face with a kerchief. He dropped the kerchief, and a second after it hit the floor, a scream rippled through the air.

Shaye turned to where the scream had come from, just in time to see a courtier fall to the ground. The man who had stabbed the woman was not one of Allerick's rebels. It was one of Duke Brayham's private guards. Shaye's stomach dropped as all hell broke loose. King Idor's guards and court-appointed Magi turned on the rebels, who could do nothing but defend themselves. Shaye shook her head in disbelief.

The room faded once more, and Yrlissa and Shaye were once again alone, back in the library. Shaye breathed in the scent of the books, trying to regain her train of thought and ground herself after such a jarring change in scenery. She had to remind herself that she was safe here, that what she'd just witnessed had already come to pass.

She turned to her mother with tear-filled eyes, "What am I to do with all of this? Why are you showing me this, *now?*"

Yrlissa raised her chin. "Because you are lost. With each use of your dark magic, you risk losing another piece of yourself. I need you to know the entire truth so that you can move on. You and Sorin both deserve to know what happened in the past, so that you can understand it, and heal from it." Yrlissa was pleading with Shaye, "The past is just that. You have all the facts and can put it behind you now. You can heal... Together."

"Heal? How can you say that? After what the Nefari have done? After what *I* have done? There is no coming back from that."

Yrlissa took Shaye's face in her hands—they were cool on Shaye's skin. Her mother's lips trembled as she spoke, "Forgiveness is the only path. You must forgive Bastian for his misguided beliefs. You must forgive the mortals for their misguided fears. And more than anything, you must forgive yourself for the part you have played. Once you do that, you will find peace. The nightmares will no longer control you. They will no longer fuel you. And once that happens, Asterion will stand a chance at surviving what is to come tomorrow."

"Bastian will make me kill Sorin tomorrow. I—I cannot fight the power he holds over me."

"You can and you will. Your father and I believe in you, but we need you to believe in yourself. Tomorrow you will fight harder than you have ever had to fight before. But you will do it through *love*, not hatred. It is the only way." Shaye did not feel as sure as her mother sounded.

Shaye crossed her arms over herself protectively. "What if I'm not strong enough?"

Yrlissa hugged her tightly, and Shaye closed her eyes as warm tears fell down her cheeks. Her mother whispered in her ear, "May The Mother guide you."

When Shaye opened her eyes her mother was gone, and she was once again in the dark war tent. Erebus snored loudly at her side. She turned toward him and clung to his large body, rubbing her black fingers through his rough fur. No matter what the morning brought, she was determined to make her mother and father proud.

CHAPTER SEVENTEEN

Sorin

Sunlight leaked through a small tear in the tent. Sorin was glad for the break from the darkness. His eyes burned, and his head throbbed from yet another night with Umbra. She had arrived sometime after Brina, and Sorin had done everything he could to keep Umbra's attention on him, and away from Shaye's best friend. Umbra had not taken kindly to the insults he had spewed her way, in an attempt to protect Brina, and she had been more malicious than ever.

He and Brina were alone now in the tent, and he could hear the Nefari army readying for battle. Shouts and the clanging of weapons drifted to Sorin's ears. He searched the space to find Brina laying still on the hard ground. She had been sick all night, but now she did not stir.

Sorin's heart dropped at the sight of the woman lying alarmingly still. He couldn't tell if she was breathing. "Brina..." His voice grew more urgent as he called to her, "Brina, wake up, please, wake up."

She stirred; it was a small movement, as she tried to turn her head to him. Relief washed over him. Her voice was hoarse as she answered him, "Sorin... I can't..."

"Save your energy. I'm going to get us out of this." Sorin pulled at his restraints and looked around for anything he could use to free himself. Bastian would be sending for him soon, to take him to his execution. As afraid of death as he was, he was more afraid of what it would do to the woman he loved. He did not doubt that Bastian would order her to carry out the execution, and Sorin knew that she would never forgive herself.

Sorin let out a frustrated groan, "I need to get out of this damned chair."

"Perhaps I can untie it?" Brina moaned in pain as she tried to crawl to him.

"They're enchanted. There is no way you will be able to untie them."

"We could cut them?"

Sorin shook his head. Bastian had been clever in keeping the tent empty of anything, save for the chair he sat in, and the table nearby. If he could break the chair itself, then perhaps he could wriggle his way free. He rocked hard in the sturdy chair—pausing only when he made a loud noise at the effort and looked around to the tent's entrance to see if the guards outside had heard. To his relief no one came. The bustle of the camp had drowned out the sound of his attempts. He threw himself side to side again, harder this time, until the chair fell over to the side.

His face hit the ground hard, blurring his vision, but the chair remained intact. Sorin used all the strength he could muster, trying to break the chair on the ground, and prayed for a miracle. A low growl rumbled from the corner, and he froze. A shadowy creature slinked out from the darkness. A sliver of sunlight cut through the tent, casting a glow onto the shadows that made up the beast's body. The shadows shied away from the light as if its body had trouble holding form. Much like Umbra's did. Sorin wondered if they both hailed from the same place.

Bastian's Black Shuck stood nose to nose with him now, and Sorin stilled. He knew Bastian would not allow the beast to kill him where there was no audience to witness the Asterion king's destruction. Bastian was a showman, and this would not be his style. But that would not prevent the hellhound from doing a number on him beforehand. Sorin steadied his breathing as the Shuck stalked around him to where one of his arms was tied to the chair.

With one swift gnash of its teeth, the canine tore the ropes from his arm. Sorin sat in place, stunned as the beast went to work, removing the rope from his other arm and legs, freeing him completely. He scrambled back in the dirt to where Brina was laying, shielding her from the attack he expected would come next. To his surprise, nothing happened. The Black Shuck sat down in the dirt, and looked at Sorin expectantly.

Sorin was baffled. "Is this some sort of trick?"

Brina spoke for the Shuck, "His name is Erebus. And I believe he has just changed sides."

"How is that possible?"

She tried to sit up, and Sorin lent her a hand, pulling her into his side so that she could lean on him for support. She smiled at Erebus. "Because Shaye is kind and Bastian is not. It seems Erebus is more taken with her than I thought." She reached out a hand, and Erebus stalked over to her, nuzzling his face into her touch. His shadowy body vibrated like a cat purring in pleasure.

"He is not the only one." Sorin thought of the hateful glares the two guards had shot at Bastian when he had punished them. "The guards... The ones who were assigned to keep watch over the Stave—how loyal are they to Bastian?"

"It is hard to say, I do not know much about them. All I know is that they have never harmed Shaye. Most of the guards who have spent time with her have even become friendly in their interactions. I do believe the twins who are assigned as her personal keepers have given Shaye a declaration of loyalty of sorts; though she would not give details, for fear of being overheard."

"Do you think you are strong enough to find the twins?"

"For you and Shaye, I will try."

"Go to them. See if you can indeed turn them to our side, and ask them to get you the antidote. Then find the others. Mavka, Bron, and Ingemar will be nearby, I have no doubt."

Brina nodded, and kissed Sorin on the cheek. "May The Mother keep you, King Sorin."

"And you, Brina."

Sorin helped her to her feet, and Erebus offered support as she stood. The three of them left the tent together out of the back, tearing it more so that they could fit through. Sorin followed behind; he was a wreck, and knew he would not make it through the camp unnoticed. He parted ways with Brina, who limped off with Erebus following her obediently. Sorin hoped they would make it in time. He felt guilty about leaving her on her own, but knowing that the ferocious canine was at her side made him feel better.

Sorin ducked into an empty tent, in hopes of finding clothes that would shield him from recognition. It was odd to him how bare the tent was. There was nothing more than a neatly made bed and a trunk. He had spent enough time in the Asterion military barracks, and camping with the Mortal Knights while on patrol, to know that this was vastly different from the way his men lived. In an Asterion soldier's tent you could find playing cards or various other games to pass the time.

When he had been sent to Skag with Bron, Anik, and Elijah, his own tent had been piled with books and letters from friends and family back home. Elijah had brought with him a guitar for strumming on cold nights, and even Bron had brought his favorite wine. In contrast, this tent showed no sign of the man who lived in it. There was nothing to set him apart from another. Did they really enjoy living this way? Living without any small comforts or reminders of home? Sorin could not help but wonder if it was their own choice, or if it was a result of Bastian's need for complete devotion and obedience. If his men were distracted with comforts and comradery then there would be less room for mindless loyalty to him. It was a dictator's way of thinking, and would make sense, considering the sort of leader Bastian was.

Sorin opened the plain trunk, and sifting through the contents inside, he found a dark green cloak. Not his style, but he shrugged, putting it over his clothes and raising the hood to cover his face. The fabric was roughly woven, and he was looking forward to getting it off of him. He couldn't imagine how the Nefari could stand to wear the uncomfortable garments, especially with the days growing hotter. Sorin smoothed out the robes—wearing the clothes of his enemy made him cringe. He left the tent with the intention of making it to the tree line, where he hoped the Forest Dwellers were lying in wait for the battle that would soon begin.

The sun was rising higher above the hill, and he knew the Nefari guards would soon notice his absence. He ducked behind the tents leading back to the forest line, walking casually so as not to draw attention. The trees were within view now and he sped up his pace. He just needed to make it across the open space separating the camp and the forest. As he rounded the corner, he slammed into a large, hard body. He looked up into the face of an angry Orc. It snarled at him, showing large yellow fangs dripping with saliva. They really were a disgusting bunch.

"Apologies." Sorin bowed his head and stepped aside, but the beast grabbed him by the collar. Sorin's hood fell from his face, and the Orc roared in recognition. Sorin cursed the Nefari whose tent he had raided for not having a weapon for him to steal. It had been a long time since he'd been without a sword strapped to his side or his back. Without one, he was defenseless against the Orc's brute strength.

The Orc's voice was deep and throaty, with a thick accent Sorin could barely understand. "Look at what I've caught... A runaway." It bellowed out a laugh as its friends joined them. Four massive Orcs surrounded Sorin, each foaming from the mouth, and squinting through their beady eyes.

"Listen fellas, I see you've got your hands full, what with the upcoming battle and all. So, I won't keep you—" He tried to pull free of the Orc's grasp, but it was no use. These beasts were known for their monstrous strength and stupidity. Though Sorin could not match them in muscle, he could outmatch them in wit.

One of the Orcs lifted Sorin up by the collar of his cloak, dangling him above the ground. It snorted in his face, and its sour breath filled Sorin's senses as it spoke, "Master will reward us for bringing you to him." The other Orcs grunted in agreement.

"Ah, but I am already a king with vast riches. Let me go, and you may name your price."

The Orc looked Sorin up and down. "It does not look like you have anything to give us."

Sorin wanted to roll his eyes, but held back for fear of offending the goblin-like creatures. "No, not *with* me now. But I promise to send for whatever you desire."

While the Orcs contemplated his offer, Sorin wracked his brain for a way to escape if they chose not to fall for his bribe. It was empty in this part of camp, save for the gang surrounding him. There were no witnesses, but also no weapons within reach. The group of Orcs began to argue in a language Sorin did not understand. The smelly one holding him seemed to be outvoted.

The Orc relented under the pressure from his friends. "They do not want to wait for a reward. They want a prize now."

Sorin cursed under his breath, before the Orc dropped him on the ground. He felt his shoulder pop on the impact. He sucked in a breath between his teeth, and winced at the pain as the Orc dragged him by his leg through the camp. There was no use struggling to free himself from the intense strength of the grip. Nefari soldiers stepped aside to let them pass, as they made their way to the highest point on the hill that overlooked the valley below.

The Orc dropped Sorin's leg and bowed. Bastian stood before them in a black studded tunic with the Stave of Leto strapped to his back. On his head he wore a crown of smooth obsidian, similar to the one in the pendant he wore around his neck. He smiled when he saw Sorin lying wounded in the dirt. The Orc stood, eagerly waiting for his reward, but none came. It huffed as Bastian dismissed it with a careless wave of his black hand.

Sorin chuckled, and shouted at the Orc's back, "Should have taken my offer!"

Bastian quipped, "Sorin. Nice of you to join us."

"Always aiming to please," Sorin sneered at the arrogant man standing before him. Bastian acted as if he had already won this war, but Sorin had faith in his men and their plan. They would not give Asterion up, even if Sorin was not there to stand with them.

"Let us continue as planned, then." Bastian snapped his fingers and Shaye stepped forward. She looked every bit the fierce warrior Sorin had always known she could be. She was stunning in a silver dress coated in glittering armor. The bodice was beaded similarly to the gown she had worn to Bastian's ball. Chainmail began at her breasts, running up to her neck, with a sheer silver cape attached at her shoulders. Black lines marred her skin, but her warm autumn hair still shined in the light of the dawn. It was braided back and topped with a crown to match Bastian's. Sorin knew in his heart that this was still the woman he had come to love over the course of their journey together.

He was surprised to see the Sword of Roth strapped to her side, gleaming in the early morning light. Her chin was raised as she stood obediently at Bastian's side; but Sorin did not miss the glimmer in her eye as she looked down at him, or the wrinkle of worry on her brow. Sorin smiled gently up at her. Whatever came next, he did not doubt that she was still fighting for Asterion; still fighting for him.

Bastian, too consumed with his self-importance, did not note the exchange as he turned toward the valley below. "Your general has arrived with the cavalry, Sorin. Would you like to see?"

When Sorin did not respond, Bastian hurried to him, grabbing the back of his cloak, and dragging him to the edge of the hill. He kicked Sorin in the back of the legs, forcing him to his knees for the Asterion army below to see.

From here he could see his men, the soldiers he had grown up with, readied below for battle. Their armor glimmered in the early morning light. It was a significant show of force, but Sorin knew that their total numbers were far greater than what currently stood in the valley. Under General Tyrell's orders, the rest of the force would be flanking the sides of Bastian's army now, staying out of sight until the right time. He suppressed a smile. Sorin was careful not to give anything away to Bastian—the element of surprise was vital if his men were to gain the upper hand.

Sorin looked up at Bastian. "It is not too late to stop this madness. Order your men to retreat into The Beyond, to live in exile."

Bastian struck him in the face. The blow stung, but Sorin had seen it coming, and had prepared himself for the assault. He spat blood into the dirt at Bastian's feet. Bastian was running out of patience, and Sorin was enjoying it. Seeing Bastian lose his composure felt almost as good as when he had been pummeling him in the tree line. Though Sorin would rather be beating him to a pulp, he'd take what he could get. He glanced back to see the Nefari army standing on the hilltop with them now, awaiting their orders.

Bastian addressed them, "Brothers and sisters. Today is the dawn of a new era. One where only the worthy hold the power.

Where the weak kneel at our feet." He pointed to Sorin on the ground, and shouts sounded from the power-hungry men in the crowd, fueling Bastian on. "For too long we have been at the mercy of mortal men. Men who were not born to rule the ancient power of Asterion. Today, we take back what is ours, even if we have to spill every last drop of mortal blood in this Mother-forsaken country." The Nefari army went wild, stomping their feet into the ground, and clanging their swords against their shields.

Shaye stood silent and unmoving, but Sorin noticed her hands clenched at her sides. As Bastian continued to rile up his men, she inched closer to Sorin and whispered, "Did you see Brina?"

"She got away. I sent her to find help."

The tension in her shoulders relaxed slightly, and she let out a heavy breath. "This is not over Sorin. I need you to trust me."

"I have trusted you since the first moment I saw you."

CHAPTER EIGHTEEN

Shaye

Bastian finished his speech as the sun dawned on the horizon. Shaye knew what was coming next—she had been awake for hours readying herself. She'd practiced calling on her power, engulfing her mind with it. She hoped to be able to block Bastian out. Repeatedly, she built a wall up in her mind, locking it in place, and lowering it again. She wasn't sure it would be enough, but it was better than sitting around doing nothing.

She was filled with anxiety after she had sent Erebus to free Sorin. So when she had seen him dragged to the hill by the Orc, her heart had dropped. She had been foolish to hope that he could get away, so she would not have to fight Bastian's command to execute the man that she cared so deeply for. All she could do now was to believe in herself and the strength that her ancestral land would grant her.

The ground where they stood was dead from the blight; but since the visit from her mother, things had felt different. It was as if Asterion was pooling the last of its power at her feet, ready for the taking. The Sword at her side strummed with overwhelming magic, as if it, too, was ready to do her bidding. She set a steady hand on its hilt—the steel was calling to her and she itched to unsheathe it.

The Nefari army's roar simmered down to a low rumble. They were all looking at her now. Bastian smiled viciously as he took his place back at her side. Erebus' shadowy form appeared from the crowd, which parted to let Bastian's favored servant pass by. Bastian smirked at the hellhound, who stalked over to them in all his mighty power. Erebus approached, and paused a moment before taking his place at Shaye's side.

Noting his beast's choice, Bastian spoke under his breath so that only Shaye could hear, "Interesting."

She ignored him and continued to stare back at the Nefari army. She knew Erebus choosing her had left a small crack in Bastian's pride. She scanned the crowd for Gorm and Ulf, finding them almost immediately. They were standing beside the scarred guards she had saved. The other soldiers who stood with them were familiar faces as well—men that she had played cards with the night of Bastian's celebration. She rocked on the balls of her feet as adrenaline wracked her body. Would these men fight for her when the time came? Gorm met her eye and gave her a curt nod.

Bastian spoke louder for all to hear, "Over a decade ago, a pretender took the throne. A mortal man who thought to rid us of the magic that is rightfully ours. His son kneels before us now, at our mercy. It is with the spilling of his blood, that we reclaim Asterion and our magic as our own. As it was at the beginning."

The army dispersed, taking their places on the hillside leading down to the valley, and to Sorin's men. Standing at attention, they left a path cleared down the middle so that the Asterion army could still see their king on his knees, at the mercy of Bastian and Shaye. Shaye was concerned to see how organized the Nefari were. It was as if they had undergone formal military training. Something she feared that Sorin had not counted on.

Umbra lingered nearby, keeping a watchful eye on Shaye. She was clothed in her signature black dress and veil, shrouding her true face. Shaye looked at her in irritation, scoffing at the towering black crown that Umbra had taken to wearing. It was made of long, jagged black bones intertwined high above her. It looked like it was not of their world, shining in the sunlight like a snake's scaly skin.

Bastian raised his voice so that it carried down to the Asterion army in the valley, "Your King has failed you. Today you die because of his failure."

The hair on Shaye's arms rose when he turned to her. His eyes were filled with malice as he gave her the command: "Kill him."

His power swept over Shaye like a storm in her soul. Her hand gripped the hilt of the Sword, and she unsheathed the magnificent weapon, holding it up for both armies to see. Her breath quickened as she fought Bastian's command. She closed her eyes, calling on every ounce of power that the land could spare. It pooled into her, filling her veins, and overtaking the black magic. She welcomed the familiar feeling of divine magic and felt more alive than she had known possible. Careful not to let Bastian see that his power over her was no longer effective, she looked at him pleadingly. "Please, my lord, do not make me do this. You promised to wait until the battle was over."

Bastian scoffed at her, "You do not hold the power here, Shaye. I do." When she did not move, he grabbed her roughly by the arm, pushing her toward Sorin and snarling, "Kill him."

Sorin knelt at her feet, his dark blue eyes clouded with sorrow. "Listen to my voice, Shaye, you are more powerful than he is. The nightmares do not control you... *He* does not control you."

Bastian moved into her line of vision. "I can feel you fighting me. You know it is pointless. You will *always* obey me in the end."

She held the Sword out in front of her, realizing it, too, had magic that she could draw on. She gripped it tightly in her hands, reveling in the immense power flowing from it, and into her.

Bastian roared in anger at her, "Kill him! It is my command!"

Seizing the momentary distraction, Sorin slammed his full weight into Bastian's side, causing him to stumble. Shaye panicked; she could still feel the draw of Bastian's magic. Every muscle in her body ached as she fought the urge to plunge the Sword into Sorin's heart. She looked at Gorm and Ulf, who stood watching the altercation. They did not move to help Bastian.

Bastian swore, and reached out to grab Shaye by the arm—gripping her tightly, he shouted in her face, "Kill him, or I will rip every single person you care about limb from limb! I will force you to watch as I gouge out their eyes and feed them to my *dog!*" He pointed to Erebus, who was still standing by Shaye's side.

Shaye knew Bastian well enough to see that this fit of rage was a result of the control he knew he was losing. She smiled sweetly at him, looking into his black soulless eyes as she spoke. "I know what you did to my mother." She leaned in close to him. They were near enough to kiss, his breath hot on her lips. She spoke low so that only Bastian and Sorin could hear: "You are a hateful, deceitful, monster. And you are going to get everything you have ever deserved."

Bastian looked like he could spit venom. He shouted at the Nefari who were standing nearby, "Seize her! If she will not kill him, then I will." He gave her a smug look, until he realized his men were not answering his command. Gorm and Ulf stood between Shaye and the other Nefari on the hill. They showed no emotion, standing as tall and still as the ancient trees of the Raven Wood.

Shaye snickered, drawing Bastian's stunned face to her again. Fire was still coursing through her veins, as she struggled to keep still, and away from Sorin. She did not show it, though, as she spoke to Bastian, "These men see you now for what you really are."

She slammed her head into his face and heard the crunch of bone as she broke his nose. Dazed, he stumbled back. He gaped at her, and his eyes went ablaze with madness. He turned to his army and shouted, "Charge!"

Gaining their composure, and looking at Bastian in utter terror, they charged into the valley. Chaos ensued as the first of the Nefari ranks charged forward. The Asterion cavalry met them with great force, as they collided together at the midpoint on the hill. Bastian scrambled away from Shaye with a triumphant smile on his face, but not before she had pulled the Stave from his grasp. He slapped her hard in the face, but she ignored the sting of it. Her magic swelled, and she released it into him with all the fury she had been holding onto since coming to his camp.

His body skidded across the ground, and she took the opportunity to run to Sorin. Shaye looked at him in a panic, and he let out a gasp of pain as she touched his injured arm.

"You're hurt?"

Before he could answer her, Bastian hit them with an overwhelming force of magic. They tumbled to the ground in a tangle of limbs. Sorin howled out in pain, and Shaye shifted her body over his to protect him from another attack. When none came, she looked back to where Bastian stood.

His arms were extended as he muttered words she could not hear. He was stretching his magic beyond its natural limits, and straining under the pressure. Shaye couldn't believe her eyes as she witnessed eight Nefari soldiers, taking a stance between her and Bastian's wrath. They held their ground under his power, pushing back with their own. Gorm and Ulf were at the head of the small rebellion; and beside them were the two guards she had intervened for in the tent.

Gorm shouted over his shoulder so that she could hear him, "Get out of here!"

He didn't have to say it twice—Shaye grabbed Sorin by his

uninjured arm and helped him up, leading him into the valley below, and into the heart of the battle. If they could lose Bastian amidst the chaos, they might stand a fighting chance. She would gladly face an army of swords, rather than risk Bastian's gaining a hold on her again. She had been so close to carrying out his order to kill Sorin, it had taken all of the power that she and the land could muster to resist the first time around.

They were nearly to the heat of the battle when Sorin grabbed her arm, pulling her back to him. His dark blue eyes burned into hers as he said, "We stay together. Protect one another as we always have." He kissed her then, passionately. It was different from the tender kiss in the library; there were a thousand promises in this kiss.

When they parted, Shaye smiled as she asked, "You have a plan?"

"You're gonna love it."

Sorin let out a loud whistle in the direction of the Nefari camp on top of the hill. Bron, Mavka, Ingemar, and to Shaye's relief, Brina, appeared from the forest on horseback. Brina rode in on Finn, looking stronger and healthier than ever. The dapple-gray gelding snorted in excitement as he ran straight for Shaye. They surpassed the Nefari who were still standing on the hill, fighting back against Bastian's magic.

When they reached Shaye, she embraced Finn's thick, muscular neck, while Brina dismounted. Shaye took the reins and whispered into Finn's wild mane, "I have missed you." She then hugged Brina tightly as she added, "Both of you."

"We are here now." Brina grinned and pulled an axe from the side of Finn's saddle. "And we are ready for a fight." Shaye hugged her again tightly, thanking the Fates that Brina was okay.

Behind her, she could hear Bron giving Sorin a detailed report on the Dwellers waiting in the tree line. Mavka took one look at Sorin and went to work on his arm. He let out a yelp as the small girl stood on her tippy toes, popping his arm back into place.

Bron hovered over them, searching for any other sign of injury to his king. He smiled warmly at Shaye. "It's good to have you back." Shaye returned the smile before he went on, "As I was saying, the Dwellers are in place. They await your command."

Sorin grinned ear to ear. "Mavka, will you do the honors?"

"With pleasure." Her moths fluttered away in a hurricane-like flurry.

Sorin led Shaye and the others to a cluster of stones in the valley, allowing them a full view of the battle. It gave them a vantage point to see both the valley, where Nefari and Asterions were going sword to sword, and the forest that stood tall behind them on the hill.

The Asterion army was struggling to hold their ground as the Nefari steel cut through their armor like butter. Shaye felt a stab of guilt as she watched the mortal men fall. "This is all my fault."

Ingemar put a hand on her shoulder. "Do not dwell on the past, we must face this now, together." She raised her hands, and her magic flared to life. It extended through the valley, shielding the Asterion soldiers that were nearest to them.

The magic held strong under the Nefari swords, protecting the mortals in their path. Shaye watched in awe at Ingemar's power. "How long will it hold?"

"As long as I hold." Sweat began to bead at Ingemar's temple.

"I need to break the magic between the Stave and the Sword." Shaye held the Stave in one hand, and the Sword in the other. Closing her eyes, she called on her divine magic. She whispered an incantation, hoping to draw on stronger magic by using the Sorcerer's tongue: *"Bre-t-nk."* The ground rumbled beneath them, and the sky clouded, blocking the summer sun.

The valley turned dark as Asterions were slaughtered under the Nefari, out of reach from Ingemar's protection. Shaye felt a small hand on her other shoulder and turned to see Mavka standing at her side. Ingemar moved closer, grabbing Shaye on the other side. She felt their power flowing into her; it was a beautiful feeling, like warm sunlight after a long winter. It was so unlike the lightning she had felt at Bastian's touch, and she relished the difference. She welcomed the divinity of the Forest Dweller's and the Ceasg's magic, given to them by The Mother.

Embracing the power they were lending to her, she threw the Stave to the ground. With one swift blow, she struck the Stave with the Sword. Power blasted on the hilltop, blinding Shaye and the others with the magic that erupted from the relics as they collided. When the light ebbed away, Shaye and her friends cried out in victory. The Stave lay before them, split in two. The Sword had cut through it.

They ran to the edge of the stones, looking out into the valley. Nefari shouted out in confusion as their swords met mortal armor; the impact of their steel was meaningful, but it did not slice through. The mortal soldiers used the Nefari's surprise to their advantage, attacking ruthlessly with newfound courage. The Nefari weapons had lost their ability to cut through anything in their path. Shaye had done it. She had turned the tide of this battle.

Taking that small victory as their cue, Anik and his forces swooped in from the east and the west. The soldiers that had been lying in wait flanked the Nefari on three sides, forcing them back up the hill toward the forest. Bron and Sorin had already drawn their weapons, ready to meet any Nefari who dared advance on them and their small group.

Bron shouted to Sorin, "This is it!"

"I'm ready when you are!" Sorin gave him a wicked grin, wild with the anticipation of joining the other soldiers on the battlefield.

Ingemar released her shield and reformed it around herself and the others. As the Nefari retreated toward the woods, a line of Forest Dwellers on horseback revealed themselves. They sa tall, coated in armor the color and texture of tree bark. Their faces were streaked with blue and black paint surrounding their eyes—it was a fearsome sight. With a war cry, they charged on the Nefari. Shaye looked at Sorin in disbelief. She knew Sorin had made an alliance with the Magi creatures in the north, but she had never imagined such a vast number of fighters.

He shrugged his shoulders casually. "We made a few friends while you were away."

Shaye scanned the hill for any sign of Bastian, but he was gone. She could see bodies lying in a crumpled heap, and she prayed that Gorm and Ulf were not amongst them. She turned her attention back to the scene unfolding in the camp—just before the Dweller cavalry reached the Nefari, they turned away, retreating into the tree line. The Nefari cried out in victory, giving chase into the forest. Shaye was confused. "Why are they retreating?"

Mavka gave her a toothy smile. "Wait for it..."

Shaye continued to watch, unable to see the Dwellers in the density of the trees. Crows still circled above Shaye where she stood, but she noticed that they had gone silent. It felt as if Asterion itself was holding its breath as it waited. That was when she heard the first scream—it was an ear-curdling sound. Shaye imagined it was what death would sound like if it were a person. Nefari began to run from the forest, stumbling and trampling over one another, to escape the terror that had met them in the trees.

A second unit of Forest Dwellers emerged, right on the Nefari soldiers' heels, slaughtering those that had been foolish enough to chase them into their domain. Shaye felt the adrenaline in her veins rush at the sight. Nefari around them in the valley paused when they heard the dying cries of their men on the hill. But they did not have a chance to send assistance, as they defended themselves from the Asterion soldiers that had flanked them down below.

Shaye wanted to kiss Sorin right then and there. His plan had been brilliant, and his men were executing it perfectly. It would now be impossible for the Nefari to pin down the Asterion forces. Sorin stood silently, with a sly smile on his lips as he watched his handiwork. Shaye thought he had never looked more magnificent than he did in that moment.

That moment didn't last long, however, as Sorin and Bron were soon engaged in battle with the Nefari who had retreated from the forest, blocking their escape back into the valley. The two Mortal Knights fought in perfect harmony. It was like a dance that they had been practicing for their entire lives. Standing back to back, Sorin and Bron cut down anyone arrogant enough to challenge them.

The smell of blood and sweat overwhelmed her. It was mixed with the smell of Nefari magic, like sulfur and rotting earth. It was chaos down here, and Shaye felt a stab of fear. Not for herself, but for the mortal men who were going hand to hand with the dark Magi and the creatures who stood alongside them.

She watched in horror as a massive Orc crushed an Asterion soldier's skull beneath its boulder-like fist. She shot her magic at the beast, sweeping him up in a wind that broke his neck as he hit the ground.

A pack of Fenrir gnashed their teeth, tearing flesh from bone. The giant wolf-like creatures turned their molten eyes on Shaye and Sorin. She braced herself for an advance, but Erebus jumped between them. He had conjured himself from thin air, his shadows dancing wildly in the slivers of sunlight that were peeking through the clouded sky. His growl rippled through the air, sending a cloud of black smoke into the pack of Fenrir. Their yelps were silenced as the smoke consumed them.

Shaye whistled, calling him to her. "Well done."

Amid the fighting, Shaye spotted Forest Dwellers holding strong against the black Nefari magic, countering it with their own divine magic. Though the mortals were at a disadvantage against the Nefari, the Dwellers were evening the odds. They defended the Asterion troops and sent their own magical creatures after the opposing forces. Shaye caught glimpses of creatures she had not seen in over a decade: an eerily beautiful Banshee screamed at a group of Nefari who were descending on a Mortal Knight, blasting them back and rendering them unconscious. A Chimera slammed into several Orcs, burning them alive with fire from its lion-like face.

Shaye panicked as she turned to see a Nefari on horseback charging toward them. Before Shaye could lash out with her magic, an arrow struck the man through the eye. He fell from his horse with a thud. Shaye turned to thank the archer, and was surprised to see Runa grinning at her from behind one of the large rocks. She ducked back for cover and continued to fire her arrows. They hit their mark every time. Shaye felt her confidence grow, knowing that Captain Thorsten and his crew were nearby.

Sorin shouted to a towering man in shining armor. Six dead Nefari lay at his feet, and he bowed in Sorin's direction. The defeat of so many Nefari was an impressive feat for a man who looked old enough to be her father.

The older knight called out to Sorin and Bron, "Hell of a fight, boys!"

Sorin shouted back, above the noise of battle, "We can't take all the credit!" He nodded to Shaye and the girls on the rock. The old knight regarded Shaye suspiciously.

The battle was raging on around them, and Shaye did not care to stand there being scrutinized by this stranger. Sorin and Bron must have held the same sentiment, because they turned from the old man, resuming their roles in the battle. They remained close to the rocks, where Shaye and the other women stood, taking on attackers from every angle. Finn reared at anyone who came close enough for him to strike, and Brina was using all of her strength to swing her axe. Their little band was a fearsome sight to behold.

Mavka called out as a Nefari soldier charged toward them. Black magic was forming between his hands as he began to speak. Ingemar held fast to her power, bracing herself for the attack that was headed for her shield. It slammed into them, knocking Shaye back into Mavka. They steadied one another and shouted. Shaye was stunned by the hit, a force that would have been fatal, had Ingemar not been there to shield them from the brunt of it.

Sorin charged at the man, sprinting, as Ingemar lifted her magic enough to let him pass safely. He ran his blade through the Nefari, roaring as he ended the man's life. A small group of Nefari noticed the commotion and ran toward them to join in on the fight. Bron took his place at Sorin's side as they went sword to sword with the enemy. One of the Nefari began speaking under his breath, and Shaye knew another magical blast was headed toward Sorin and Bron.

She jumped from the rocks, calling on her divine magic again. She lashed out with it, steering clear of Sorin and Bron, just in time, as the Nefari man unleashed his spell. Her magic hit its mark, landing a killing blow to the man. Sorin looked for the source of the counterattack, and smiled when his eyes met Shaye's. She continued to defend them from where she stood. Sorin and Bron were unstoppable, cutting down anyone in their path. Blood covered them as they tore through the dark Magi advancing on them.

A murder of crows screeched from above, eagerly awaiting Shaye's command. Recalling the many times she had been visited by the creatures, she extended her magic to them, connecting her to the group of sleek, black crows. She closed her eyes and whispered, "Descend."

CHAPTER NINETEEN

Shaye

The crows did as she bid, diving down toward the Nefari. It was a brutal sight as they tore away at the dark Magis' hands and faces. The crows were wild with bloodlust. Distracted by the attack, the Nefari did not see Bron or Sorin coming. The Mortal Knights finished what the crows had started, wiping the remaining Nefari out.

The battle raged on, as more Nefari came at them, and Shaye felt exhaustion creeping in as she protected Sorin and Bron from being outnumbered. Shaye was so distracted with keeping them safe that she did not notice an ambush from behind her.

Bastian struck the women with explosive power. Shaye landed a few feet from Sorin, and he rushed to help her stand. He was searching her for any sign of injury, when she shoved him away.

He reached for her, but she pulled out of his grasp. Over the sound of battle, he shouted, "Where are you going?"

"To finish this." Before she left, she shoved the Sword of Roth in his direction. "Take it!"

"No, you need it."

"I have my magic. Just take the damned thing."

He grabbed it from her hands, and she immediately felt the absence of its power. Her instincts screamed at her to take the power back, but she ignored the feeling. She turned back to the rocks where Bastian stood. His face was a picture of vengeance itself. Like his ancestor before him, he was full of rage—blinded by it. So much so, that he did not expect what came next.

As he lunged for Shaye, she met his force with her own. Their magic collided in a flurry of darkness and light. She held fast to her power, willing it into him. Bastian was relentless—he shouted a dark spell at her: "Br-her!"

It was enough to break through her magic, and she was thrown to the ground. She coughed, trying to catch the breath that had been knocked out of her at the impact. Her body screamed in pain as she tried to rise, and her vision began to darken at the edges.

Sorin was shouting at her, but he was too far away to reach her before Bastian did. Bastian grabbed her by the throat, digging his fingers into her until she couldn't breathe. Her vision faded in and out as she struggled under his hold. She kicked him in the gut, and he released her long enough for Sorin to get her attention.

He let out a whistle, and when she turned to him, he threw the Sword. It hit the ground within arm's length of her, and she scrambled for it. Bastian grabbed her ankle, dragging her back to him and away from the Sword, but something hit him. Shaye reached the Sword and clung to it for dear life, its sharp steel edges cutting into her hands. With blood dripping down her black fingertips, she readjusted her grip, grabbing onto the hilt, and standing for another round with Bastian.

He was recovering from the blow he had taken from Ingemar, who was standing behind him, surrounded by golden dust. In the blink of an eye, he was upon Shaye again with a murderous rage

This was it. One of them would not walk away from this, and she was determined that it be him.

As he reached for her with his jet-black arms, Shaye plunged the Sword into him with every ounce of strength she could muster. She grunted as she pushed it deeper, relishing the look of shock on Bastian's face. He let out a sickly choking sound as she pulled the Sword back slowly. She wanted him to feel every bit of agony as the Sword sliced through his insides. He gripped her dress as he fell to the ground, tearing it to reveal her leg, lined with black from his connection to her.

She stood tall and unmoving as he slumped to the ground, blood pooling from the wound in his stomach. Shaye knelt beside him. She could feel his power over her slipping away.

He choked as he tried to speak, "You traitorous *bitch*."

"You are the traitor; and for that, you will die *powerless* in this valley. You have failed, Bastian, and I will not make the same mistakes as you. I will find forgiveness in my heart. Forgiveness for you and for the dark Magi who stand amongst us... And perhaps one day, I may even be able to forgive myself."

Bastian's eyes fluttered as he struggled to hold onto his life-force. Through gritted teeth he said, "You should have chosen me."

Shaye felt a pang in her heart at the words. He sounded like the boy she had once known and loved. She watched as the black pools faded from his eyes, revealing warm brown irises. She grieved for the man that he could have been. "You should have chosen forgiveness, Bass."

She grabbed his hand—it was cold as he gripped hers back. They had once loved one another. But she would never forget what he had done to her mother, or to Asterion. Now all those warm memories from their childhood would forever be tainted by the horror he had inflicted. Perhaps in another lifetime things could have been different for them...

Shaye struggled to find the words. Her voice was a hoarse as she said, "If it's any consolation... I forgive you, Bass."

His grip on her hand tightened in response, but he said nothing. Instead, he closed his eyes, and took his last breath. Bastian was gone. She looked up to see Sorin, holding out a hand to help her up from the ground where Bastian's blood seeped into the land. Before she took it, she reached down to untie the Obsidian hanging around his neck.

Sorin was breathing heavily when she stood to look at him. "Shaye, your face."

She raised a hand to touch her cheek, unsure of what he was seeing. "What is it?"

"The black, it—it's gone." He took her cheek in his hand. "The darkness is fading."

She looked down at her arms, then to her leg, showing through the tear in her dress, all of which were once covered with the sickening marks of Bastian's control. They were clear—her smooth, pink skin shone brightly under the risen sun. But to her dismay, her hands were still black. Her face fell in disappointment, but Sorin raised her chin to him gently.

"It will all be okay." He took her hands in his and squeezed them tightly.

Shaye dropped his hands, and reached to cover her ears, as a screech sounded from behind them. Umbra stood, seething in anger at the sight of her master lying defeated and dead. She lunged for them, but Erebus blocked her path. She shot out one of her shadows, knocking the canine back into the dirt. The Nefari soldiers near them stood still in shock and confusion, looking at their leader lying dead in the grass.

Still, the battle raged on, Asterions and Dwellers were keeping the pressure on the Nefari army from all sides in the valley. The Nefari defended themselves the best they could, but it was no use. The Asterions were too great in numbers and power now. Shaye noticed a few Nefari dropping their weapons and clasping their black hands behind their back, in a show of surrender, at the sight of Shaye standing over Bastian's body. More Nefari followed suit.

Sorin raised his voice high above the battle, addressing the Nefari force like the king he was. "Surrender now, and live. Or die fighting."

At his words, the Nefari looked around nervously. They noted the state of their army, and that their numbers had significantly diminished in the battle. No longer powered by the Stave, their weapons were no match against the disciplined Asterion army— and their magic was matched with that of the ancient Magi creatures fighting for Sorin. They conceded. Shaye could barely contain her pride. Had they really just won? She could not help but hope that the worst was over. She grabbed Sorin's arm and squeezed it affectionately. When she looked at him, he was beaming with triumph.

Umbra screamed at the Nefari in a voice that sounded like the gates of hell opening, "Don't just stand there, you imbeciles! Kill them all!" They hesitated, and Umbra allowed her power to explode into them.

Shaye stood tall, and shouted at Umbra, "It is over!"

Mavka let out a piercing scream, as Umbra used her shadows to grab her. Umbra sneered at Shaye as her shadows snaked out around Mavka's small face, caressing it.

Shaye chose her words carefully, "Umbra, you do not need to do this. You are free now, don't you understand? Bastian can no longer control us."

Umbra scoffed at her, "Control *me*? You think I am so weak as to be controlled by a mere man?"

Shaye was confused. She had witnessed with her own eyes the obedience Umbra had shown Bastian. She had tortured mortals at his command, had used her powers to create the man-eating fog that had terrorized them and the citizens of Asterion... Shaye furrowed her brow, "I don't understand. Why are you here, if not by his hand?"

Umbra released a wicked sound from her throat, it was like a fire crackling. She narrowed her eyes at Shaye through her thin veil. "I am here to do what I have always done. To devour this pathetic world of yours. It has been a long time since I have tasted destruction, and I am not leaving until I have had my fill."

Both the Nefari and Asterion armies stood still as they watched the scene unfold before them. Shaye took a step toward her, but Umbra tightened her hold on Mavka, making her cry out in pain. Shaye stopped in her tracks. She could not risk Mavka by getting any closer. All she could do was keep this monster talking. She needed to stall long enough for one of the others to come up with a plan.

Shaye gestured to the battlefield. "Then look around. You got precisely what you wanted, men lay dead and dying all around us. Please, let Mavka go. She is of no significance to you. Release her and we will step aside to let you return to wherever it is you came from."

"Silly girl. You remind me of the man whose blood runs in your veins. Leto also thought he could talk his way out of defeat. His world made for a magnificent meal when I feasted upon it."

Shaye bristled at the confession. The war that had driven the brothers from their land in The Beyond had been Umbra's doing. They had fought, and had failed to save their people. Shaye's hands shook. How could they defeat this ancient beast, when so many others had failed before them?

Umbra must have enjoyed the doubt on Shaye's face, because she continued, "Now, Baal and Bastian, on the other hand, were quite eager to aid me in my quest. Just like their predecessor, Pris. Foolish men, to think that they were in control, when it was I who was guiding them to this moment."

Shaye had heard enough. She burrowed her magic into the ground, sending it to where Umbra stood. If she could call on the roots below, then she could take hold of her. Out of the corner of her eye, she saw Bron lunge toward them—but he was too late. Umbra sensed the attack and snaked her tendrils around Mavka's head. Glee filled Umbra's eyes as she snapped Mavka's neck.

Bron let out a roar of despair as he charged at Umbra, but she was gone. Black smoke and a broken Mavka was all that was left behind in her wake. He fell to the ground with a sob. Shaye reached him before Sorin. Ingemar held Shaye back, allowing Bron to pick Mavka's small frame up, rocking her body as he cried out. Shaye felt sick to her stomach. Everything had been going right and, in her confidence, she had been careless to have not seen this coming. She would make Umbra suffer for this.

Sorin caught her as she turned to hunt down the shadow monster, "Shaye, where are you going?"

"I should have ended Umbra's reign of terror the moment I met her."

"No. We stay together. We will kill that Witch, but we will do it together." He looked sadly at his grieving friend on the ground. "Right now, Bron needs us."

Shaye conceded. Sorin was right. If they were going to get through this, they needed to stand united. Umbra was an ancient creature from The Beyond. It would take every ounce of power and strength Shaye could muster to defeat her.

Shaye looked around now at the bloody battlefield. The fighting had ceased, and Asterion soldiers were now gathering the remaining Nefari force. Some of the mortal men shouted out in victory, while others looked around the valley in grief. The older knight that Sorin had shouted to earlier did not waste his time on celebrating; instead, he got to work barking out orders for the Nefari army to be rounded up and taken for questioning. They could afford to leave no stone unturned. If there were more Nefari in hiding, they would need to sniff them out.

Shaye could tell Sorin was struggling between his need to take his place as king, and what he really wanted, which was to go to his friend. The latter won out in the end, and he followed Shaye to Bron and Mavka's side.

Shaye spoke softly to Bron, "We need to take Mavka's body back to the forest. We'll use Finn to get her there."

Finn pawed his hooves into the ground, and Shaye put a hand on his velvet nose. "Let's get her home." The horse calmed, allowing Bron to lift Mavka's body onto his broad back.

"W—where are you going?" Ingemar's tear-filled eyes reminded Shaye of how much they had lost, even though they had won the battle.

Forest Dwellers gathered at their sides, weeping for the loss of one of their own. Shaye had no words to comfort them. She was barely holding it together herself. They walked up the hill toward the forest in a silent procession. As they left the valley, Shaye watched the tired Asterion soldiers wipe the blood and sweat from their faces before gathering prisoners.

She asked Sorin, "What will happen to them?"

"They will be taken back to the Summer Palace to stand trial for their crimes."

"Will their lives be spared?" She knew Sorin to be a good man, but she did not know his council or his generals. She feared the worst.

Sorin looked into her eyes, worry furrowed his brow. "We will keep our word. The guilty will be exiled. The next moves we make will set the tone for the future of Asterion. I have no intention of starting my reign with unjust retaliation."

The clouds parted in the sky. Shaye knew she should be smiling brighter than the sun reappearing above them at their triumph here, but she failed to muster even a hint of one. She could barely feel the sense of victory as she walked beside Finn and Sorin.

The old knight fell into step beside them and cleared his throat. "King Sorin. We need to return to camp. There is still much to be done." He eyed Shaye warily as she walked by Sorin's side. She felt uncomfortable under his scrutinizing gaze. He reminded her of the no-nonsense Mages who had taught her as a child at the Winter Palace. She fought the urge to shift uncomfortably.

Sorin nodded to him, "Of course, General Tyrell. We will meet you at the camp once we have tended to our friend."

General Tyrell shifted his eyes between them impatiently, but did not argue with his king. Even Sorin seemed like a young boy ready for a scolding in the presence of the General, but he kept his voice steady, "We will join you shortly." The general caught Sorin's dismissing tone. He bowed and took his leave, shouting more commands at the men left standing on the battlefield.

Sorin took Shaye's hand in his, leading her through the empty Nefari camp. As they passed the mess of tents, despair still clouded the thrill of their victory. Not only was she grieving the friend they had just lost, but she had not caught sight of their other friends since she had spotted Runa. She whispered a silent prayer that they had all made it through the battle in one piece.

A pale green man fell into step at Sorin's side. His face was covered in red and blue, and Shaye could not tell which was paint and which was blood. He bowed deeply to Sorin, and Sorin returned the honor.

He acknowledged the Dweller, "Chief Einar."

The chief spoke, his voice a low rumble, "My daughter fought bravely. I only wish I could have told her how proud I was."

Shaye's heart skipped a beat. His daughter... Mavka. There was an uncomfortable silence as they escorted the Dwellers into the forest.

Chief Einar grabbed a large horn from his side. He sounded it, breaking the quiet air that now filled the battlefield below. Every Dweller and creature from the Raven Wood answered his call, following obediently behind as Sorin led the way back to the tree line. They walked so silently that Shaye could hear her own heartbeat. She tried to remind herself to breathe steadily, but all she could think of was the sight of Umbra snapping Mavka's small neck.

When they reached the trees, they were met by Captain Thorsten and his crew. Shaye searched frantically for any signs of significant injury, but found none. They sported bruises and cuts but nothing fatal. She had no time to feel relief as they cleared a path, settling Mavka's lifeless body onto a bed of brown leaves.

Bron sat at her side, gripping her small hand tightly. He looked like a giant beside her small body. Her moths were no longer dancing around her; but rather, sat on her arms and legs in mourning. Chief Einar knelt at Mavka's other side; his face fell and he began to weep. Shaye turned away, it was too much for her to take in.

The Dwellers gathered around the fallen princess, dropping to their knees. They bent down low so that their heads touched the ground. Though they had won the battle, and defeated Bastian, it seemed that the land had not yet healed. The Dwellers dug their hands into the cold, rotting earth and began to whisper in a language Shaye did not recognize.

Their hushed chants rose through the trees, and a cool breeze blew Shaye's loose hair into her tear-filled eyes. Sorin kept hold of her hand as they witnessed the Dwellers in mourning. Their voices began to rise—it was like music, as it drifted through the forest around them. Shaye swore she could see the glisten of magic in the air, as if the words themselves were filled with it. She kept her eye on it as it flowed toward Mavka.

Shaye released Sorin's hand and knelt to the ground. Putting her hand to it, she could feel the pulse of the land, as if it was answering the Dwellers' call. Sorin knelt beside her with confusion in his eyes. "What is it?"

Shaye whispered to him, "This is going to sound crazy, but I think they're asking Asterion for help."

CHAPTER TWENTY

Shaye

Shaye couldn't believe her eyes as she watched the scene unfolding around her. Crouching beside Sorin, she could sense the change in the atmosphere in the forest. The Dwellers were chanting in an ancient language, and the land seemed to be awakening because of it. Sunlight streamed through the trees and highlighted Mavka's body, laying still beside Bron.

Chief Einar sat on the other side of her, his head pressed into the ground like the Dwellers that surrounded them. Shaye, unsure of what to do, and too afraid to disrupt what was happening, sat silently beside Sorin. His presence was a powerful thing; it felt like she had gotten back a piece of herself. She could not help but steal glances at him, afraid that if she took her eyes off him for too long he would disappear.

Shaye leaned into Sorin and began to whisper a prayer. She placed her hands on the ground in front of them and closed her eyes. Her heavy lashes kissed her cheeks as tears ran down them. She reveled in the heat radiating from Sorin at her side, as she called on her power. The ground beneath them rumbled in response to her call, and she felt Sorin tense as the crowd around them chanted louder. The dead leaves around Mavka began to change. They came to life, green and healthy, just as the flowered trees had done in the forest, the day she had sung the ancient Druid ballad.

Bron noticed it, too. His voice wavered, "Mavka?"

The magic around them was undeniable now. Something otherworldly was happening here; something that was not meant for mortal eyes. Shaye peeked over at Sorin, who was not used to such a display of powerful magic. Mavka's moths began to stir as something shimmered above her body. Bron jolted back in alarm as Mavka's spirit took form and wavered above. Shaye watched as he reached out tenderly, trying to brush shaking fingers through her vine-covered hair. Tears came tumbling down his cheeks when his hand met only air.

Shaye could sense Sorin holding his breath. She could not blame him—she too was having a hard time believing what she was seeing. Mavka's spirit smiled down at Bron. She was no more than a thin veil, teetering between their world and the next. The Dwellers stopped chanting, but the magic still lingered in the air.

Mavka's voice was a faint echo on the wind, "Bron." Her head tilted to the side, there was so much sorrow in her voice that Shaye had to hold back a sob. "I do so wish we could have gone to that ball together."

Bron balled his fists at his side, and collected himself before answering her through his tears, "I would have liked nothing more than to have taken you to as many balls as your heart desired." He struggled to choke the words out, "Hell, I'd have even thrown one in your honor." He hung his head low in despair, and Shaye's heart broke for him.

"It was a great honor to have been in your presence, even for a short time." She held both hands to her heart, showing her sincerity.

"The honor was all mine, Mavka." Bron held a fist over his heart in return, and shut his eyes tight.

They stayed like that for some time, as the Dwellers gave them time to speak the words that had been left unsaid. Chief Einar caught Shaye's eye. The ancient Dweller was smiling sweetly at the scene unfolding before him. When he noticed Shaye's attention on him, he nodded to her, acknowledging her role in calling on the powerful magic that was helping to hold Mavka's spirit in place.

Sorin's face was pale. "How?"

Chief Einar smiled sympathetically, "It is a rare gift... but our ancestral land has chosen to answer our call. It is not for us to question."

Mavka regarded them, tilting her head, and giving Sorin and Shaye an endearing smile. "I do not have the words to fully express what you all mean to me. I have lived a fulfilled life, thanks to you all." More urgently, she added, "Unfortunately, we do not have much time, and there is work to be done."

Shaye knelt in front of Mavka's spirit, wishing she could take her small delicate hand in her own black, tainted ones. "Mavka, the battle is over. The Nefari have surrendered."

Mavka looked at Shaye as if she were the one visiting from a fatal slumber. She shook her head and giggled, "I know that, silly. It is what comes next, that concerns me."

"Y—you knew?" Shaye fumbled for her words.

Shaye glanced at Chief Einar, who did not look surprised, as he stood silently to the side with his hands clasped in front of him. Mavka smiled softly at him, and replied to Shaye's question matter-of-factly, "Of course. I could see everything from where I am. Now listen carefully, it is vitally important that you get going."

"Going where?" Shaye felt exasperated by Mavka's vague words. "I don't understand." She searched Mavka's sweet face and held back the tears threatening to fall.

"Oh please do not cry." Mavka reached a ghostly white hand out to Shaye.

"Mavka, you died. We *watched* you die."

Mavka held her hand to her heart. "I know, and I am sorry for the grief you all felt, and the heartache that will follow when I leave you; but your mother is very insistent on what you must do."

Shaye's heart thudded in her chest. The forest suddenly felt small, and far too warm. Through her shallow breath, she whispered, "My mother? You saw her when you were…"

"Yes. She says that killing Bastian did not destroy the blight. She explained that it was far too late for that, and that what must be done now is up to you."

Shaye knew it would sound crazy to the others, but she had only just dreamed of her mother. It wasn't out of the realm of possibility that her mother would have found Mavka on the other side, wherever or whatever that might have been. Mavka had her full attention.

Shaye stood tall to face her. "Tell me everything."

Mavka launched into a condensed version of her story, skipping over the details of her journey to the other side, to the part where she encountered Shaye's mother. Sorin shifted beside her; she knew he was growing anxious. Mavka could see it, too. "I know this is difficult, Your Majesty. These things are often beyond our understanding."

Satisfied with his compliant silence, she continued, "Yrlissa Wistari believes that the relics must be returned to where they came from. You must take them north and destroy them. If you do not, you risk this realm falling to a fate worse than anything you can imagine."

Shaye looked at Sorin. His jaw was clenched, and he looked like he was ready for an argument. Shaye tugged nervously on her long hair. "I believe her. Look around. The blight is still here. We need to finish what we first set out to do."

He shifted on his feet and looked around the forest. Shaye thought for a moment he might argue with her, but instead he said, "Then we do it together. Just as we planned before."

Bron rested his hand on the hilt of his sword, "We will ready the horses."

Sorin held a hand up, "No. Shaye and I will go. You will stay here. My mother will need help to sort the aftermath of the battle out."

Mavka's ghost-like form faltered, she was losing her foothold on their world. She spoke quickly before Bron could protest, "King Sorin is right. You are needed here. Shaye and His Majesty will keep one another safe as they make their journey into The Beyond."

Sorin and Shaye spoke in unison, *"The Beyond?"*

Mavka giggled uncomfortably, "Did I leave that part out?" Her moths were back to their lively selves, fluttering around her iridescent head. They seemed to be keeping closer than usual to her, as if they too were afraid she would drift away at any moment. "The relics of the three brothers must return to where it all began. That is, they must return to where the brothers came from... to The Beyond." She shrugged, attempting to look casual. Shaye knew better—she could see the way Mavka's shoulders were drawn up, and the way she shifted her eyes nervously.

"Is there something else?" Shaye didn't want to push, but they needed to be ready if they were to go to a land that no mortal had ventured into, and returned from, in centuries.

Mavka shook her head and looked down at the ground, as her spirit began to fade. "I wish I could tell you more, but that is all I know. I am here to give you the puzzle, but it is up to the two of you to solve it."

Before Shaye could say a word, Mavka bid them farewell, looking at Bron first, "I will truly miss you..." Then to Shaye, Sorin, and the Dwellers surrounding them, "All of you."

Mavka's spirit blinked out from the forest, with no sign that she had ever been there to begin with. Her moths fluttered away in a sad swirl of motion. Shaye fought back the tears and reached for Bron. He joined her and Sorin, and the three of them stood in silent mourning for Mavka.

Shaye turned to Sorin. The memory of the night at the *Brass Blossom*, after Leif's funeral, lingered in her mind. It felt like ages ago since Sorin had stood by her side, waiting for her to agree to help him. He had not forced her to go with him; it had always been her choice to make. Now she needed it to be his choice if he would come with her on yet another hopeless quest.

She held her hands nervously at her sides, gripping her filthy, torn dress. "I can do this alone, Sorin. No one would judge you for staying here and taking your place on the throne."

He reached for her hands, settling them into his own. Giving her a sly smile, he repeated the same words she had said to him when she had first agreed to help: "Tell me what I have to do."

CHAPTER TWENTY-ONE

Sorin

Shaye made haste in preparing for their journey. Sorin watched her and Bron gather supplies and ready the horses. He knew that Bron was angry with him for ordering him to stay behind, but there was no one he trusted more with cleaning up the mess the Nefari army had left in the wake of battle. He knew that he could rely on his best friend to oversee the trials, and to find any Nefari deserters who may have gotten away. More than that, Bron needed to take time to grieve for Mavka. Her loss was a heavy blow to all of their hearts, but Sorin had known Bron long enough to recognize that his friend had been in love.

Bron and the rest of the palace would be left with quite a mess; there was sure to be discord in the city of Aramoor. Their capital would soon be buzzing with word of the battle. The last thing Sorin wished, was for Magi and mortals to turn on one another, when what they needed most was a united front. Though it would be difficult for his friends to sit out this journey north, he knew that their help would be invaluable to the next steps Asterion needed to take.

Bron was using Sorin's orders as a distraction from his grief, and joined Sorin in talking with the clan chiefs to make sure their delicate alliance would not falter while he was away. The clans were buzzing with excitement after their victory on the battlefield, and the miracle they witnessed with Mavka's brief visit from the afterlife—but the chiefs were wary. They did not know Sorin's mother or the council, and were having a hard time believing that the other mortals would be as willing to work with them as Sorin was.

The chiefs were growing louder in the heated debate amongst themselves. They were ignoring Sorin entirely before Chief Einar stepped in, "Friends, how can King Sorin prove his word and his loyalty if you will not give him the chance?" Chief Einar sighed, stepping between the clan chiefs, each still wearing their armor and paints, and ready for a brawl. Sorin knew it was best to stay quiet and allow Chief Einar to take control of his people.

The exasperated chief bellowed above the noise, "It is our duty to allow the young king the chance to prove himself." He addressed Sorin now, "We will meet with the Queen Regent and your council." He added, "And we will be gracious in doing so." He gave a pointed look to the other chiefs, and Sorin suppressed a smirk. Chief Einar acted more like a stern father than a clan chief amongst this rambunctious lot.

In the end they agreed, and with the reassurance that Bron would be the bridge between the Asterions and the Forest Dwellers, Sorin felt confident that the treaty would hold until he could return. Now there was the matter of getting his mother and the council to agree. He knew it was time for him to take his seat on the throne, but he could not let Shaye venture into The Beyond alone.

He bid farewell to the Forest Dwellers, thanking them sincerely for their service and sacrifice, then walked with Chief Einar, Shaye, and Bron to the Asterion camp on the other side of the battlefield.

Sorin's heart ached at the sight of it; a vast number of bodies littered the dead, brown grass. Men, women, and creatures laid lifelessly, with their blood seeping into the land. He frowned each time he passed a face that he recognized, taking a moment to close their eyes, and saying a silent prayer for what this war had cost them.

General Tyrell's men had worked quickly, rounding up the injured and any Nefari who had surrendered. The camp was cramped with soldiers tending to their wounds, and Asterion women worked on those too injured to help themselves. Shaye called his attention to a clearing between the tents where the Nefari prisoners were being held. They sat in chains, some with a look of disdain on their faces, and others with a look of sorrow and defeat.

Sorin called to the General, "Have you recorded the numbers?"

General Tyrell handed him a small stack of papers, and Sorin sorted through them, noting the tallies of dead Asterions, Nefari, and creatures, along with the number of prisoners taken. He nodded, satisfied with how meticulous the general's men had been.

Shaye shifted beside him. He knew she was anxious to see how this would play out for the Magi. There had been Nefari who stood between them and Bastian's wrath on the hill, and Sorin would not forget the enormity of that.

He addressed General Tyrell, "It is my official decree that each and every one of the prisoners be given a fair trial."

General Tyrell nodded, "Of course, Your Majesty."

Shaye chimed in, "How are you keeping them from accessing their magic?"

A familiar, raspy voice answered from behind, "I have enchanted the chains. I've been working on the spell for some time." Anselem chuckled, "Turns out I've still got a little pizzazz in these old bones."

Sorin grinned at the old councilman, surprised to see that he looked younger than before. He was still an old man, but he no longer appeared drab and ancient, as he had before Sorin left the palace. Perhaps it was a sign of his magic being returned to full strength with the Stave destroyed.

"It seems we all do." Sorin's mother, Queen Evelyn, strode up to them with a smile. She reached for Sorin, and they embraced. She whispered into his ear, "Your father would be so proud of you."

"We're not finished yet, mother."

She pulled from the embrace and tilted her head, "Spoken like a true king."

Still, Sorin felt a sense of pride swell within him at her words. He had doubted himself so often—and still feared the journey ahead—that he had not considered the enormity of what they had accomplished these last weeks.

He guided his mother to where Shaye stood patiently. "Mother, allow me to introduce you to the last Druid, Shaye Wistari."

Shaye started to bow, but his mother swept her up into a hug. Shaye's eyes went wide as she looked at Sorin, and he chuckled.

His mother spoke, "Shaye, you have done this country a great service. There are no words grand enough to thank you for your selflessness."

Shaye shifted uncomfortably and there was a blush on her beautiful face. "Queen Evelyn, I cannot take the credit. I nearly lost myself to the darkness and cost Asterion many lives in the process."

Sorin's mother shook her head, "We all lose ourselves from time to time. It is what we do to make up for it that counts in the eyes of The Mother."

Sorin stepped in, "That brings us to our next conversation. May we?" He gestured to a large military tent, and his mother led the way.

Before they could reach the tent, the ground jolted beneath their feet. Sorin looked at Shaye with confusion. "Did you feel that?"

Shaye nodded in response and then shouts came from the battlefield. Soldiers began to scramble away from the center of the valley as the ground quaked again. This time it was even more noticeable. The ground rolled and shuttered as it began to cave in. The men still left on the battlefield tried to run, but those closest to the quake disappeared as they were swallowed up by the opening earth.

The smell of fire and brimstone filled Sorin's senses, and terror flooded his heart. He shouted to General Tyrell, "We need to get them out of there!"

Most of the soldiers who had been in the valley moments ago had now made it back to the camp. But no sound came from the men who had fallen into the cavernous hole. Shaye bolted to the valley and Sorin followed her lead. The earth had stopped shaking and the battlefield was silent once again.

Shaye was ahead of him as he shouted to her, "Careful! The ground could still be unstable."

They slowed as they neared the hole in the earth. The grass surrounding it had blackened as if it had been burned, but there was no sign of fire where they stood. They inched closer, and Sorin sensed his men close behind him. He held up a hand to signal for them to stand back. He would not risk any of them.

He and Shaye crept further until they could see down into the treacherous depths that had opened up in the heart of the valley. Sorin felt dizzy, looking down. There was no sign of life. How could there be? The hole ran deep into the earth, revealing a thick, rolling liquid. It was red and popped with heat. Like liquid fire.

Sorin startled as he felt the ground rumble under his feet. He shouted, "Shaye! Get back!"

He was too late, loose rocks surrounding the hole began to

crumble and fall. Shaye lost her footing as the land beneath her began to slide. She hit the ground hard and Sorin dove toward her. The ground was falling quickly, taking Shaye with it. He grabbed hold of her hand, gripping it tightly with both of his.

Shaye was hanging over the ledge and Sorin could see her struggling to find footing in the side of the earth. The soldiers that had followed them out onto the field came to Sorin's aid. Two men joined him, grabbing hold of Shaye, and pulling her up onto solid ground.

They scrambled back quickly, trying to clear themselves of the danger. Sweat was beading on Sorin's forehead and he wiped it away with his sleeve. He could hear Shaye trying to catch her breath beside him, and he put a steadying hand on the small of her back.

She swore under her breath. "That was too close."

Sorin shook his head in disbelief. "I'd say that's an understatement." He patted one of the soldiers on the back as he added, "Thank you."

The soldier gave him a lopsided smile. "Of course, Your Majesty."

They all rose to leave, wanting to put as much distance between them and the falling earth as they could.

Sorin closed the distance between himself and Shaye as they walked. She was no longer shaking from the adrenaline of nearly falling to her death. He had to give her credit for keeping her composure. He paused a moment before asking, "Do you think this is the blight's doing?"

"I think we are running out of time." She stopped so she could turn to face him. There was fire in her eyes as she said, "Mavka was right. If we do not stop this, our world will cease to exist as we know it. If this isn't enough to convince the council then I don't know what will."

It was quiet when they returned to the camp. Sorin called on General Tyrell. Giving the command, he said, "General, we need to clear the area. You need to get the men packed up and ready to head south immediately. Take any of the surviving prisoners and go." General Tyrell nodded curtly to him and began barking out orders to his men.

Sorin spotted the councilmen in the crowd and noted their trembling hands. The quake had shaken them all, but it was his duty as their king to present a strong front. He set aside his own grief and fear as he faced them now. He gestured for them to follow him to an unoccupied tent, and they did so without argument.

The tent was set up simply, with a massive war table in the center of the room. The council entered soon after Sorin, Shaye, Bron, and his mother did. Chief Einar stood to the side, observing, like a fly on the wall. He eyed the generals who joined them next, warily. There was still distrust lingering in their eyes, and Sorin felt the weight of how important this meeting was. They would all need to band together for what was to come next.

Sorin took the lead, no longer the princeling who had sat idly by during a council meeting. "Today we changed the course of our world. Our forces have fought valiantly and defeated our enemies in battle, but we have not yet won the war. The blight still threatens our land and our way of life. What just happened out there may be proof of it."

Nervous murmurs filled the tent, and Sorin gave them only a moment to register what he was saying. He held an authoritative hand high, "If we're right, and the blight is growing more powerful, then it is only a matter of time before it reaches every corner of this kingdom." He took a deep breath before continuing, "With that said... I will venture north to rid our world of the relics and restore the land, with the help of Shaye Wistari." He gestured to Shaye, who stood beside him, and she gave him an encouraging smile.

"You mean to leave? Again?" Cerwin balked at him. He was dressed in his usual garb and it was clear that he had not taken up arms to fight in the battle. Sorin did not judge him, as he had many times before. This man was no warrior and likely would have gotten himself killed if he had gone into that valley.

Sorin had expected this reaction. "I mean to finish what I started. It is my wish that my mother continue to act as Queen Regent, and, with the help of the council, to begin the trials and the rebuilding of our country. With North Asterion in such a delicate state, you will need to find a way to set up housing for those who cannot return home." He looked around at the faces of his councilmen, who bowed their heads in agreement.

Sorin took a deep breath, preparing himself for the next matter at hand. "Chief Einar, if you would?" He motioned for the Highland Chief to step forward. "This is Chief Einar of the Highland Forest Dweller clan. He is the one responsible for having formed ties between our forces and the Magi from the Raven Wood. He is a hero to this country, and we owe him a great debt."

Queen Evelyn was the first to bow in respect, and the rest of the room followed suit. The air in the tent was tense as she stepped forward to take Chief Einar's hand in her own. "There are many wrongs that need to be righted. Allow me to be the first to say that I am deeply sorry for what your people have endured."

Chief Einar grinned at her. "It has been a pleasure to work alongside your son. Though, he has made promises to my people. Promises we do hope he will be able to keep."

Sorin interjected, "Promises I *will* keep. In my absence, I have asked Sir Bronimir to coordinate relations between our peoples. Will the council support him?"

The military commanders in the tent bristled, and one of them spoke up, "Relations with Magi?" His face was battered, and he looked like he needed to be tended to.

Sorin needed to use his authority before the man said anything he might regret. "Yes. In case any of you missed it, these *Magi* fought beside us today when they did not need to. They have sacrificed their lives for Asterion, and for that we will show them the respect they deserve... The respect they have deserved all along, but have not received."

The men around the tent listened in quiet respect for their king, as Sorin continued, "Things are going to be different. We cannot and will not go on the way we have been. The relic is broken, and with that, magic has returned to the Magi of Asterion. With the council's support, I will see to it that a Guild be formed for the Magi. It is my hope that, with rules and regulations, they will be inducted into society for the greater good of *all* our people."

Sorin's nerves finally caught up to him as he waited for their response. This was what he had dreaded the most, having known it would be no easy task to change the minds of these people—they had been brutalized by magic in the past, and had faced the very worst of it only hours ago.

Larken, the fierce Skagan councilman, stepped forward. He scratched at his long, unkept beard, and huffed before he spoke. "It could be done, King Sorin; but I warn you, it will be no easy feat."

"I did not expect it would be." Sorin addressed everyone in the tent, "This is not about what is easy... It is about what is *right*."

He saw a few reluctant nods in agreement in the small crowd. *One step at a time*, Sorin thought. Shaye must have agreed because she wrapped her fingers tightly around his and did not let go. Her hand was clammy, and he knew she had been as anxious about their response as he had been.

His mother raised her chin. "That settles it then. General Tyrell, you and your men will escort the prisoners back to the palace, where they will be held until their trials. Sir Bronimir will work diligently with myself and the council to set forth the preparations to integrate Asterion's Magi back into society, and..." She turned to address Chief Einar, "I do hope you will join us. Repairing Magi relations will include mending the broken relationship with the Magi in the north."

"It would be an honor." Chief Einar bowed to her.

She turned to Sorin and Shaye with the hint of a smile on her face as she looked down at their hands, which were still locked together tightly. "As for you two… Make haste on your journey. I do so hope to be able to retire from this duty as acting regent." She winked at them. "It is quite exhausting."

Sorin laughed, "Of course, mother." He scanned the tent; the faces staring back at him would be the forefathers of the new society he wanted to build. It took everything in him to put his trust in them, but he had no choice. There was much work to be done; but here in their presence, he felt hope returning. They were on the path to healing and peace.

Before taking his leave, he bowed to the people he was leaving behind. It was a bow worthy of royalty, because he needed them to know how grateful he was to them. Many in the tent looked shocked at the gesture, and returned it with deep gratitude.

With Shaye's hand still in his, they left the tent. Behind him he heard Anselem say, "May The Mother carry you both."

Sorin squinted at the sunlight outside in the cramped encampment. Men were rushing around, packing their things in preparation for their return to the south. A hush fell over the crowd, and someone shouted, "Long live King Sorin!"

Shouts of triumph and respect sounded throughout the men and women standing around him, "Long live King Sorin!" The words hit him with an impact he did not anticipate, and he felt his cheeks warm with a blush.

Shaye nudged him in the shoulder and whispered, "Long live King Sorin."

He smiled down at her, "With you by my side, I have no doubt about that."

He closed the distance between them, pressing his lips to hers. When he pulled back, she laughed at the troops grinning and whooping around them. One eager soldier was even clapping in applause. Shaye blew a stray hair from her face and rolled her eyes. Anik was standing before them, with an injured arm. It was a superficial wound, and did not stop him from embracing both Shaye and Sorin in greeting.

Sorin was glad to see his friend alive and as well as could be expected. It had been weeks since he had parted with Anik at the Winter Palace and he had missed having the small, but fierce knight at his side.

Anik wiped the sweat from his face, leaving a smear of dirt on his dark skin in the process. Sorin patted him heavily on the back. "Well done, Anik. You executed the plan perfectly."

"Ah, perfect enough to get a promotion?" He winked in Shaye's direction.

Sorin laughed, "I'm sure we can arrange something when I get back."

"Back? Where are you going?"

"To The Beyond." Sorin waited for Anik's reaction.

Anik laughed so hard that he winced from the pain of his wound. "You can't sit still for a moment, can you?"

"One grand adventure after the next." Sorin steered Shaye toward the horses that were awaiting them, packed and ready, beside Ingemar, who stood hand in hand with Signe.

He shouted over his shoulder to Anik, "Take care of Bron while I'm away!"

Bron, who had left the tent to join Anik and the others, shouted back, "He can help me work on my new ballad! *The Tale of King Sorin and His Knightly Ass!*"

Sorin laughed at the reference to their conversation, from when they had left the Summer Palace to collect Shaye at the spring festival. It was hard to wrap his head around how much had changed since then. They had battled deadly creatures, and had made new friends, forming unlikely bonds in the process. They had won and lost love, had defeated an army, and had changed the course of their futures. They had struggled with their own darkness, and had chosen forgiveness over vengeance.

If their journey thus far had taught him anything, it was that his and Shaye's quest to The Beyond would be met with many challenges. But Sorin did not have a doubt in his mind that they would emerge triumphant, together.

He gave Shaye a moment to say her goodbyes—she was hugging Ingemar and Signe and thanking them for everything. Sorin shook their hands. "I do hope you will return to Aramoor one day. It would be an honor to host you in the palace."

Shaye interrupted, "Before we go, there is the matter of breaking the magic that forces your people into granting wishes." She closed her eyes and Sorin watched as she called on her magic. It was a wonder that she could still wield her power after the strain of battle; but when Shaye was determined, there was nothing that could stop her.

Her brow furrowed and her breath quickened as she struggled to hold the magic she needed for such a big spell. Her body swayed with the strain and Sorin turned to Ingemar. He did not know the limits of Shaye's magic and he did not want to find out. Ingemar must have read the fear on his face because she joined Shaye at her side.

Ingemar locked fingers with Shaye's and gave her an encouraging smile. Their magic collided in a cloud of bright light and Shaye began to chant. Her words carried on the wind in a whisper, "G-em-free."

The magic extended toward Signe and the other Ceasg, who were gathered in the clearing. Shaye continued to chant and Ingemar allowed her to draw on her for strength. Both women looked as if they were struggling to extend their magic out far enough to reach all of the Ceasg. Sweat was beading on their brows and their eyes were closed tight in concentration.

Sorin had an idea. He shouted for the old Sorcerer "Anselem!"

Anselem appeared with rosy cheeks and a smile on his face "Yes, Your Majesty?"

"They need help." Sorin pointed to Shaye and Ingemar.

"Breaking curses, are we?" Anselem looked ecstatic. "I remember when the Ceasg were first cursed, you know. It was a messy business, a Sorcerer scorned by his Ceasg lover—"

Sorin interrupted his rambling, "Anselem, can you help them?"

Anselem looked offended at the insinuation that he might not be able to help. He scoffed, "Of course I can, young man." He moved to join the women who were still trying to gather the power to do such an impossible thing.

As Anselem linked hands with the two of them, forming a circle, magic burst through the camp. It whirled around Signe and the other Ceasg who had survived the battle. It encompassed them completely, shining like stars in the northern sky. As the magic ebbed, Signe cried out in celebration.

Ingemar dropped Shaye's and Anselem's hands and ran to Signe, pulling her closer and holding her face. They looked deeply into one another's eyes as Ingemar spoke, "We are free now..." She glanced over to Shaye and Sorin, "Thank you, friends. Thank you. Words cannot express what this means to us. Know that you will always have friends in the sea."

Shaye argued gently, "We could not have done any of this without you. We owe you far more than we can ever give." She still swayed slightly, exhausted from the surge of power the three of them had called on together.

Anselem shook Ingemar's hand and started in again on his tale of the scorned Sorcerer and the Ceasg who had turned him away. Ingemar looked at Sorin with wide eyes, unsure of how to escape what was sure to be a very long story from the old man. Sorin smirked at her and turned to give Shaye a boost onto Finn before mounting his own horse. His gaze lingered on their friends' faces one last time. Bron and Anik, Ingemar and Signe, Brina, and even Thorsten's motley crew; they were all there... all except one. Mavka had risked everything to help them, and they would honor her sacrifice through their actions moving forward.

Shaye clicked at Finn, and Sorin followed her lead. They rode up the hill, veering toward the east. They would ride along the coast of the Living Sea, around the Raven Wood, and into the North Pass.

He looked at Shaye, who had tears streaming down her determined face, and, raising his voice above the wind, assured her, "We'll see them again, you know."

She smiled sweetly at him, wiping the tears with the back of her linen sleeve. Sorin was glad that she'd had a moment to change once the battle was over. She looked like she had the day they had left Aramoor, strong in her leather jerkin and breeches. Her skin was no longer tainted by Bastian's hold on her. She caught his eye, "I am still plagued by the black magic I used." She lifted an inky hand to show him.

"One step at a time, Shaye." He wanted to reassure her, but he knew it would take time.

As they passed the trees on the hill, Dwellers held hands to their hearts in respect and well wishes against the dangers they had yet to face. Shaye and Sorin continued on their way until they could see the Living Sea. It was clear and sparkling, and the sun shone brightly on the horizon.

But the air was still stinking with the smell of fire and brimstone. It was a humbling reminder of what they were leaving their people to face. The blight would not stop until they completed their mission. Sorin had no idea what would come next, but he prayed to the Fates that he and Shaye would pull through stronger than ever. He held tight to the hope blossoming in him, and kept his eyes on the path ahead.

CHAPTER TWENTY-TWO

Shaye

Shaye looked up at the rocky terrain ahead and tried to ignore the unwelcome pit in her stomach. It had taken them only a few days to reach the North Pass that led to the mountains. The coast had given them an unhindered path around the Raven Wood, and without the density of the forest, they had been able to cut time from their ride.

Along their way, they had seen the dangers of the blight more frequently. There were no more signs of broken earth like they had witnessed in the valley, but the presence of the blight was there all the same. The closer they came to the mountains, the worse the conditions became. Creeks were dried up completely, and the grass which had been brown and dying, was scorched. The barren dirt was giving off the sickening smell of decay, making Shaye worry that it would never again give life. Would stopping the blight even be enough to save Asterion, when it had already done so much damage?

Now that they had reached the northernmost tip of Asterion, Shaye had new concerns to add to her list. It was now the trek they faced through the jagged mountain ridge that worried her.

"It's…"

"Terrifying," Sorin finished for her.

She nodded in response, too speechless to find the words. Finn sensed her fear, prancing around from side to side. She placed a hand on his neck, running it along his soft fur. "I know boy, I know."

They rode on until they came to the very edge of a small mountain pass. The mountain range was a formidable barrier between Asterion and The Beyond—one that very few had tried, most of whom had failed, to pass through. The small trail between the two mountain peaks was their best, and really their only, chance to reach the magical realm that awaited them on the other side.

"Ready?" Sorin was beside her on Bron's warhorse, Altivo. The stallion's coat glistened with sweat under the early light of the morning.

"As ready as I'll ever be." She tried to give him a smile, but failed to conjure one.

Sorin led the way. The pass was barely the width of a horse, allowing only one of them to squeeze in at a time. Shaye followed behind, and gazed up at the mountain walls on either side of them. She was grateful for the open sky above; if it had not been for that, she would have felt utterly trapped. She reached for her magic, comforted to feel it within her grasp. It gave her a sense of control over the situation.

She could see Sorin's hand on the hilt of the Sword of Roth ahead of her. His knuckles were bone-white from gripping onto it so tightly. It was the only sign of stress he was showing. He had been like this since they had left the valley, when she had told him the details of the visit from her mother. It had been a big revelation for him to find that it was not his father's men who had landed the first blow during the Winter Solstice ball.

Tears had filled his eyes as he said, "He'd been telling the truth when he said he meant to take them without bloodshed, but I didn't believe him."

Shaye had felt so helpless in that moment, watching his old wounds open up. After that, Sorin had avoided the subject. He needed time, and she knew he was trying to stay strong for her, but she wished he wouldn't hide how he was really feeling.

She supposed they were both hiding from each other in a way. They hadn't spoken of his declaration of love in the tent while under Nefari captivity, but the words Shaye had left unsaid lingered between them. Whenever they had stopped to make camp for the night, he would lay his bedroll within her reach, just as he had done many times before. Only now, she felt the constant need to reach out for him, and to touch him. They had laughed and told each other stories throughout their days of traveling, but the tension they felt didn't leave much room for anything else.

Being so close to The Beyond made her nervous, and she wanted to say something to him before it was too late. Anything could go wrong, and she did not want to die without saying those words back to him. "Sorin," she called to him up ahead, "there's something I should have said to you... I..."

Footsteps from behind interrupted her, and the hair on her arms stood on end. If they had been followed into the mountain pass then there would be no way to defend themselves, no way to turn the horses around. She whirled around from where she sat firmly in her saddle to see who the unwelcome visitor was.

She slumped in relief when she saw the familiar shadowy body. "Erebus! You horrid creature, what are you doing here?" The Black Shuck lowered his head, and Shaye softened, "You scared me half to death."

"Seems he did not want to leave his new master." Sorin was twisted around in the saddle with his sword drawn.

Erebus tucked his large, shadowy tail between his legs. Shaye had no desire to be anyone's master, but she would not turn him away after all that he had done for her.

"Fine. You can come with us." He popped his head up eagerly; it was hard for her to believe she had been so terrified of the creature; he was more like one of Brina's hounds than the demon everyone believed him to be. He was just… misguided.

Sorin chuckled and mumbled under his breath playfully, "Sucker."

"I heard that!" Shaye threw up a vulgar gesture, though he could not see her as he rode on up ahead.

Erebus followed them loyally as they continued through the tight passageway. It took longer than Shaye liked to get to the opening on the other side. She focused on calming her breath and keeping her magic on the surface and within reach.

Beyond the pass, she could see a small, flowing, jewel-blue stream, and more mountains. She groaned. The valley here at the bottom of the mountain ridge was small. They could stop to rest for the night, but after that it would be a perilous trek.

They made camp beside the water, allowing the horses to drink and rest. Erebus sat nearby; he was curled up in an attempt to shield himself from the sun. It was clear that he preferred the dark, and Shaye wondered if the light pained him. She took the blanket that she used under Finn's saddle and laid it gently over him. He purred gratefully at the gesture.

"You really do care for him." Sorin was in the middle of starting a fire for them. He had left nets in the stream, hoping to catch fresh fish for them so they could save their pack of provisions for the mountains.

"He's just misunderstood, that's all. We know all about that don't we?"

Sorin grunted in response. "Here we go, a nice warm fire." He held his hands out to display his handiwork.

"I could have done that for you." Shaye called on her elemental magic, making the flames grow bigger.

"Let me feel useful." He smiled ruefully at her.

She took a seat by his side, close enough that their legs brushed. He reached down for her hand and she laced her fingers between his. This was the moment she had been hoping for after finally working up the courage in the mountain pass to tell him her true feelings. She looked into his dark blue eyes—they reminded her of the night sky when lit up by the Northern Lights.

"Sorin, in the Nefari camp... when you told me you loved me..."

"Shaye, you don't have to—"

"No, Sorin, I do." She shifted so that she was on her knees facing him. "*I love you.* I couldn't say it then, for fear of who was listening, but I love you and I will do everything to make it up to —" Sorin cut her off with a kiss.

When he pulled away, he brushed the hair from her face, and she melted into that touch. She giggled, and the giggling soon turned into a fit of laughter. The horses looked up at the commotion before going back to grazing on the green grass.

Sorin's eyes went wide. "What is so funny?"

"I just..." The laughter continued, "I just told the k*ing* that I am in love with him."

He laughed then, too, "We make quite the pair, don't we?"

Shaye wiped the tears of laughter from her eyes and nodded. They sure did—a Druid smuggler and a mortal king. Sorin laid back onto the grass with one arm behind his head and the other around Shaye. She laid back with him, breathing in the fresh air of the mountains around them. She rested her head on him and closed her eyes, drifting off into a peaceful sleep.

The peace did not last long. A screech pierced through the quiet night sky and she jolted awake. Sorin was already up and alert. His eyes were wide as he held a finger to his lips, signaling for her to remain quiet. He pointed above with his other hand.

A faceless creature circled high above them, winding its way through the valley. It was headed back the way they had come and seemed not to have noticed them camping below. Shaye watched in horrid fascination as the creature passed by them. It was remarkably large with wings that looked too small to be holding such a heavy weight. The wings were like old leather and beat heavily, blowing a small wind in their direction.

Shaye did not speak for fear of drawing its attention. The dying fire beside them popped and she held her breath. She felt her magic pool within her on instinct, ready to defend against whatever this horrible creature was.

Its wings shifted in the air, and the creature paused, flying in place. It turned its head to where Shaye and Sorin were, and she could see that it had no eyes or nose. Only a long snout covered with taut skin. It felt as if time was slowing as Shaye readied herself for a fight.

But before the creature could descend on them, something across the field caught its attention. An unwitting deer had wandered into the clearing and Shaye watched as the faceless creature turned toward it. In a fluid motion, the creature flew over the deer, reaching out sharp talons to grab a hold of it.

The creature's claws pierced into the deer's skin and swept it up into the air. Shaye let out a sigh of relief as the creature carried the deer out of sight and away from the valley.

Sorin broke the tense silence. "Shit. What the hell was that thing?"

Shaye shook her head in wonder. "I have no idea. But I can wager a guess that it came from the direction we're headed in."

"It was headed toward Asterion..."

Shaye thought so, too. It was clearly flying in the direction of their home. It infuriated her that they were allowing something so dangerous to venture so close to the Asterion border.

She cursed. "I should have killed it."

"We have no idea what that thing was. Or what it was capable of." Sorin added, "And anyways, there is nothing to b done now. All we can do is keep an eye out and keep moving north."

Shaye relented, but the pit in the bottom of her stomach remained. They did their best to rest again, but sleep did not come easily. Shaye spent the rest of the night restless. When she did drift to sleep, her mind was filled with images of the creature and the look of anguish on the deer's face as it was carried away.

When she awoke in the morning, the air was wet with dew, and there was a chill in the air. The smell of fire-roasted fish filled her nose, and her stomach growled. When she sat up, she stretched out her limbs, aching from sleeping on the hard ground all night beside Sorin. She did not want to mention the creature from the night before, willing herself to forget the whole encounter and focus on the journey ahead.

Sorin smiled from across the fire, "Rise and shine. Unfortunately, I don't have a magnificent feast to present to you... only fish."

Shaye yawned, "Oh how I miss the muffins that Rolland bakes every morning."

"He'll have to teach me how he does it, when we return home."

"*You're* going to bake muffins?"

"Why not?" He handed her the fish and shrugged, "If I remember correctly, you made me brew tea for you at the inn."

"And you did a horrible job of it," she teased. "I sure hope you're a better baker than you are a brewer."

They both laughed, and the sound echoed through the empty valley. Erebus broke through their good humor when he let out a low growl in the direction of the mountains that stood opposite of those they had just left. There was nothing out of the ordinary, just phantom-white mountain tops looming high above.

Sorin drew the Sword of Roth. "He's seeing something that we don't."

Shaye grew nervous again. "Do you think the creature circled back?"

She grabbed the horses and stood behind Sorin. The sun was just beginning to rise over the ridge, and she shielded her eyes, trying to get a better view in the direction of whatever it was that had Erebus on edge. She wished the Black Shuck could speak, to tell them what was wrong.

They walked slowly in the direction he was looking; it was the only safe pathway up the mountain, so they had no choice but to go toward the potential danger. Shaye extended her magic toward the ridge, hoping to feel or sense something.

It wasn't until they reached the base of the mountain range that it hit her. It was an intense feeling of power, but it wasn't coming from her or the land. She grabbed Sorin's arm. "Something is definitely wrong."

Her breath hitched in her throat when she saw the threat. Finn and Altivo reared up as a man rode up on horseback... no, not a man... a Centaur. His upper body was bare, revealing a muscled chest—but from the waist down he had the body of a horse.

Erebus jumped in front of Shaye and Sorin to defend them, his hackles raised. He bared his teeth at the warrior standing between them and their only way to The Beyond. The Centaur did not acknowledge him; instead, he looked directly at Shaye.

"You seek passage?" His voice was rich and smooth.

Shaye answered him, "We do."

"Many have tried, and have been found unworthy. What makes you so different?"

Shaye did not know how to respond; her first instinct was to say "nothing." She did not fancy herself better than those who had come before her, and she wasn't sure she would even survive this new quest they were on. What she did know was that she was not ready to give up before they had a chance to try.

"It is our cause that is worthy. We seek to return something to where it belongs."

That answer had not been the one the Centaur was looking for. He stamped a hoof into the ground and a horde of Centaurs appeared from various positions on the mountainside. They brandished spears and bows; she and Sorin were vastly outnumbered and out armed.

"We are the guardians of what lies beyond. To get through the great North Pass means getting through us first."

Sorin spoke up, "We are not looking for a fight."

"Then you should not have come here, *mortal*." The Centaur spat the word.

"Enough." Shaye could see that there would be no reasoning with these ancient warriors. It was clear that they would not listen to words. Instead, she would have to show them.

She raised her chin high and closed her eyes, soaking in the rising sun. Holding her hands out she thought of the Northern Lights that she missed so much, and let her power bloom around her and Sorin. It began as a beautiful mist, filled with colorful light, but erupted into something more. She opened her eyes as darkness fell over the valley—she then replaced it with a curtain of light, cascading around them. Lights of purple, blue, and green sparkled in the sky; it was magnificent.

She held onto the magic proudly, and looked around at the Centaurs. Their leader was stunned into silence, fueling her to make the display even more grand. She spread the veil of lights throughout the entire valley, reaching it high above to the mountain peaks.

She was amazed by the strength of her magic as she held it without strain. It felt like every fiber of her being was awakening with it. There was no sting, no guilt, and best of all no darkness, like that which had accompanied the Nefari magic she had used before. It was as if every element of the universe was coming together, *for her*.

When she released the veil and allowed the sunlight to return to the valley, the Centaurs were kneeling on their front legs. Each of them crossed an arm in front of their chest, bowing to her.

Their leader broke through the heavy silence, "It has been many an age since we have been presented with one worthy of the power you wield. If The Mother has seen fit to bless you with such a gift, then we are not to stand in your way."

He bowed again, nearly touching his head to the ground. Shaye took that as their cue—she did not want to test the patience of these creatures. She led the horses forward, with Sorin and Erebus close on her heels, past the Centaur leader. She hadn't even realized she'd been holding her breath until they had passed him.

Sorin gave her a boost onto Finn, and they rode away at a full gallop, refusing to slow until they were well away from the valley, and the threat they had just faced there.

Once they reached the range, they were met with a new sort of threat. The elements on the rocky terrain seemed to be in place to stop them as well. They were hit with rain, sleet, and snow. Sorin was quiet but calm as they made their way up the steep slopes. They stayed close to the body of the mountain, and every so often one of the horses would cause the rocks that made up the narrow path to fall, sending them toppling down the dangerously steep height to where more dangerous stones awaited.

Shaye shut her eyes tight when the threat of falling became too much for her. It felt like time was slowing, and she desperately wanted to be back on flat ground. She pulled her jacket tightly around her, trying to block out the dropping temperature as they traveled. Snow was beginning to fall rapidly, and it was becoming increasingly more difficult to see. As night fell, it became impossible to see the path ahead.

"Sorin!" She shouted to him and hoped that he could hear her through the wind. "The horses need to rest!"

Rather than shout back to her, he pointed up ahead to a break in the stone wall. She squinted through the snowflakes that were stuck on her lashes, and it wasn't until they were upon it that she realized it was a cave.

The talus was a small opening just big enough for them to slip inside. The horses snorted in discomfort until they reached the larger opening past the mouth of it. They tended to the horses and Erebus first, giving them much-needed food and water.

Shaye rubbed her hands together, trying to rid them of the tingling sensation that the cold had brought to them. Sorin embraced her, holding her tight to his chest and sharing any shred of warmth he had left.

Shaye looked around at the jagged, rocky walls of the talus. "Sorin," she gasped, pulling back and turning to get a better look at what she was seeing.

The walls were covered with scenes of death and destruction, painted in hues of red and blue. From the way they had faded in some places, they must have been nearly ancient. She ran her fingers along them, seeing Centaurs standing tall at the mountain's edge, spears in hand. As she continued, the paintings grew more graphic in detail.

They told the story of a war, and the death of a people—but worse were the depictions of pain and suffering. Small figures were strewn about in the mural along the wall: men trapped in a pool of blood, and women forced to dance until their feet broke from under them. It was more terrifying than any nightmare Shaye had ever dreamt.

She shivered, though she wasn't sure if it was from the gruesome paintings or the cold. Rubbing her arms, she said, "I'll start a fire."

Sorin continued to gape at the walls. "It's incredible… Do you think this is the war that drove the brothers into Asterion?"

"It's possible." She got to work laying out the sticks they had brought with them. It took her several tries before her magic sparked, the cold making it difficult for her to concentrate. Once it was lit, she and Sorin sat together with their bedrolls pressed side by side. He put his arms around her, rubbing the cold from his arms.

Erebus laid close to them, offering the warmth of his body. He was hot to the touch, and it seemed that the cold did not bother him as it did the rest of them. They ate, and sat for a while, until they could no longer fight the exhaustion. They had barely said a word to each other since leaving the valley, but Shaye welcomed the silence, comforted by Sorin's mere presence.

She moved to lay down, but Sorin stopped her. "It will be safer if we share our body heat..."

She blew into her cupped hands, trying to warm them, and paused to consider what he was suggesting. After a moment, she agreed, removing her jacket and her shirt to reveal the thin linen undergarment she had on underneath. Sorin did the same, taking each piece of clothing off until he was in nothing except for knee-length linen pants. She let her gaze linger on him for a moment, reveling in the way his broad, muscular chest looked in the firelight, before removing her pants, and standing in a similar fashion. He smirked at her, raising his eyebrows suggestively, and she stuck her tongue out playfully in return.

They crawled under the blankets together, pressing their bodies close. Shaye shifted around, taking off her shirt so that nothing stood between them. She rolled to her side so that her back was pressed against his chest, and snuggled in closely. The warmth from his body hit her immediately, and she sighed at the relief it brought to her ice-cold skin.

It was getting late, and she knew she needed her rest to face the morning. But as much as she willed it, sleep did not come. Shaye could feel Sorin's breath rising and falling in his chest, and he still smelled of citrus and sandalwood. She welcomed the familiarity of it.

He held her in his arms, and his hot breath tickled her shoul der. This was the closest they had ever been to one another, and she was surprised that she did not feel a small hint of self-consciousness, as she had with lovers in the past. Unlike other relationships she'd had, this one was deeply rooted in mutual trust and friendship.

Sorin was not a man you could spend the night with, and then forget afterwards. They had done everything in their power to protect one another, and that was something that meant more to her than any roses or love ballads.

Shaye shifted again so she could face him. His eyes were open, and he was smiling at her under the dim light of the fire, which danced across his face. She put a hand on his chest and whispered, "I know it was you that night in the ballroom. I am sorry I ever doubted it."

He took her hand in his and kissed it. His lips lingered on her palm, and there was a faraway look in his eyes. "I dreamt of you for years after that night. Wondered where you were and what you were like."

"I dreamt of you, too... Of your eyes, and of how strong and safe your hand felt as you pulled me into that stairwell."

"I wish I could have saved them all." His eyes were misty, and Shaye pressed her lips to his. There were years of unspoken words in that kiss, she would forgive him, even if he could not forgive himself. She would spend the rest of their lives making him feel worthy of that forgiveness if he would give her the chance.

Sorin's fingers tangled into her hair, pulling her deeper into the kiss. She welcomed the feel of his hands on her, letting the world around them fall away. Nothing mattered in that moment except the two of them, together at last.

Her hands drifted lower, pulling at the string of his linen pants. The fabric was soft and thin, the only thing standing in their way now. Sorin followed her lead, pulling hers down as well. His eyes darkened as they melted into one another. Sorin whispered her name, and she gave into her desire, moving so that their bodies fit as one. Shaye gasped, hungry for more. Every ounce of the pain and sadness of the last weeks was long forgotten as he settled over her. Her body screamed in pleasure; they were like two stars colliding in the night. It was better than any magic she had ever felt.

CHAPTER TWENTY-THREE

Shaye

In the morning Shaye woke from a dream. Not a nightmare... But an actual dream. She stretched out beneath Sorin's arms and smiled at the memory of it. They had been walking through Aramoor, arm in arm, with Bron, Ingemar, and Anik. Mavka had been there too, dressed in a beautiful emerald gown. They were on their way to the Summer Palace for a ball that was being thrown in their honor. Her friends had laughed and sang love ballads as they stumbled through the city. It was a wonderful sight, all of them together, and Shaye hadn't wanted it to end.

Sorin moaned something in her ear, drawing her attention back to the mountain cave where they had spent the night. She moved until they were nose to nose. She smiled. "Too bad we can't stay in this cave forever and forget the whole world."

"That would certainly be easier than what we actually have to do." He kissed her on the forehead, and sat up. "I'll get us packed up and we can get going."

Shaye shivered in the absence of his warmth, and he held out hand to help her up. They packed their things and ventured back out to the mountainside, leaving behind the foreboding cave paintings, but bringing with them the memory of what had happened between them the night before. Shaye blushed as Sorin gave her a knowing smile.

The weather was mild, compared to what they had braved the previous day. There were no flurries in the air, and as the day went on, the sun grew warmer. They were making good time, and the horses had grown more comfortable, keeping their footing on the rough path they were following. By evening they were on a winding slope descending from the mountains, and Shaye released a sigh of relief when she spotted a small valley in the distance.

The horses trotted along with newfound confidence, and with Erebus in the lead, they were on flat, grassy ground in no time. Sorin let out a whoop of victory as Shaye jumped down from Finn and into his arms. He spun her around before setting her down, and she pushed her windblown hair from her face.

The warm air in the valley was vastly different from the bitter cold they had faced in the mountains, and Shaye tipped her face back, soaking in the summer sun. They sat down to eat, trying to regain some of the energy they were lacking.

"Not much further and we'll be reaching what has been described in the history books as the wall." Sorin kicked at a rock as he tore into the stale bread they had brought from the camp.

"I wonder what it's like."

"If the stories hold any truth, it's a place of nightmares."

"Well, I should feel right at home then." Shaye laughed.

They spent the night lying beneath the stars, talking about their dreams for Asterion. Sorin spoke excitedly of the possibilities that came from having a Guild for the Magi, and of the things he wanted to change at court. Shaye shared her own ideas and hopes for the future, and Sorin listened intently.

She was excited about the prospect of the Magi having their own Guild and wondered if they would have a place for her in it

She wasn't sure what her future looked like in Asterion, but she could not imagine running away again. Returning to Sagon with Thorsten and his crew felt wrong after everything that had happened to her home.

She knew she would have a place with Brina and her family at the inn, but something told her it would not be enough. She had changed over the course of her journey with Sorin. Before, she allowed her nightmares to influence every action she had ever taken: from running away to take up a life of smuggling, to spending her sleepless nights gambling and fighting. None of it had helped. Since meeting Sorin and the others, she had found a new sort of family. One who did not make her want to turn back to old habits.

There was a new purpose to her life now and the power that she wielded. She knew that Sorin valued her opinions and that gave her the opportunity to influence change. She could forgive the mistakes the previous kings had made, and with that forgiveness, she could finally move forward. She could make her parents proud.

Fueled by the possibilities that the future could hold, she decided to enjoy the moment with Sorin. That night they made love again. The rest of the world melted away as they embraced one another.

He must have felt it too, as he did not hold anything back. Shaye dug her fingers into his shoulders, calling his name out in pleasure as she clung to him tightly under the night sky—different from the tenderness of the night before. The previous night had been an exploration, taking their relationship to another level; but tonight it was a wild release of their need for one another. With The Beyond looming on the other side of the valley, they needed to make these moments count. If this was Shaye's last night with him then she would make it one to rival all others.

They fell asleep in a tangle of limbs, and awoke just before the dawn. Erebus was waiting for them on the other side of the lush green valley, patrolling it like a watchful guardian. When they reached him, Shaye's power flooded her senses. The "wall" that stood before them was a glimmer of powerful, ancient magic.

It stretched as far as the eye could see; but when Shaye peered directly into it, she could see nothing past the silver pool of magic. The way the wall glistened, it reminded her of the third relic. She reached a hand into her pack, feeling for the smooth Obsidian gemstone she had taken from Bastian's neck. It burned to the touch, and she hissed, pulling her hand back.

"Are you okay?" Sorin's brow was furrowed with worry.

"Fine." Shaye jumped from Finn's back and led him on foot to the edge of the wall.

She reached her hand out, dipping her fingers into the magic. It was cool and strange to the touch. There was nothing she could compare it to—it was thick and vibrating with power. Sorin took his place at her side. He held his arm out to her, and she took it, holding onto him tightly with one hand and onto Finn's reins with the other.

She smiled, trying to appear more confident than she felt. "Together?"

Sorin kissed her cheek. "Always."

They stepped through the barrier, feeling the magic flow all around them. It was like walking through the heavens, but nothing could have prepared Shaye for what she saw when they emerged on the other side.

She gasped at the beauty of the landscape they were met with. The clearing before them was like a painting come to life, aglow with sunbeams breaking through a blue and purple sky. It highlighted a sparkling, crystal lagoon beneath a cascade of glistening waterfalls. The sounds of birds and other wildlife filled her ears and she thought that this must truly be what paradise looked like.

Sorin stood beside her, speechless. It took him a moment to find the words: "Well, this is...unexpected."

"That's an understatement." She poked at his side, making him shout with laughter.

Erebus whined, drawing their attention to him. Shaye reached down to soothe him, but the whining only grew more urgent. Shaye's concern for him grew. "Erebus, what's wrong?"

Sorin tugged at her shirt. "Shaye, do not make any sudden movements."

Her heart dropped at the fear in his voice, and she watched as a beautiful black horse emerged from the water. It stalked toward them slowly, and Shaye's breath caught in her throat as she watched it transform. Its sleek, muscled body shifted elegantly into human form, leaving a naked woman standing in front of them, with a wild mane of black hair reaching down past her hips. Her eyes were dark and strange, and her lips were as red as blood. When she smiled at them, her razor-sharp, white teeth flashed.

Finn and Altivo reared up, causing Shaye's heart to leap in her chest—she was terrified that their sudden movements would provoke the water spirit standing before them. She tried to soothe the horses, and leaned in to Sorin to whisper, "It's a Kelpie. Sorin, these are very dangerous creatures who prey on humans. Get behind me."

He refused, staying rooted at her side. "I don't think she means us any harm."

The Kelpie spoke then. Her voice was like music in the air. "Shaye Wistari and King Sorin of Asterion. We have been waiting for you."

She gestured beyond the stream, to where a path between the trees loomed, dark and foreboding. Shaye looked to Sorin with uncertainty. She gripped his hand, unwilling to let go.

"Shall we?" The Kelpie licked her lips and tilted her head to the side. It seemed like she was there to make a meal of them, rather than to guide them through this strange new world. But before Shaye could ask her anything, the Kelpie turned, disappearing into the shade of the trail.

Shaye and Sorin followed hand in hand. They had come this far, and there was no turning back now. As they stepped onto the soft dirt of the path beneath the trees, the shadows folded in on them, enveloping them in the darkness.

READ ON FOR A SNEAK PEEK OF BOOK THREE IN THE LEGACY OF DARKNESS SERIES:
A LEGACY OF DESTRUCTION

CHAPTER ONE

Shaye

Shaye was once again consumed by darkness; only this time it wasn't from within her. The trees surrounding the path blocked out any sliver of sunlight, leaving them no choice but to weave their way through the woods behind the Kelpie. Shaye jumped as she heard a scream in the distance, followed by deadly silence.

The Kelpie, who had shed her horse-like form to take on the form of a beautiful woman with wild black hair that flowed down over her naked body, didn't flinch at the sound as Shaye had. Instead, she continued on her way, leading them to an unknown location.

"You said, 'We've been waiting for you.'" Shaye's voice rang loud in her own ears, disrupting the silence in the forest. "Who are you? And who is this *we* you referred to?"

Shaye narrowed her eyes at the Kelpie's back, thinking the water spirit would ignore the question. Sorin shrugged beside Shaye, dragging Altivo behind him. The horses were not enjoying this any more than the two of them were. Shaye did not blame their reluctance. They were in uncharted territory now.

Nobody in the history books had gone into The Beyond and returned.

The Kelpie finally responded, her voice echoing in the trees, "I am Nevia, and the others will reveal themselves soon enough."

Shaye blew a stray hair from her face and thought, *great, more puzzles to solve.* It was bad enough that Mavka's spirit had given them vague instructions to return the relics of the three brothers to The Beyond, but now their guide was keeping vital information to herself.

An owl hooted from above, causing Shaye to stumble on a fallen tree branch. She was not prepared for what she saw when she looked up to find the source of the call. Two dozen sets of wide eyes were staring back at her. She held back a yelp, and grabbed Sorin by the sleeve, making him come to a halt.

"Nevia... What in The Mother's name is that?" She pointed to the trees where an absurd number of owls sat around a strange girl. The girl wore a long, feathered cloak, and sat smiling down at them with a cup of tea in her dainty hands.

Nevia looked up and frowned, clearly exasperated by all of Shaye's questions. "Ignore her."

The owl-girl clucked her teeth, "That's no way to treat me. Did you even get permission to pass through the Darkening? With guests, no less?" She sipped her tea and crossed her legs, sitting with remarkable confidence, considering she was on a narrow tree limb.

Nevia hissed, "I do not need permission from the likes of you, Gaia."

Shaye crossed her arms uncomfortably at the exchange, but said nothing. She was an intruder to this strange world and unfamiliar with the customs of its residents. All she knew was that they desperately needed to rid themselves of the relics, and fast. The fate of Asterion rested on their success. If they failed, the blight would surely overtake the land and the battle they had just won against Bastian would have been for nothing.

Gaia turned her attention to Shaye and Sorin. "She will not like you being here, you know?"

Shaye's brow furrowed, "Who?"

"The maiden of the old world."

"Maiden of what?" Shaye turned to Nevia, who had conveniently left out the details of what waited for them at the end of the forest path—or, the Darkening, as Gaia had called it.

Gaia answered for her, "Of the world this once was. She is the keeper of what is left of the realm. She will not like—"

Nevia's eyes flashed in anger. "Enough!"

Gaia went silent at the tone of Nevia's voice. Shaye wanted to ask more of the strange, owl-like girl, but she did not get the chance before a hair-raising screech came from behind them. Like a reflex, Shaye's magic flowed into her hands. The land in this place was incredibly potent and breathed life into her power. Sorin drew the Sword of Roth from his scabbard, lighting up the forest with its magic.

Gaia giggled, "Someone seems to agree with me." She looked at Shaye, adding, "If I were you, I'd run." And with that, she closed her cloak around her and was gone before Shaye had a chance to spit back a retort.

Before Shaye or Sorin could react, the source of the screech was upon them. Shaye felt it before she saw it. It was like a void in the air. It was what she imagined death would feel like… Nothingness. Her mind told her to run, but her body would not respond. Sorin's breath quickened beside her, and she wanted to reach for him, but her hand would not cooperate.

The monster appeared from thin air, as if conjured from the darkness itself. Now, standing between them and their guide, was a ghost-like creature. Her face was withered, revealing skeletal bone, and her hair flowed around her in ash-gray whisps. When she tried to speak, her jaw clicked.

It was the only sound that came, but Nevia seemed to understand. "I seek passage with the Curse Breakers."

Shaye's chest tightened. *Curse Breakers?*

The spirit clicked her jaw again and released a high-pitched whine from her throat. Nevia shook her head, and responded in a language Shaye did not understand. She'd had enough of this. Nevia seemed content to leave them in the dark, but she wasn't about to step another foot further on this path without answers.

Shaye advanced on Nevia, ignoring Sorin's heated whispers for her to stop. She addressed both Nevia and the spirit: "I think it's about time you tell us what's going on."

Nevia held a finger up to Shaye and turned to the spirit again, speaking slowly, "I will say it one more time. Step aside or face their wrath."

The spirit looked both Shaye and Sorin up and down with a scrutinizing glare. Apparently somewhat satisfied with whatever it saw, it turned and flowed back into the trees. With it went the sense of dread that had overwhelmed Shaye moments ago.

Nevia rounded on her. "You nitwit. Do you have any idea the sort of peril you were in? Had it not been for me—"

Shaye cut her off. "Peril happens to be our specialty—isn't that right, Sorin?"

"I'll admit, we have some experience in it." He shrugged casually, as if they had not been on the brink of death.

Nevia pressed her lips into a thin, white slash before speaking, "You have no idea what is at stake here."

Shaye wanted to shout at her, to tell her that their entire world was at stake, but the Kelpie did not give her the chance. She quickened her pace, leading them onward until they saw a clearing in the trees. Shaye and Sorin followed obediently, ready to face whatever came next.

But nothing could have prepared them for the horror that awaited them beyond the Darkening.

ACKNOWLEDGMENTS

I'm still in awe at the fact that I have not one, but two books out in the wild. When I began this journey, I never anticipated finding such a welcoming community of authors and readers who wanted to lose themselves the stories that have been running amuck inside my head. I am deeply humbled by all the love and support from my readers, friends, and family.

First, to my husband, Zach, who has supported all my whims. You are the most patient and supportive man I have ever met, and I could not have done this without you. From entertaining the kids so I could write uninterrupted, to waiting up for me on late editing nights, and letting me vent when the imposter syndrome kicked in. Thank you, honey, for helping to make a lifelong goal of mine possible.

To my kids. Thank you for bringing me out of my daydreams for reminding me to enjoy playtime and sunshine. I love you both more than the Northern Lights of Asterion!

To my mom. You have shown me what a strong, female character should look like. You have taught me to grow from the trials in life, and how to persevere. Thank you, for encouraging me to fuel my imagination and for telling me anything i possible.

To my best friend, Catherine... The Brina to my Shaye, who was the first to talk about my story with me like we were in a book club! Thank you for inspiring me to write about fierce friendships. (And for letting me use your dad as inspiration for Rolland and his cooking!)

To my family: my dad, stepmom, and grandparents. Thank you for supporting me through all the twists and turns, and for never skipping a beat in supporting me when I announced I wanted to become an author.

To my mapmaker, Melissa Nash. Thank you for bringing the world of Asterion, Sagon, and Skag to life. You took my messy sketch and turned it into something tangible. Without you, my readers would still be trying to figure out where Shaye and Sorin were going.

To my betas: Ardena, Catherine, Diana, Lisa, and Stephanie. You were the first people that I entrusted my characters and world to. Thank you for being the first steppingstone in this process, and for making me smile at your reaction notes as you read!

To my final editor, Aunt Suzie and her bundle of red pens. Thank you for the corrections, and for the late-night pep talks. Without you, my stories would never be ready to set free into the world.

To all of the writers who have come before me. Thank you for shaping my world with your stories and inspiring me to create worlds of my own.

To my readers and fans. Thank you for your support and encouragement through your sweet messages, posts, and reviews. I am immensely thankful for each, and every one of you. It is because of you, that I have the drive to continue sharing these stories with the world. Truly, *thank you*.

Lastly, to our Father in Heaven, who has blessed me with an imagination filled with endless possibilities. Thank you.

ABOUT THE AUTHOR

J.M. Wallace is a proud military wife. She has spent much of her adult life moving from place to place with her husband and their two children, making stories of their own. As a young girl, J.M. was fascinated with stories that she read and that she dreamed up on her own. Even when she was horseback riding, she was never in her own yard; instead, she was in an enchanted forest or riding into battle alongside brave knights. Today, she puts those stories to paper, to share with the world. She does this in the little pockets of her day between giving her kids snacks, naps, baths, and putting them to bed. *A Legacy of Darkness* is her first series.

Follow J.M. Wallace's writing adventures on:
Instagram @j.m.wallaceauthor Tiktok @jmwallace.author

Made in the USA
Middletown, DE
22 May 2022